Class of '59

Class of '59

American Journey Series

Book Four

JOHN A. HELDT

ISBN-13: 978-1-09-190146-9

Edited by Aaron Yost

Cover art by LLPix Designs

Novels by John A. Heldt:

Northwest Passage Series: The Mine, The Journey, The Show, The Fire, The Mirror. American Journey Series: September Sky, Mercer Street, Indiana Belle, Class of '59, Hannah's Moon. Carson Chronicles Series: River Rising, The Memory Tree, Indian Paintbrush, Caitlin's Song.

Follow John A. Heldt at johnheldt.blogspot.com

To Matthew Erik

CONTENTS

Acknowledgments 9

1	Mary Beth	11
2	Mark	16
3	Mark	20
4	Mary Beth	23
5	Mark	27
6	Mary Beth	31
7	Mark	37
8	Piper	40
9	Ben	43
10	Piper	47
11	Mary Beth	51
12	Piper	56
13	Mary Beth	59
14	Mark	62
15	Piper	66
16	Mark	73
17	Piper	76
18	Ben	80
19	Mary Beth	83
20	Piper	87
21	Mark	92
22	Ben	95
23	Mary Beth	99
24	Mark	103
25	Mary Beth	107
26	Piper	110
27	Mary Beth	116
28	Piper	121
29	Donna	127
30	Mary Beth	131

CONTENTS (CONT.)

31	Mark	135
32	Ben	140
33	Mary Beth	146
34	Piper	150
35	Mary Beth	155
36	Piper	161
37	Mark	165
38	Mark	168
39	Piper	173
40	Mary Beth	176
41	Piper	181
42	Mary Beth	186
43	Mark	191
44	Donna	195
45	Mary Beth	199
46	Piper	203
47	Dennis	208
48	Mark	211
49	Ben	214
50	Mary Beth	217
51	Piper	223
52	Ben	226
53	Mary Beth	229
54	Mark	233
55	Ben	236
56	Mary Beth	239
57	Mark	244
58	Mary Beth	251

ACKNOWLEDGMENTS

Near the end of *My Cousin Vinny*, one of my favorite movies, Marisa Tomei warns Joe Pesci, her go-it-alone lawyer boyfriend, that he may actually have to thank people who help him succeed.

Pesci frowns at the prospect. He laments the fact he was not able to win his first case without the assistance of others. Tomei sarcastically describes his "dilemma" as a "nightmare." Needless to say, I can't relate. I love thanking people. I love getting their help. For without their assistance, I would not be able to bring quality novels to the reading public.

Some of the people who helped bring *this* novel to the public are veterans. Aaron Yost has edited every book. My wife, Cheryl Heldt, and brother-in-law, Jon Johnson, have *read* every book. I am deeply indebted to them and others who offered their time, talents, and insights.

They include Morgan Coyner, Leslie Teske Mills, Christine Stinson, and Craig Stoess, who read the early drafts; Mary Heldt, Cathy Hundley, Esther Johnson, and Becky Skelton, who read the later drafts; and Maureen Driscoll, John Fellows, and Kristin Wogahn, who provided expertise on a variety of subjects. Driscoll is the author of twelve novels.

I am also grateful to cover illustrator Laura Wright LaRoche and several individuals who provided research assistance and guidance. Among the most helpful were staff from the Library of Congress, Los Angeles Public Library, Nevada Gaming Control Board, Pasadena Public Library (California), and University Libraries (University of Nevada, Las Vegas).

When researching and writing this novel, I consulted several books. They include *The 1950s*, edited by Stuart A. Kallen; *The American Drive-In Restaurant* by Michael Karl Witzel; *Fashions of a Decade: The 1950s* by Patricia Baker; *Fragments: Poems, Intimate Notes, Letters* by Marilyn Monroe; *Futures at Stake: Youth, Gambling, and Society* by Howard J. Shaffer, Matthew N. Hall, and Joni Vander Bilt; and *Las Vegas: City without Clocks* by Ed Reid.

I also learned much about the Fabulous Fifties by reading the *Las Vegas Sun*, *Los Angeles Times*, *Pasadena Star-News*, *Washington Post*, and *Whittier Daily News*. I encourage readers to consult these and other sources when seeking information about a truly remarkable era.

1: MARY BETH

Los Angeles, California – Saturday, May 27, 2017

Mary Beth stopped when she saw the gun. She didn't need to see more to know that her carefree Saturday evening had taken a serious turn. Men in nylon masks didn't point pistols at convenience store clerks unless they meant business.

"Put the cash in the bag," the masked man said.

The clerk, a balding man of fifty, didn't argue. He pulled bills from the open register, put them in a stack, and slowly placed them in a small paper bag.

"Speed it up," the robber said.

Mary Beth watched with horrified fascination. She had never seen a robbery in progress. She had never seen an angry man hold a gun.

Standing fifteen feet to the left of the robber, Mary Beth tightened her hold on her fiancé's hand and silently prayed that the confrontation would end quickly and peacefully. She didn't get her wish. The moment another man, a policeman in uniform, pushed open the store's front door and walked into the establishment, all hell broke loose.

"What the—?" the cop asked.

The masked man answered the question quickly. He fired a slug into the officer's chest from a distance of twelve feet and then turned back to the clerk, who had used the disruption to reach for something, presumably a weapon, in a compartment below the register. The gunman didn't waste time on him either. He dispatched him with a bullet to the head.

Mary Beth froze as Jordan Taylor, her boyfriend of five years, released her hand and rushed the assailant when he turned his back. She screamed when the gunman reacted to the new threat by shooting Jordan in the stomach, dropping the former defensive end to the ground.

"No!" Mary Beth screamed again.

11

She ran toward Jordan as the robber grabbed the bag and bolted out the door. She reached him seconds later, dropped to the floor, and rolled him over.

Jordan stared at Mary Beth, winced, and lifted his head a few inches off the floor. He tried to speak but failed. He winced again, closed his eyes, and lowered his head.

Mary Beth grabbed his wrist, felt a weak pulse, and quickly scanned the store for help. When she saw an elderly man cowering behind an energy-drink display, she snapped at him.

"Get help! Please call someone!"

When Mary Beth saw the man pull a phone from his pocket and punch some numbers, she returned her attention to the only boy she had ever loved. She tore open his button-down shirt and gasped when she saw blood pulse out of a pea-sized hole near Jordan's navel.

"Please hurry!" Mary Beth barked at the man.

She quickly removed her sweater, wadded it into a ball, and pressed it against the wound. She pressed until her hand and arm began to hurt, but she pressed in vain. Blood seeped through the sweater and began to flow onto the tile floor.

"Don't leave me, Jordan," Mary Beth said. "Help is coming. Just hang in there."

Jordan groaned when Mary Beth applied pressure to the wound, but he didn't speak. He took a few quick breaths, turned his head slightly toward the woman trying to save him, and expired. Just that quickly, the gentle giant was gone.

Mary Beth shuddered. She shuddered again when a familiar voice snapped her out of a daze.

"Mary Beth?"

Colleen McIntire repeated her daughter's name.

"Mary Beth?"

"Huh?"

"Professor Bell asked you a question."

Mary Beth took a breath and pulled herself together. She had done that often since watching a common criminal murder her best friend nearly eight months earlier. She looked at the man seated at the head of the long dining table, forced a smile, and rejoined the living.

"I'm sorry, Professor. I had my mind on other things. What did you ask?"

Geoffrey Bell smiled.

"I asked, 'When do you start medical school?'"

Mary Beth gazed at her questioner.

"I start this summer. Classes at UAB begin July 25."

"Do you still plan to become a surgeon?" Bell asked.

"I do," Mary Beth said. "I may consider other options later on, but right now I want to specialize in critical-care surgery."

"I can't imagine a more noble pursuit," Jeanette Bell said cheerfully. "You'll be saving lives every day. I admire that."

"Thank you."

Mary Beth placed a cloth napkin on her lap and paused before digging into her baked salmon dinner, which Jeanette had prepared in the kitchen of her turn-of-the-century mansion. She took a moment to study the people at the table and noted their differing expressions.

The Bells, seated at the ends, looked interested. They had not seen Mary Beth in ten years and no doubt wanted to know what the studious former sixth-grader was going to do now that she was all grown up and ready to conquer the world.

Mary Beth's parents, seated opposite her, looked concerned. Brody McIntire, a retired Army colonel, often worried about his oldest daughter in the months that followed the shooting. Colleen Finley McIntire, his perceptive wife of twenty-five years, did so seven days a week.

Piper McIntire, a recent high school graduate, sat at her sister's left. She glanced at Mary Beth with eyes that reflected both optimism and sympathy. She knew more than anyone how much Mary Beth hated talking about her college life or even the future.

After an awkward silence, Professor Bell, a noted physics instructor who had gained a national following touting the possibilities of time travel, changed the subject from career plans to vacation plans. He looked at both girls.

"Have you two decided how you're going to spend next week?" Bell asked. "If you haven't, I can offer a few suggestions. There is more to L.A. than Disneyland and Universal Studios."

Mary Beth exchanged glances with Piper and then returned to her host.

"We talked about going to the beach until we saw a weather report. It looks like we brought Alabama's rain with us."

The professor chuckled.

"I apologize for that. I spoke to the weather gods just last night and requested sunshine for your entire visit," Bell said. "I confess I don't have the clout I used to."

Brody and Colleen laughed.

"That's all right," Mary Beth said. "We'll find something to do, even if we do nothing more than enjoy this wonderful house. Did you say your great-grandfather built it?"

"I did," Bell said. "He built it in 1899."

"Has the house been in your family all this time?"

Bell took a breath.

"No. In fact, it has belonged to others most of the time."

13

"Oh," Mary Beth said in puzzled voice.

"Let me explain," Bell said. "Percival Bell, my great-grandfather, died of a stroke only a few months after moving in. Though he had provided my great-grandmother with the means to hold the house, she decided to sell it. She returned to her native Boston with her young children after the funeral and never returned. Five other families occupied this place in the years that followed. Jeanette and I didn't take possession of the mansion until the summer of 2000."

Mary Beth looked at Bell thoughtfully.

"Well, for what it's worth, I'm glad you bought it *and* restored it. This is a beautiful house, Professor. I would much rather stay a week in a place like this than some noisy hotel."

"I'll second that," Brody said.

"I'll third it," Piper added.

Mary Beth laughed to herself. Though she knew Piper loved historic homes, like this Painted Lady in central Los Angeles, she also knew her sister preferred modern hotels on warm sandy beaches. She wondered how long it would be before Piper complained about the house's location. The nearest beach – in Santa Monica – was twelve traffic-filled miles away.

Bell had offered the mansion to Brody, a good friend, after hearing that he intended to bring his family to Los Angeles in late May. The professor had already made plans to entertain other guests at his second home in Santa Barbara and welcomed the opportunity to help out the colonel, whom he had met at a physics conference in 2005.

"We haven't heard much from you, Piper," Bell said. He zeroed in on the teenager plowing into a chef's salad. "What do you plan to do this summer and fall?"

Piper smiled.

"I intend to work on my tan."

The Bells laughed. The colonel frowned. Colleen shook her head.

Mary Beth looked at her host.

"What my sister meant to say, Professor, is that she will work as a lifeguard at a pool in Huntsville this summer and then study art history and dance in Knoxville."

Bell chuckled.

"Thank you for the translation, Mary Beth. I thought that's what she meant."

This time everyone laughed.

Jeanette looked at Piper.

"I commend you on your choice of subjects, Piper. I majored in art history in college and took a few dance classes. I also commend you for bravery."

"Bravery?" Piper asked.

14

"Yes," Jeanette said. "I'm sure it took guts to commit to Tennessee."

"What do you mean?"

"I mean your father, mother, and sister are graduates of the University of Alabama. Isn't Tennessee one of Alabama's sports rivals?"

"It is."

Jeanette cocked her head.

"Didn't your family take issue with your choice of colleges?"

"They did at first," Piper said. "But I quickly gained their blessing."

"How did you manage that?"

Mary Beth smiled. She knew where this was going.

"It was simple, Mrs. Bell."

"Oh?" Jeanette asked. "How so?"

Piper grinned.

"I threatened to go to Auburn."

2: MARK

Saturday, March 21, 1959

Mark Ryan yanked on the handle and swore when he could not get the drawer to budge. He had tried to open the drawer of the antique desk five times in five minutes and had failed miserably each time. He knew there were better things to do at six fifteen on a Saturday morning – like sleep or reread the newspaper he had pulled from the porch and left on the kitchen table – but he did not want to do any of them. He wanted to see what was inside this desk.

The college senior retreated to a double bed, the only other furniture in what was now his bedroom, and plopped on the mattress. He decided he needed to think things over before tackling the drawer again. No challenge was worth a broken wrist.

Mark laughed to himself when he thought about his circumstances. He was spending every weekend in his new home because his mother had asked him to and not because he wanted to live in a creaky mansion or sleep on a lumpy mattress. He had vowed at his father's funeral in October that he would do anything to make Donna Ryan happy.

Mark took a moment to assess his surroundings. This wasn't a bad room, he thought. It was just a little bland. It needed more furniture, a few wall hangings, and perhaps a plant or two. He made a mental note to spruce up his quarters as soon as possible.

The twenty-two-year-old had moved into the mansion, a Painted Lady in the West Adams district of Los Angeles, over Christmas break. With the help of his mother, brother, and several friends, he had managed to move most of his family's belongings from their rambler in South Pasadena to the stately manor in only two days.

Mark still considered Zeta Alpha Rho, a fraternity four miles away, to be his primary residence, but he knew he wouldn't call it home for much

16

longer. In less than two months, the engineering major would graduate from the university, move out of the fraternity, and reside full-time in the Painted Lady as he looked for employment in Southern California.

In the meantime, Mark planned to support his widowed mother as best he could, spend more time with his obnoxious sibling, and perhaps decipher the mysteries of his new digs. He looked again at the desk, a mahogany monolith that was built into the wall, and decided he would start with its stubborn keyless upper drawer.

Mark pondered the possibilities for a moment and then smiled when he remembered something a roommate had told him their freshman year. Some old desks had hidden locks and latches – locks and latches that could not be accessed without patience and effort.

He got off the bed, walked to the desk, and pulled on the drawer's handle one more time just for the hell of it. Then he dropped to his knees, crawled into the kneehole under the desk, and ran his hands in and around the desk's nooks and crannies. He needed only thirty seconds to discover a small metal latch on the backside of the keyless drawer.

Mark lifted the latch, which he could feel but not see, and pulled the drawer handle until he heard a click. He scampered out of the kneehole, tugged on the handle again, and this time encountered no resistance. He opened the locked compartment with one easy pull.

His heart raced when he looked inside the drawer and saw two colorless stones that resembled gypsum crystals he had once seen in a rock shop. He took them out of the drawer, placed them on top of the desk, and gave each a thorough inspection.

Mark did not know if the gems were valuable, so he conducted a test. He grabbed one of the stones, walked to the window, and pressed the rock against the glass. He tried to cut a groove but did not succeed in creating even a scratch. Whatever he held in his hand, it was not a diamond.

Mark returned to the desk, placed the rock next to its twin, and stuck his hand into the deep drawer. He quickly found two more objects: a large skeleton key and a piece of paper.

He retrieved the items, put them on the desk, and gave them a look. The key was ornate and shiny but otherwise unremarkable. The paper was something else.

Mark examined the slip and saw it was a sheet of academic stationery. He noted a name at the top of the page and a date in a corner and began reading a detailed personal letter that Percival Bell, a professor of geology and physics, had written on March 22, 1900.

Mark needed only a minute to realize he had discovered something potentially far more valuable than precious gems. He had found the musings of a man who had apparently traveled backward in time on three occasions and planned to travel *forward* in time the very next day.

He paid close attention to the back page. In the first five paragraphs, the professor, the original owner of the Painted Lady, had stated his intentions. Bell planned to test the limits of a time tunnel under his house by traveling to June 2, 2017, a date he had picked at random. He apparently intended to leave the letter for his wife in case he never came back.

Mark reread the letter and this time focused on the closing paragraph. He could not help but admire a man who had risked everything in the pursuit of knowledge.

"Please know that I do not undertake this venture lightly. I know the risks and accept them. I take them because the interests of science demand that I do. Give my best to the children should I not return. I will think of them — and you — fondly."

Mark wanted to run to the library and learn the fate of Percival Bell. He also wanted to see if there was anything to the professor's claim that he had traveled through time on three occasions.

He found the idea preposterous at face value. Yet Bell had documented how he had planned to travel to 2017 in great detail. Perhaps he wanted to do more than apologize to his wife and children. Perhaps he wanted to leave something to science in case he failed.

Mark stared into space and pondered yet another possibility. What if Percival Bell had not traveled at all? What if he had changed his mind or had a life-altering experience? What if he had died before stepping into his so-called time tunnel? Surely he had not expected his wife to find a letter in a locked drawer. Something did not make sense.

Mark looked again at the letter, the rocks, and the key, which, according to the letter, opened the exterior door of the tunnel. He had all he needed to determine whether the professor was a genius or a lunatic. Dare he act on his curiosity?

He put the four items back in the drawer and walked again to the window. He looked out at his quiet street and noticed how bland and pedestrian it was. He wondered what the street looked like in 2017. He wondered what cars, clothes, and *people* looked like.

Mark heard a noise and turned away from the window. He glanced at the door just as Charlotte, the family's three-year-old Himalayan cat, entered the room. He wondered how long it would be before his eighteen-year-old brother, Ben, an early riser, also got up.

He did not wonder about his mother. Donna was in Fresno visiting her brother. She would not return to Los Angeles until March 29.

Mark paced back and forth in his room for several minutes. He knew he should forget what he had found, make some coffee, and put a dent in the homework he had neglected for days, but he could not. He was intrigued, mesmerized, and hooked. He had something amazing within his grasp. He could not let it go. Could he? He decided he could not.

Less than an hour after finding the letter, two rocks, and the key in a locked drawer, Mark Ryan walked out of his bedroom, taking the items with him. He did not know what he would do when he reached the basement of the Painted Lady, but he did know one thing. The second-to-last day of his spring break was about to get interesting.

3: MARK

Mark wasted little time walking down a flight of stairs to the main floor and then down another flight to the basement. He had visited the lowest level of the mansion only once before. It was just as dark, dingy, and depressing the second time.

He flipped on a light and walked through the room to a nondescript door that presumably provided access to a tunnel and the backyard. According to Percival Bell's letter, the tunnel that connected the basement to the yard was no ordinary corridor. It was a time machine, a magic portal, a passageway between the present and the past and maybe the future too.

Mark retrieved Bell's letter from a pocket, scanned the particulars, and wondered again whether he was reading the words of a genius or a lunatic. If the professor was telling the truth, then all Mark had to do was step into the tunnel with at least one of the stones and wait for magic to happen. He could not believe time travel could be that simple.

Mark felt a twinge of fear as he tucked the letter away. Maybe running to the library first was not a bad idea. He wanted to know what had happened to Percival Bell on March 22, 1900. He wanted to know a lot of things. He worried about failure.

Then he got an idea. If he took a simple precaution, he could minimize the risk of an unpleasant outcome. He turned around, surveyed the basement, and looked for two heavy but portable objects he could use to keep two doors from closing behind him.

Mark found what he needed in the form of two bricks. Both looked like leftovers from the construction of the house. Each appeared to be more than sufficient. He walked to a pile of debris a few feet away, picked up the bricks, and returned to the door. He felt his fear subside.

Mark lowered the bricks to the floor and prepared to enter what he had every reason to believe was a simple passageway. He patted the shirt pocket containing the letter and the key and then the trouser pockets containing the crystals. He had everything he needed.

Deciding that he had to either act or walk away, Mark opened the door, picked up the bricks, and stepped inside a tunnel that was fifteen feet long, eight feet high, and five feet wide. He placed one brick between the door and the doorjamb and then carried the other to the middle of the chamber. He waited for something to happen. Within seconds, something did.

Mark noticed a change immediately. He lifted his head and saw a string of blue and white crystals, embedded in the ceiling, light up like bulbs on a Christmas tree. They flickered and glowed and gave an otherwise dreary space a festive feel.

Then Mark looked down and saw something else. The three-inch crystals he had placed in his pockets had also come to life. They emitted bright light that shimmered through his wool pants. Something was going on, he thought. Something was really going on.

Mark took a breath as he battled both anxiety and excitement. Dare he take the next step and actually walk outside? He checked his watch and saw that it was seven fifteen, or at least seven fifteen inside the Painted Lady. What time it was in the backyard was anyone's guess.

The would-be time traveler collected himself once again, glanced at the exterior door, and considered his options one last time. He patted his shirt pocket, felt the key, and decided to take the plunge. He picked up the second brick and walked to the door.

Mark hesitated only a moment before turning the knob and opening the door. He withdrew for a few seconds as daylight hit him hard and fast. When his eyes adjusted to the light, he stepped through the door, placed the second brick between the door and the jamb, and advanced to the first of twenty brick steps. The steps rose about ten feet to ground level.

Mark noticed something different the minute he got his bearings. The stairway looked clean and new – or at least restored. No weeds shot up between the bricks. No cracks marred the steps.

The collegian noticed something else too. It was raining. A steady drizzle fell from a light gray sky. Just minutes earlier, the sky had been cloudless, blue, and bright.

Mark took another breath and slowly ascended the stairs. Though he heard nothing unusual and certainly nothing that might cause alarm, he felt apprehensive. He was literally stepping into something new and unknown. He had no idea what awaited him.

Mark reached the top of the stairs thirty seconds later, walked to the center of the spacious yard, and stopped. He spun around, gave his surroundings a 360-degree inspection, and let the reality of the moment sink in. He raised his arms to the sky.

I did it! I really did it!

No matter where he looked, he saw something new. The lawn was plush and surrounded by a six-foot cedar fence he had never seen. A riding mower occupied a covered space near the house. Something that looked like Sputnik protruded from the roof. Even the Painted Lady looked different. It sported a fresh coat of latex and upgraded windows.

Mark saw a sign that read: THIS HOUSE PROTECTED BY SENTRY 2000. He did not, thankfully, see one that read: BEWARE OF DOG.

He felt a knot form in his stomach as the truth of his situation slowly set in. Mark Ryan, a college senior in 1959, was no longer in 1959. He was in another time and maybe another place. Percival Bell had been no lunatic. He was a man who had possessed an incredible secret.

For a few minutes Mark walked around the yard and basked in his surroundings. He noted sights he hadn't seen before and sounds he hadn't heard. He marveled at the sight and sound of a massive twin-rotor helicopter that roared over the mansion.

Mark wanted to explore. He wanted to see the world beyond the lawn of his once and present home. He looked for a way out of the fenced yard and saw two possibilities: a gate in front and a gate in back. The latter provided access to a neighbor's backyard.

Mark started toward the latter but stopped when he heard a tapping sound. He turned around, looked at a large paned window in the Painted Lady, and saw a young woman look back.

The woman frowned. When she lifted a small object, pressed it against her ear, and pointed at Mark, as if ordering him to stay put, he panicked and ran. He ran toward the house, down the stairs, and to the door he had propped open with a brick.

Mark opened the exterior door, grabbed the brick, and slammed the door shut as he entered the tunnel. When the flickering lights told him he could advance, he did just that. He opened the interior door, grabbed the other brick, and shut the door behind him.

He didn't bother to see if anyone followed. He ran through the dingy basement and up the stairs to the main floor of a home that looked comfortingly familiar.

Mark reached a recliner in the living room just as a clock on the mantle chimed and signaled a quarter past the hour. He collapsed in the chair, caught his breath, and stared at the wall. At seven fifteen on what was presumably still March 21, 1959, he took some time to think.

4: MARY BETH

Friday, June 2, 2017

Mary Beth poured herself a cup of coffee and wandered about thirty feet from the kitchen to a cozy reading room that faced Geoffrey Bell's backyard. She liked quiet spaces like this because they allowed her to relax, set her troubles aside, and concentrate on things that mattered.

She sat down on a love seat, placed her cup on a coffee table, and gazed across the room at a large paned window. She admired the window – a restored, weatherized version of the original – almost as much as the wicker furniture and the seashell-themed paper that covered the walls.

Mary Beth glanced at her cell phone, noted the time of eight o'clock, and curled into her seat. If she did nothing else on the second-to-last day of her rainy California vacation, she would enjoy an exquisite cup of French roast, relish a rare moment of peace, and ponder her future.

She didn't worry much about professional fulfillment. She knew she would enter the medical school at the University of Alabama at Birmingham in seven weeks, begin a series of degree programs and residencies, and emerge from the chaos as a capable surgeon.

Whether she would emerge as a happy woman was an open question. Mary Beth had never imagined life without Jordan, the boy she had dated since the eleventh grade. Now that he was gone, she refused to take the long view of anything. She measured happiness in terms of good days and bad. The distant future was a murky swamp she was not yet ready to explore.

Mary Beth retrieved her cup, took a sip, and placed the cup back on the table. The coffee was hot, piping hot, unlike the weather of the past seven days. A storm front had brought a week of cool air and rain to Southern

California and forced the McIntire family to seek refuge in museums and shopping malls instead of amusement parks and beaches.

Brody and Colleen had adjusted well to the weather. So had Mary Beth. Each had enjoyed the J. Paul Getty Museum, the California Science Center, and the Dorothy Chandler Pavilion.

Piper was another matter. She had moped all week about the gray skies, chilly winds, and persistent drizzle. She insisted that a Los Angeles vacation was not complete without a visit to the beach, Disneyland, and Dodger Stadium. She had spent a disproportionate part of the week reading mysteries in the antique-filled bedroom the Bells had provided her.

Mary Beth started to reach for her coffee again but stopped when she heard someone open an outside door. She knew it couldn't be her sister. Piper didn't rise before ten unless she had to.

Mary Beth knew it couldn't be her parents either. They were in Beverly Hills attending a lecture on investment opportunities. Unless the Bells had returned home a day early, someone else was moving about their property. Did they employ a groundskeeper? Mary Beth picked up her phone, got up from the love seat, and stepped toward the window.

She reached the window a few seconds later, peered through the rain-streaked glass, and scanned the yard. She saw nothing of interest. Then just that quickly a man wearing a white button-down shirt and cuffed gray slacks walked into view. If he was a groundskeeper, he didn't look the part. He looked more like a college student from the 1950s.

Mary Beth dialed Geoffrey Bell's cell-phone number, tapped on the glass, and glared at the man, who was almost certainly a trespasser. She pressed the phone to her ear, waited for Bell to answer, and pointed at the man when he looked at her. She wanted him to know that she had seen him and was in the process of checking him out.

Mary Beth frowned when Bell did not pick up the call and panicked when the trespasser, who appeared startled and frightened, ran toward the house and down a stairway that led to the basement. She felt her stomach drop when she heard the basement door slam.

She started to leave a message but ended her call when she realized that leaving a message would do no good. She did not have time to wait for the professor to call back. She had to deal with the situation now.

Mary Beth raced out of the room, ran down a hallway, and made a beeline for an interior door that led to a basement she had never seen. A moment later, she threw the door open, flipped on the lights, and started down a stone staircase that looked almost medieval.

She felt a little uneasy as she descended the steps. She did not know what waited in the basement. She doubted the wisdom of her actions. A smart person, Mary Beth thought, would run upstairs, lock the door, and call the police. A smart person would carry a weapon.

Mary Beth hesitated for a moment, took a deep breath, and braced herself for an unpleasant confrontation. She did not know what she would say when she encountered the man. She did not know what she would do. She knew only that she had to act quickly and decisively.

Mary Beth entered the basement expecting to find a man. She did not expect to find a thirty-by-forty-foot space that looked like a heavenly lobby. White lights illuminated a chamber with white walls, white carpeting, and a white ceiling. A glass-and-brass coffee table stood between two large white couches near the back of the room.

"Hello?" Mary Beth asked. "Is anyone in here?"

No one replied. Then again, no one else was in the room. If a man had entered this basement, he had either raced out of the house at the speed of light or vanished into thin air.

Mary Beth walked around the room looking for clues. She found nothing useful. Then she saw a nondescript door that almost blended into the wall facing the backyard.

She gathered her courage once again, stepped toward the door, and opened it. She found a drab, narrow, unlighted tunnel that led to another door. She did not find a man.

Impossible.

Mary Beth walked to the other door, opened it, and saw what she expected to see: a brick staircase that led to the backyard. She ascended the steps, stepped onto the lawn, and scanned the property for young men in white shirts and gray slacks. She didn't find anything more interesting than a riding mower. For the first time since tapping on the window of the reading room, she began to question what she saw. She needed more coffee.

Mary Beth walked down the brick stairs, shut the self-locking exterior door, and returned to the basement. She almost hoped to find the trespasser waiting for her. Better to lose her life, she thought, than lose her sanity. She laughed to herself. What a morning.

As she ascended the medieval steps, reentered the main part of the residence, and worked her way back to her French roast, Mary Beth pondered her next action. She considered calling Professor Bell again but ultimately decided against it. She did not want to interrupt his morning by reporting phantom trespassers. If he returned her aborted call later in the day, she would simply tell him she had a question about accessing his satellite television service.

Mary Beth returned to the reading room and the love seat, picked up a magazine, and read about an actress who had adopted three children from Africa. Then she perused an article about a Mississippi family that lived on thirty dollars a week. She read mindless fluff until she heard a clock chime nine times in the adjacent room and decided it was time to do something else.

Mary Beth finished her cold coffee, got up from the love seat, and stretched her arms. She stepped toward the door but stopped when she heard a loud and persistent bark. She walked to the window, wiped condensation from a pane, and peered through the glass. She needed only a second to see why the neighbor's dog, a German shepherd, was making such a fuss. College boy was trying to climb over Professor Bell's back fence.

Mary Beth did not bother tapping on the glass this time. She did not bother picking up her phone. She instead bolted from the room and raced toward the basement as fast as she could.

She did not know why the man had returned. Nor did she know why he had decided to enter the yard by climbing over the fence rather than walking through the unlocked front gate.

She knew only that when this daring individual tried to reenter the Painted Lady, he would have to first get past a *protective* lady. Mary Beth McIntire would be waiting for him.

5: MARK

The elderly woman stared at Mark, offered a kind smile, and finally asked a question that had no doubt been on her mind since she had joined him in line.

"Are you auditioning for a movie, young man?"

Mark felt his stomach flutter.

"No, ma'am."

The woman widened her smile.

"I just thought I'd ask. I haven't seen a haircut or clothes like yours since I was in college. Back then, of course, all the boys looked like you."

Mark looked around the small grocery store for eavesdroppers. He didn't mind chatting with a woman who had to be pushing eighty, but he didn't want to invite additional scrutiny. He had already drawn his fair share of hard stares and raised eyebrows.

"When did you go to college?" Mark asked in a soft voice.

"I graduated in 1959," the woman said. "I know that's ancient history to young folks like you, but to me it seems like yesterday. The fifties were the best days we've ever had."

Mark smiled.

"I agree."

The woman nodded but said no more. A young person had agreed with her nostalgic view of the past. What more did she need?

Mark approached the checkout counter and handed the cashier, a young Latino woman, a magazine he had pulled from a nearby rack. He watched in fascination as she dragged the periodical over a tinted glass plate and three lighted numbers popped onto a small screen.

"That will be five thirty-eight," the cashier said.

Mark gave the clerk a five-dollar bill and a fifty-cent piece bearing the image of Benjamin Franklin. He held his breath when the woman gave the bill and the coin a cursory inspection and exhaled when she handed him a dime and two pennies minted in 2017.

He thanked the cashier, nodded to the elderly woman, and headed for the door. A moment later, he stepped into a busy parking lot, tucked the magazine under his shirt to keep it dry, and started toward the Painted Lady three blocks away.

Mark had wanted to do more than buy a magazine from a local grocery store. He had wanted to spend the entire day in Los Angeles and see more of the twenty-first century, but he had decided even before accessing the tunnel a second time to take it slow.

As he headed down the first block, Mark thought about Percival Bell's letter, the crystals in his pockets, and the woman in the window. He had more questions than answers. Who was she? What had she held in her hand? Did she live in the mansion? Was she alone? Did she know about the time tunnel? Had she reported him to the police?

Mark suspected that she had told someone. *He* would have told someone had he found a stranger milling about his property.

Despite the obvious risks of going back, Mark had not hesitated before committing to another trip. He had wanted to satisfy his curiosity and satisfy it before Ben got up and started asking a lot of questions. So he jumped back in. He grabbed the colorless rocks and what was left of his sanity and forty-five minutes later accessed the tunnel and the backyard again.

This time he had not walked to the middle of the yard, where he could easily be seen, but rather toward the mansion itself. He had moved quickly to the front gate, a windowless side of the house, and the street. To his knowledge, he had not drawn the attention of others.

Mark had then gone about exploring the neighborhood. He had visited a park, an unoccupied elementary school, and finally a small grocery store, where he noted the difference between the time on a clock and the time on his watch. Both seemed out of whack.

Once in the store, a place that offered more pop and potato chips than fruits and vegetables, he had gone straight to the magazines. He searched the racks for something useful and found it in the form of a news magazine's seventy-fifth anniversary edition. He concluded he would be able to learn a lot about the world after 1959 by simply thumbing through some pages.

Mark picked up his step as he crossed a street and started down the last block, but he stopped when he saw two women talk and laugh on the sidewalk in front of the Painted Lady. Neither seemed eager to exit the scene. Both no doubt would view him with suspicion if he walked past them to the front gate and gained entry to a property he no longer owned.

He retreated a few steps to the street corner, pondered his options, and then remembered the gate in back. If he could reach the gate unnoticed and uncontested, he could access the mansion's backyard and run to the time tunnel before any nosy girls could tap on a window.

Mark stepped away from the women and walked around the block until he reached the house that stood behind his one-time home. He studied the residence for a moment and didn't see anything that might cause alarm. The driveway was empty. Curtains were drawn. No humans or animals prowled the premises. At nine o'clock local time on what Mark knew was Friday, June 2, 2017, the property looked positively inviting.

Mark checked again for onlookers and then stepped toward a gate that provided access to the backyard. He lifted the latch, opened the gate slowly, and walked inside. He listened for voices or barks, heard neither, and proceeded through the side yard to the grassy patch in back. He smiled when he saw the Painted Lady in the background and the gate the properties shared.

He looked up at the sky and noticed a new bank of dark clouds rolling in from the Pacific. He made a mental note to bring a light jacket or an umbrella on his next visit.

Mark patted the magazine under his shirt, saw that it was firmly secured, and stepped toward the fence. He reached the gate as the wind picked up and the drizzle turned into a steady rain. He tried to lift the latch but found that he couldn't. Rust and neglect had apparently rendered it useless. So he gave up on the latch and decided to climb over the fence instead.

He placed two hands on top of the six-foot barrier and started to pull himself up when he heard a bark. He lowered himself to the ground, glanced over his right shoulder, and saw a complication he didn't need. A German shepherd had detected his presence.

The canine exited the far side of a covered porch, ran around a fountain, and raced toward the trespasser from the 1950s at breakneck speed. The dog looked hungry.

Mark didn't need another reason to move with haste. He quickly pulled half of his body over the top of the fence and lifted his feet just as the German shepherd lunged at them. The dog missed his target and tumbled a few feet but quickly regrouped. He charged again and this time sank his teeth into the intruder's right foot.

Mark winced at the pain. He eventually shook himself free but not before Fido bit into his foot a second time and chewed off a chunk of his gray slacks. He swung both feet over the top of the fence and landed on all fours in a patch of petunias.

Dazed, shaken, and unnerved, Mark stood up, brushed dirt off his pants, and stepped into the yard. As he walked briskly toward the stairwell, the Painted Lady, and 1959, Mark glanced at the large paned window. He saw no one behind it. Thank God for small blessings, he thought.

Mark stuck a hand in his shirt pocket and reached for the skeleton key. He retrieved it when he reached the top of the stairway, held it out when he started down the steps, and dropped it when he saw a woman with folded arms standing in front of the door.

"Hello," the woman said. "Are we having fun yet?"

Mark dropped his head and sighed. He berated himself for not trusting his instincts. He should have waited a day before traveling again. He looked at the woman.

"Who are you?"

She narrowed her eyes.

"Perhaps I should ask *you* that question."

"I'm Mark Ryan. I live here."

"That's funny," the woman said. "I'm a guest here. I know the man who owns this house. I know his wife. You don't look like either one. Shall we try again?"

"Please let me pass," Mark said. "I mean you no harm. If you let me pass, I promise you'll never see me again."

The woman dropped her hands to her hips and laughed.

"You're a regular comedian."

"Please," Mark said. "Just let me in."

"No."

"I could force my way in."

"I could also scream," the woman said. She hardened her stare. "I don't think you want me to wake the neighbors. Do you?"

"No."

"Why don't you be a good boy and return to your movie set or frat party or wherever you came from?"

"I can't," Mark said.

The woman's face softened.

"Why not?"

"I'm not from here."

"What do you mean you're not from here?" she asked. "You just told me you live here."

"I do," Mark said. He took a breath. "I live here in 1959."

6: MARY BETH

Saturday, March 21, 1959

Ten minutes later, Mary Beth stared at a copy of the *Los Angeles News* – a March 21, 1959, copy of the *Los Angeles News* – and then at the strange man she had captured in Geoffrey Bell's backyard. For the second time in less than an hour, she questioned her sanity.

"Let me get this straight," Mary Beth said. She sat across from the home invader at a small table in the kitchen. "You've done all this with two rocks and a key?"

Mark nodded.

"The rocks activate the tunnel downstairs. The key opens the exterior door from the outside. I was about to use the key when I ran into you."

Mary Beth smiled as she revisited the encounter in the stairway. She had not believed for a minute that Mark was from 1959, but she had let him enter the basement anyway because she believed him to be harmless and in need of help. Now that she was sitting in a venue that tested even her fertile imagination, she did not know what to believe.

"I'm sorry for startling you," Mary Beth said.

"That's all right, Miss—"

Mary Beth extended a hand.

"I'm Mary Beth McIntire. It's nice to meet you, Mark Ryan."

Mark shook her hand.

"It's nice to meet you too."

Mary Beth paused to inspect her surroundings. She recognized the kitchen but almost none of its trappings. The table was different. So were the oven, the refrigerator, and cabinets. Pastel pink had replaced stainless steel. A percolator and a blender stood in place of an espresso machine and a toaster. Fancier paper covered the walls.

Mary Beth had noticed other things as well. The heavenly basement she had explored in 2017 was now a dingy dump. The living room and the dining room sported furniture from *Leave It to Beaver* and *Father Knows Best*. Bright sunshine spilled through clear windows. A black telephone with a rotary dial sat atop a counter.

"Where are the rocks?" Mary Beth asked.

"Right here," Mark said.

He reached into his pants pockets, retrieved two colorless crystals, and put them on the table next to a skeleton key. Each rock was three inches long.

Mary Beth picked up one of the stones, held it up to the overhead light, and then placed it beside its twin. She tapped her fingers on the Formica tabletop as she thought of something to say. She still was not convinced this wasn't a dream brought on by undercooked food.

"How did you know about the rocks and the tunnel?" Mary Beth asked.

Mark reached into his shirt pocket and pulled out a folded sheet.

"I read this. It's a letter from Percival Bell, the man who built this house, to his wife."

"May I see it?"

Mark nodded and handed Mary Beth the letter.

"He intended to travel to June 2, 2017, but I'm pretty sure he never did. I found the letter, the crystals, and the key in a locked drawer upstairs."

Mary Beth read the letter.

"I've heard of this man," she said. "He was the great-grandfather of the professor who invited my family here. Geoffrey Bell, our host, said that Percival died of a stroke only a few months after moving into this place. I'll bet he died right after writing this letter."

"That makes sense," Mark said.

Mary Beth glanced again at the letter.

"It says here that you need only one crystal to make the tunnel work."

Mark nodded.

"I haven't tested Percival Bell's claim, but I have no reason to believe it's false. I took both crystals just in case I needed them."

Mary Beth smiled sheepishly.

"Can I have one?"

Mark put a hand to his chin and studied her.

"Can I trust you?"

"No," Mary Beth said.

Both of them laughed.

"In that case, take one," Mark said.

Mary Beth grabbed one of the rocks and placed it in a pocket. She felt conspicuously underdressed in a crimson University of Alabama T-shirt, yoga pants, and flip-flops.

"Thank you," she said.

"You're welcome."

Mary Beth gazed at her new friend and noticed that he was not just kind and humble. He was also strikingly handsome. He had thick brown hair, brushed up in a pompadour, and a chiseled, shaven, boyish face that would turn heads in any century.

"Has anyone ever told you that you look like a young Warren Beatty?"

"Who's Warren Beatty?" Mark asked.

Mary Beth laughed.

"He's a famous actor. Or at least he *will* be a famous actor."

Mark took a breath.

"You probably know a lot of things about the next fifty-eight years."

Mary Beth nodded at Mark and then glanced at the newspaper. She noted headlines that seemed torn from a history text. Nikita Khrushchev had fired one of his advisors. China's Red Army had put down a rebellion in Tibet. California was preparing to play West Virginia in the title game of the NCAA men's basketball tournament.

"How much do *you* know about the future?" Mary Beth asked.

"I know almost nothing," Mark said. He reached under his shirt, pulled out a magazine, and placed it on the table. "That's why I bought this. I wanted to read about the future."

Mary Beth picked up the periodical, a special edition that touted its news coverage between 1942 and 2017, and quickly flipped through its pages. She noted a dog-eared page that featured photos and information on the Apollo program, the moon landings, and the space shuttle. She slid the open magazine across the table.

"I see you like rockets," Mary Beth said.

"I hope to build them someday," Mark replied. "I'll graduate with an engineering degree in a few weeks and hope to find a job at the Jet Propulsion Laboratory or another research facility. My dad worked at JPL until he died last fall."

Mary Beth looked at him thoughtfully.

"I'm sorry to hear that. Do you have any other family?"

Mark nodded.

"I still have my mom and a brother. Mom is in Fresno for the next several days. My brother, Ben, is upstairs sleeping. This is our spring break."

"Do you attend the university?" Mary Beth asked.

"I do. I live there most of the time too. I come home on weekends to look after my mother and do odds and ends around the house."

"Have you lived here long?"

Mark shook his head.

"We moved in three months ago. Mom thought about selling the place after my dad died, but she decided to keep it. This was their dream home.

She wanted to hold onto the dream even if she couldn't share it with my father."

"I see."

"What about you? Do you really attend the University of Alabama?"

"I used to," Mary Beth said.

"I figured as much from your shirt and your accent," Mark said. "I don't hear southern accents around here very often. It's pretty."

"Thank you."

Mary Beth blushed. She didn't know whether he was sincere or simply trying to weasel something out of her, but she accepted his compliment at face value. She liked compliments. She hadn't received many from handsome young men since that awful night in Tuscaloosa.

"So you *used* to attend Alabama," Mark said. "Does that mean you graduated?"

Mary Beth nodded.

"I graduated a few weeks ago – or fifty-eight years from now," she said with a laugh. "I'm still trying to get a handle on this time-travel thing."

"That makes two of us."

Mary Beth smiled.

"That's good to know. If I'm going to lose my mind, I would at least like some company."

Mark laughed and shook his head. Then he took a closer look at his new acquaintance. It was clear from his puzzled eyes that *he* still had a lot of questions.

"Did you say you were a guest in this house in 2017?" Mark asked.

"I did."

"So are you on vacation?"

"I am," Mary Beth said. "We are. My parents brought my sister and me to Los Angeles as sort of a graduation present. My sister, Piper, graduated from high school about a week ago."

"Do you live in Alabama?" Mark asked.

Mary Beth nodded.

"We live in Huntsville. That's in the northern—"

"I know where it is," Mark said. "The Army develops missiles there."

Mary Beth beamed.

"What a coincidence. So does my father."

"Your dad develops missiles?" Mark asked.

"He does. He's done a lot of things."

"What do you mean?"

"I mean he's worked on everything from ground-based interceptor missiles to a new space launch system," Mary Beth said. "He retired from the Army as a colonel five years ago and now works full-time for NASA."

"What's NASA?"

34

"It's the National Aeronautics and Space Administration."

"I've never heard of it," Mark said. "Maybe it's new."

Mary Beth smiled.

"It isn't where I come from."

"I feel really stupid," Mark said.

"You shouldn't. You just don't have the benefit of hindsight," Mary Beth said. She looked at him closely. "I'm sure you're very smart – smart enough, in fact, to answer a question that's been on my mind since you brought me here."

"What's that?"

"Will these rocks enable me to go back to June 2, 2017, as if I had never left?"

Mark nodded.

"I think so. I've only traveled to the future twice, but on both occasions I exited the tunnel around eight in the morning. I think the time machine is set to a particular date and time."

"That reminds me of a movie I once saw," Mary Beth said.

"Oh?"

Mary Beth nodded.

"The main character, a TV weatherman, checked into a motel on Groundhog Day and kept repeating the day over and over. Every day was February 2 and began at six o'clock."

Mark laughed.

"That sounds like a nightmare."

Mary Beth smiled.

"He thought it was."

"I'm pretty sure you're safe from a similar fate," Mark said. "Even if you go back to June 2, 2017, you won't have to repeat the day over and over."

"That's a relief," Mary Beth said. She paused for a moment. "Does the time machine work the same way on return trips? Did you return to a fixed time?"

"No. I didn't," Mark said. "I came back to the time I left. I left the house – and March 21, 1959 – about seven fifteen the first time and eight o'clock the second."

Mary Beth laughed.

"I think this is where my head explodes."

Mark smiled.

"I don't understand it either. I just know I need at least one of the crystals in my possession to travel to the future and the key to access the outside door."

Mary Beth started to say something but stopped when she heard footsteps in the hallway. She glanced at the entry just as a younger version of Mark walked into the kitchen.

The new arrival yawned, rubbed his eyes, and tightened the belt of his bathrobe. Then he turned his attention to the people at the table and stared at Mary Beth.

"Who are you?" Ben Ryan asked. He looked at his brother. "Who is *this*?"

Mark chuckled.

"This is Mary Beth McIntire. She's a visitor."

Ben gave his brother a look of annoyance.

"I can see that," Ben said. He looked at Mary Beth again and then at Mark. "Why is she here on a Saturday morning? Is she your newest girlfriend or something?"

Mary Beth noted the word "newest," smiled at Mark, and then looked at Ben. She couldn't help but notice that the brothers had sharply differing temperaments.

"She's just a visitor," Mark said. He turned back to his new acquaintance. "Mary Beth, this is Ben, my brother. He's not always this way around people. He just needs some coffee."

"Hi, Ben," Mary Beth said.

Ben looked at her shirt.

"Are you from Alabama?"

Mary Beth nodded.

"Then how did you meet my brother?" Ben asked.

Mary Beth giggled.

"He tried to break into my house."

Ben glared at his sibling.

"What's going on, Mark? Don't mess with me."

"I won't," Mark said. "I'll tell it to you straight."

"Huh?"

Mark smiled.

"Take a seat, Ben. We have a lot to talk about."

7: MARK

Thirty minutes and a dozen questions later, Mark walked out of the kitchen, pulled a light jacket from a nearby closet, and returned to the others. He put on the jacket, pushed in his chair, and looked at Mary Beth.

"Are you ready to go?" Mark asked.

"I'm ready," Mary Beth said.

"Can I come too?" Ben asked.

Mark shook his head.

"I want you to stay."

"Why?"

"I want to test a theory, that's why," Mark said. "Take a shower. Get dressed. Eat breakfast. Make coffee. Or, better yet, stay put. Just don't follow us."

"That's not fair," Ben said.

"It may not be fair, but it's what I want you to do. If my theory is correct, we'll be back in less than a minute. Then you can do whatever you want. OK?"

Ben huffed.

"OK."

Mark glanced at the kitchen clock and then at his watch, which had never stopped running. He set the watch to the time on the clock.

"Is anything wrong?" Mary Beth asked.

"No," Mark said. "I'm just getting my bearings. I'm pretty sure it's nine o'clock."

Mary Beth smiled.

"It's eight where I come from, mister."

Mark laughed.

"I suppose it is. Shall I set my watch again?"

"No," Mary Beth said. She giggled. "We're confused enough."

"I agree. Let's go."

Mark waited for Mary Beth to pass and then followed her into a hallway, through a door, and down the stone stairs to the basement. A minute later, the two passed through the tunnel, opened the outer door, and walked up the brick steps to the backyard and the morning of June 2, 2017.

Mark followed Mary Beth to a spot in the middle of the lawn, stopped, and then took a moment to assess his new friend. She was kind, he thought, and incredibly open-minded for someone who had been asked to believe the impossible on short notice. With long brown hair, blue eyes, a button nose, and a dash of freckles, she was also very pretty. Mark pondered his good fortune until a soft voice pierced the moist air and brought him back to the present.

"What do we do now?" Mary Beth asked. She looked at the mansion and then at Mark. "We can't go back through the tunnel. We'll just end up where we started."

"I know," Mark said. "We have to go through the front."

"What if the door is locked? I'm pretty sure it's locked."

"Isn't your family in the house?"

"My sister is," Mary Beth said. "She's sleeping upstairs."

Mark smiled.

"Then it's time to wake her up."

"I was afraid you would say that."

The two walked in a light rain to the front gate, the one Mark had accessed on his second trip to 2017, and passed through unnoticed. No women talked or laughed on the sidewalk directly in front of the Painted Lady. No neighbors peeked out their doors or windows.

Mark followed Mary Beth around a sleek Ford in the driveway and up a dozen brick steps to an imposing front door that hadn't changed much in nearly six decades. He smiled at Mary Beth when they stopped on the small porch and looked at each other.

"I'll let you do the honors since I haven't met your sister."

Mary Beth stared at him.

"Thanks."

She rang the doorbell and waited for someone to stir. No one did.

"Is she a heavy sleeper?" Mark asked.

Mary Beth nodded.

"She once slept through a war movie at a theater."

Mark laughed.

"Are you kidding?"

Mary Beth shook her head.

"She values sleep as much as food."

Mary Beth rang the bell again. Silence followed.

Mark smiled.

"Maybe she went for a walk."

Mary Beth glared at the joker.

"I don't think so."

She rang the bell a third time.

Mark listened for noises within the house and this time heard some. He heard a door slam and someone walk through the hallway toward the front door. He grinned.

"Sleeping Beauty has risen."

"Try the bride of Frankenstein," Mary Beth said.

Mark started to laugh but stopped when a young woman, wearing a pink bathrobe and long brown hair tied in a ponytail, opened the door. The girl looked a lot like Mary Beth and even Sleeping Beauty, but she wore the scowl of Frankenstein's bride.

"Did you forget your key?" Piper McIntire asked.

"I did," Mary Beth said. "I went for a walk and locked myself out."

Piper gave Mark the once over and then looked at her sister.

"Who is this?"

Mary Beth smiled.

"This is Mark Ryan. He's a movie extra I met on my walk."

Mark laughed.

"It's too early for jokes," Piper said to her sister. She turned around and started to walk away. "Shut the door behind you. I'm going back to bed."

"Piper?" Mary Beth asked.

Piper turned around.

"What?"

"Stick around for a minute," Mary Beth said.

"Why?"

"We want to talk to you."

Piper glared at her sibling.

"I'm tired and grumpy, Mary Beth. I don't want to do anything but sleep."

"Trust me," Mary Beth said. "You *want* to hear what we have to say."

Piper put her hands on her hips.

"You have ten minutes."

Mary Beth smiled.

"We'll only need five."

8: PIPER

Friday, June 2, 2017

Piper muttered to herself as she followed Mary Beth and the movie extra around the front of the Painted Lady to a gate, the backyard, and a stairway that led to the basement.

She did not want to traipse around the grounds in her bathrobe. She did not want to visit. She wanted to sleep. She had agreed to put off that sleep only after Mary Beth had made a fantastic claim and offered to pay Piper a hundred dollars if she could not *prove* that claim.

Mark led Mary Beth and Piper down the stairs, opened a door with a skeleton key, and then led the sisters into a dark, gloomy, tunnel-like chamber. A moment later, Mark shut the door, leaned against a wall, and looked at Piper as a string of overhead lights started to flicker.

"This will only take a few seconds," Mark said.

Piper stared at Mary Beth.

"I want the money before lunch."

Mary Beth smiled.

"You haven't earned it yet."

"I think we're good to go," Mark said. He opened the inner door, stepped into the basement, and flipped on some lights. "Please enter, ladies."

Piper followed Mary Beth into a basement that looked nothing like the one she had seen when Jeanette Bell had given her a tour of the mansion. The room had a concrete floor, hanging light bulbs, and drab, unpainted walls. It did not feature wall-to-wall white carpeting, two large sofas, and a glass-and-brass coffee table. Talk about a reverse makeover.

Piper felt a knot form in her stomach as she followed Mark and Mary Beth through the basement and up some primitive steps to the main floor of the residence. She felt the knot tighten when she stepped into a hallway and noticed even more changes.

"This way," Mark said.

Piper picked up her step as she approached what she knew to be the mansion's kitchen. She did not know what surprises awaited at the end of the hallway, but for the first time since walking out the front door, she suspected that Mary Beth was going to keep her money.

A few seconds later, Piper McIntire, a young woman of sound mind, stepped into a kitchen that looked like the set of a 1950s sitcom. She stopped when Mark and Mary Beth stopped and turned their attention to a young man seated at a small table. Like Piper, the boy wore a bathrobe. Like Piper, he looked like he needed at least another hour of quality sleep.

"Piper, this is my brother, Ben. He's a high school senior," Mark said. "Ben, this is Piper McIntire, Mary Beth's sister and a recent high school graduate."

Ben stared at Piper for several seconds but did not say a thing. He seemed as perplexed by the situation and the sudden turn of events as his teenage counterpart.

Piper looked at Mark and then at Mary Beth. She found a thoughtful expression on the former's face and an I-told-you-so smile on the latter's.

"Is this a joke?" Piper asked.

"It's no joke. At least I don't think it is," Mary Beth said. She walked to the table, picked up a newspaper, and handed it to her sister. "Look at the date."

Piper felt her head lighten as she scanned headlines with crazy words like "Khrushchev" and "Communist." This was a dream, she thought. This was her subconscious playing a trick. This was a sign that, at the tender age of eighteen, she was going insane.

She appealed again to Mary Beth.

"Will you please tell me what's going on?" Piper asked.

"I already have," Mary Beth said. "We've traveled to the past. We're standing in the same house we've occupied for a week. We're just doing it in 1959."

Piper closed her eyes for a moment and tried to process the unusual start to her morning. She had wanted to do something different and exciting on her California escape. Now, on the second-to-last-day of that escape, it appeared as though the vacation gods had granted her wish.

Piper glanced at the newspaper in her hands and tried again to make sense of the date, the headlines, and the photos of people with goofy haircuts. She looked at Mark.

"Can I keep this?"

"Be my guest," Mark said. "I've already read it."

"Thanks."

41

No one in the room said anything more for nearly thirty seconds, which Piper considered a blessing. She wanted to think this over in blessed silence. She needed time to ponder what she had seen and what two strange men and her normally levelheaded sister believed was real.

Mark finally broke the quietude. He stepped forward, placed a hand on his brother's shoulder, and said something that made no sense.

"It looks like you haven't done much since we left."

"How could I?" Ben asked. "You left a minute ago."

Mark looked at the clock and smiled.

"Thanks for confirming my suspicions."

"What suspicions?" Piper asked. "What are you talking about?"

Mark turned to Piper.

"Your sister and I returned to the same moment we left in 1959. Even though we spent fifteen minutes walking around the property and talking to you in 2017, we came back to the exact same time we left. Time stood still, as I thought it would," Mark said. He looked at Mary Beth, who returned his smile. "That opens up a whole new world of possibilities."

"What do you mean?" Piper asked.

"I mean the four of us are in a great position to spice up our vacations. Ben and I can travel to 2017 and return as if we had never left 1959. You and Mary Beth can do just the opposite. You can do anything you want."

Piper looked at Mary Beth.

"Is he serious?"

Mary Beth nodded.

"I don't like this," Ben said.

"What's the matter?" Mark asked.

"What's the *matter*? I'll tell you what's the matter. You've had fun all morning. I've done nothing but walk around in my bathrobe while you drag girls into the house."

Mark laughed.

"Is that your way of saying that you want in?"

"You're damn right," Ben said. "I want to do something today besides mow the lawn and study for my algebra exam. I want to see 2017. I want to see the future."

Piper glanced at Mark and Mary Beth and saw them exchange knowing smiles.

"I think we can arrange that," Mark said to Ben.

Mary Beth stepped forward and looked at everyone.

"I know we can," she said.

9: BEN

Hollywood, California – Friday, June 2, 2017

Ben laughed to himself as he recalled the day his father had taken him to lunch at an outdoor café in a rough part of Los Angeles. He had been fifteen at the time and completely clueless about how other Californians, particularly much poorer ones, lived.

"Keep your eyes peeled and your ear to the ground," Ted Ryan had said before they started their meal. "You can learn a lot about the world by watching and listening."

Sitting with Mark, Mary Beth, and Piper at an outdoor table at Wanda's of West Hollywood, a bakery and coffee shop, he couldn't disagree. He had learned more about the twenty-first century in eighteen minutes than he had the twentieth century in eighteen years.

Dogs in 2017 wore more clothes than their human handlers. Joggers weaved between cars in the light drizzle. People of the same gender held hands and kissed. Some pedestrians spoke into strange devices attached to their ears. Others played with gadgets the size of cigarette packs. Many sported nose rings and tattoos. One man showed off a new dress.

"You seem a bit preoccupied, Ben," Mary Beth said in a playful voice. She smiled. "Are you getting your fill of the future?"

Ben looked at Mary Beth. She sat next to Piper and opposite Mark at a sidewalk table in front of the establishment.

"I'm getting my fill of something," Ben said. "That's for sure."

Mark laughed.

"I have to agree with my brother. Life is different here. It's a lot different."

Mary Beth stared at Mark.

"Different doesn't mean worse."

"You're right," Mark said. "It doesn't."

Ben looked across the table. He wanted to see whether Piper had an opinion on the matter and was mildly disappointed to see that she did not. She tapped on one of the cigarette-pack-sized gadgets her sister had called a cell phone.

"What are you doing?" Ben asked.

"It's none of your business," Piper said.

"Are you always this rude?"

"No. Sometimes I'm ruder."

"That's good," Ben said. "I would hate to see your rudest side."

Piper looked up.

"If you must know, Mr. Ryan, I'm sending a text message. I'm telling my supervisor that I won't be able to work until Tuesday."

"What do you do?"

Piper shot Ben a pointed glance.

"I'm a lifeguard at the Madison County Aquatic Center. It's in Huntsville, Alabama, where I live when I'm not chilling with boys from the fifties."

Mary Beth turned her head.

"Knock it off, Piper."

Piper looked at Ben with softer eyes.

"I'm sorry. I'm not very nice until I've had at least three cups of coffee."

"Oh," Ben said. He laughed. "Can I get you another cup?"

"No, thank you. I think I'm set."

Ben watched Piper as she sipped some coffee and returned to her phone. He wasn't sure what to make of the spirited young woman, who had mostly ignored him, but he had seen and heard enough of her to conclude three things. She was intelligent, temperamental, and gorgeous.

He took a bite out of a pastry and sipped his own coffee. Each of the four had ordered a pastry and a cup of French roast. Piper had ordered a large cup.

Mark had offered to pay for the order until he discovered that he did not have enough cash in his wallet to do so. He had been shocked to discover that a simple cup of coffee was twenty times the price he was used to paying. Mary Beth bailed him out by producing a piece of plastic she called a debit card and handing it to the cashier.

Ben looked at Mark and Mary Beth, who talked quietly, and then at Piper, who tapped her phone a few times and tucked it in her purse. He watched with interest as she lowered her purse to the ground, sipped some coffee, and returned his gaze.

"Are you ever going to talk to me?" Ben asked.

"I haven't decided," Piper said.

"Why is that? Don't you find me interesting?"

"Oh, I find you interesting. You're a little *too* interesting."

44

"What's that supposed to mean?" Ben asked.

"It means, Ben Ryan, if that's your name, that I'm not totally convinced you're from the fifties. I'm not convinced that Professor Bell's home is not some sort of funhouse," Piper said. "I'm not convinced that someone or something is not playing a practical joke on me."

"Are you serious?"

"I'm very serious."

Mark and Mary Beth stopped talking.

"You don't believe we're from the fifties?" Mark asked Piper.

"I don't know what to believe," Piper said. "I can't explain what I saw at the mansion. I know only that it's easier to believe that you're pulling a prank than it is to believe in time travel."

Mark looked at Mary Beth.

"Do you feel the same way?"

Mary Beth blushed.

"Don't answer," Mark said. "I can see that you do."

Mary Beth put her hand on Mark's arm.

"I *want* to believe. I want to believe time travel is possible, even if my father, a physicist, says it is not. I just don't know whether I can trust my senses. People can create illusions. They can create a lot of things. This is Hollywood, after all."

"Then why are you spending time with me?" Mark asked.

"I'm spending time with you because you're nice and interesting."

Ben looked at Piper and saw her flash a self-satisfied smile. He had no doubt she found *him* mean and boring.

Mark sighed.

"What would it take to convince you we're real? What can we say or do to convince you that you really did travel through time and that 1959 is just a glowing tunnel away?"

Mary Beth offered a sheepish smile.

"I suppose we could see more of your world."

"Be specific," Mark said.

"We could walk around the neighborhood or drive around the city," Mary Beth said. "We could even take a road trip to someplace like San Diego or Las Vegas."

"We could."

Mary Beth tilted her head and looked at Mark thoughtfully.

"I don't need much proof."

Mark nodded.

"OK then. Let's do it."

"Let's do what?" Ben asked.

"Let's take a road trip. Let's go to Las Vegas," Mark said. "I'm sure we could find a lot of interesting things to do there."

Piper stared at Mark.

"We have parents coming back at six, Mark. We don't have time to run off to Vegas or San Diego or any other place. We have to pack for our return trip. We leave on Sunday."

"You still can," Mark said. "I thought I made that clear. You and Mary Beth can spend as much time as you want in 1959 and return to 2017 as if you had never been gone."

Mary Beth turned to Piper. She looked at her sister with pleading eyes.

"You haven't had fun all week," Mary Beth said. "Let's change that. Let's *have* some fun. Let's do something crazy!"

Ben laughed. He wondered if the girls could do anything crazier in the next day than he had done in the last hour. Then he looked at the street and decided they probably couldn't.

"OK," Piper said. "I still think there's a chance these two are putting us on, but I'll go. I want to see if there's more to that mansion than smoke and mirrors."

"Then it's set," Mark said. "Let's go back to the house, pack a bag or two, clean up, and take off. We left 1959 at nine thirty in the morning. We could be on the road by ten."

Ben looked at his brother.

"Where are we getting the money to take this trip?"

"I have money," Mark said.

"You have a hundred bucks in your dresser drawer. You told me that the other day. That's not enough to go to Vegas, Mark. At least it's not enough to have fun."

"We'll manage."

Mary Beth looked at the brothers.

"There's no need to manage anything. I have money. I can help out."

"You're forgetting something," Mark said. "Your debit card is no good in 1959. Neither is your cash. I've seen the currency here. It's different. The last thing any of us want to do is go to jail for passing what merchants will consider counterfeit bills."

"You're right," Mary Beth said.

"Don't feel bad. I appreciate the offer. We'll just do something else."

Mary Beth turned away and looked at a bookstore across the street. She stared at the store for several seconds. When she looked again at Mark, she did so with lively eyes.

"There's no need to do something else."

"I don't follow," Mark said.

Mary Beth grinned.

"I just thought of a way to make money."

10: PIPER

Baker, California – Saturday, March 21, 1959

Piper needed only five minutes to realize that Mark and Ben Ryan did not work for a movie studio or the producer of a new *Candid Camera*. Not even two enterprising brothers could give a city the size of Los Angeles a complete 1950s makeover.

She thought about her conversion from skeptic to believer as she stared out the right rear window of Mark's 1958 Edsel Citation and gazed at the arid fields along Route 91. She would no longer be quite as eager to dismiss fantastic claims out of hand or staunchly defend the laws of physics. Nothing, she thought, was impossible.

Piper directed her eyes to the front of the car and saw Mark and Mary Beth talk and laugh like they had been friends for years and not acquaintances for hours. She was happy to see her sister finally emerge from her self-imposed social exile.

"Mary Beth?" Piper asked.

Mary Beth peered over her left shoulder.

"Yes?"

"Are you ever going to tell me what you bought at the bookstore?"

Mary Beth smiled.

"I bought books."

Piper looked at Ben and shook her head.

"I asked a simple question."

Ben laughed and then resumed looking out his window.

Piper returned to Mary Beth.

"Well? Are you going to tell me what *books* you bought?"

Mary Beth nodded.

"I'll do better than that. I'll show you."

Mary Beth leaned forward, ruffled through a paper bag, and retrieved three thin paperback books. She turned around and handed them to her sister.

Piper placed the books on her lap. She thumbed through *Marilyn: Her Life in Letters, Old Las Vegas,* and *Sports Champions from 1876 to 2016.*

"Why did you buy these?" Piper asked.

Mary Beth shifted in her seat so that she could see the occupants in back without straining her neck. She looked at Ben and then Piper.

"I bought the first book to learn about my favorite actress and the second to learn about our destination."

"What about the third book?"

Mary Beth grinned.

"I bought it to finance our trip."

"What?" Piper asked.

"I'm betting on the Bears tonight. California plays West Virginia in the final of the NCAA men's basketball tournament. I know who wins."

"You're insane."

Mary Beth laughed.

"I like to think of myself as imaginative."

"Where are you going to make the bet?" Ben asked.

"I hope to make it at a turf club," Mary Beth said. "Your brother says there are dozens in Las Vegas and that most take sports bets."

Ben leaned forward and tapped Mark's shoulder.

"How do you know that?"

"I'm in college, remember? That's the kind of thing you learn in college," Mark said. He looked over his right shoulder and smiled. "You'll learn things in college too."

Piper laughed. She didn't doubt that. People learned all sorts of things in college. They got in all sorts of trouble. It was one reason she looked forward to her freshman year at Tennessee.

Piper handed the books back to Mary Beth and settled into her seat as the chatty couple in front went back to chatting. She thought about the books, Las Vegas, and college for several minutes before turning her attention to the mystery man at her left.

Ben had not returned to staring blankly out his window. He rested his chin on his hand and gazed at Piper in a way that made her uncomfortable.

"Why are you staring at me?" Piper asked.

"I'm not staring," Ben said. He grinned. "I'm observing."

"Well, observe something else. I don't like it when people stare at me."

Ben laughed but didn't say anything.

Piper turned away and pulled her cell phone from her purse. She flipped it on, tapped a few buttons, and accessed an app. She decided she would much rather complete a crossword puzzle than talk to Eddie Haskell.

"What are you doing?" Ben asked.

"I'm playing a game," Piper said.

"I thought that was a telephone."

"It is. It's a telephone loaded with games."

"What else does it have?"

Piper looked up from the phone and glared at Ben.

"It has a lot of things."

"Does it contain a lot of numbers?" Ben asked.

"It does."

"Does it contain a lot of numbers from *boys*?"

"That's none of your business," Piper said.

"Sure it is. I need to know what I'm up against."

"Dream on."

"You like me," Ben said. "I know you do."

"You presume a lot."

"What's your phone number?"

"Why? Are you going to call me?"

"I might."

Piper laughed.

"If you could manage that in 1959, I might answer your call."

Ben fixed his gaze on Piper.

"I'm serious though. What's your number?"

Piper told him.

"That's amazing," Ben said.

"What's amazing?"

"Your number is my birth date."

"That's impossible," Piper said. "My number has ten digits."

"You misunderstand. The last seven digits are my birth date," Ben said. "The area code – 256 – is the number of girls I've dated in high school."

Piper shook her head.

"You, sir, are insufferable."

Ben grinned.

"I try."

"Is he always this way?" Piper asked Mark.

Mark laughed.

"Yes."

Piper looked at Ben.

"You're exaggerating. I'll bet you don't have even one girlfriend."

Ben nodded matter-of-factly.

"You're half right. I am exaggerating. I have only five girlfriends – six if you count Doris Mayes. She's been sweet on me since ninth grade, but I haven't asked her out."

"You're a throwback," Piper said.

"Do you think five is too many?"

"Yes. I think one is plenty for anyone."

"How many boyfriends do you have?" Ben asked.

"That's none of your business."

"So the answer is none."

Piper pouted.

"I'm between significant others now."

"That's all right," Ben said. "It happens to everyone … except me."

Mary Beth laughed.

"It sounds like you have a live one back there, Piper."

Piper folded her arms.

"I'm taking a bus back to Los Angeles."

Ben smiled.

"You can't do that. You don't have any money."

"I'll steal some," Piper said. "I would rather risk jail than sit next to you in a car."

"Are you sure about that?"

"I'm positive."

"What if I offered to give you a ride in *my* car?" Ben asked.

"I would decline."

"What if I told you my car was a Thunderbird?"

Piper unfolded her arms.

"You drive a T-Bird?"

"I *own* a T-Bird," Ben said. "I own a red 1959 Ford Thunderbird convertible with whitewall tires, a 300-horsepower V8 engine, and leather upholstery."

"He's not rich," Mark said to Piper. "He just spent his share of Dad's life insurance money on a car rather than on college or something sensible."

"Dad would have approved," Ben said. "You know it."

Piper tried to make sense of it all but couldn't. She sighed, cocked her head, and looked at Ben as if he were the strangest thing on earth.

"Let me get this straight. You have a 1959 Thunderbird – a convertible, no less – and the four of us are driving to Vegas in an Edsel?"

Ben nodded and laughed.

"My car is in the shop."

11: MARY BETH

Las Vegas, Nevada

Mary Beth had seen Sin City a hundred times in her twenty-two years. She had seen it on television, in theaters, and even on postcards, but until Mark drove his Edsel down Las Vegas Boulevard on an unseasonably warm afternoon in 1959, she had never seen it in person.

She looked out her closed window and saw casinos, hotels, shops, and services that appeared torn from a flickering home movie. She marveled at the seemingly endless stream of props that welcomed visitors to the city.

A thirty-five-foot sultan straddled the entrance to the Dunes. A giant, blinking, rotating shoe spun in front of the Silver Slipper. A menacing raptor, perched atop a large neon sign, greeted motorists and pedestrians as they approached the Thunderbird.

Mary Beth pondered the possibilities as she admired the signs and marquees. She could see Johnny Mathis at the Sands, the McGuire sisters at the Desert Inn, or Le Lido de Paris, "the world's greatest floor show," at the Stardust. Or she could talk the others into dining, dancing, and exploring the Strip. They might like that. She knew she would.

"What are you thinking?" Mark asked.

"I'm thinking about what I want to do tonight. We have so many options," Mary Beth said. She looked at the driver. "What do *you* want to do?"

Mark turned his head.

"I don't know. We still have time to decide. What we *don't* have is time to find a turf club. The game starts in less than an hour in Louisville. We need to place a bet soon."

Mary Beth scanned the road ahead.

"Do you know where we can?"

Mark nodded.

"There's at least one club a few blocks away."

Mary Beth looked over her shoulder and saw that the combatants in back had not warmed to each other. Ben stared blankly out the left window, Piper out the right. Neither had said more than a few words since bickering over significant others and seating assignments.

"Are you two ever going to enjoy yourselves?" Mary Beth asked.

"I'm enjoying myself," Piper said. "I'm just not enjoying *him*."

Mary Beth glanced at Ben and saw him laugh quietly. She felt sorry for any boy who drew a sword against her sister. He had no idea what he was getting into.

"Can I trust you children to get along while Mark and I place a bet?" Mary Beth asked. "I'm pretty sure they won't let you in unless you're twenty-one."

"You can trust me," Piper said.

Mary Beth looked at the hapless male in back.

"Ben?"

"I'll be fine," Ben said. "Have fun."

Mary Beth laughed to herself. She didn't believe either one. She turned around and directed her attention to the street ahead just as Mark slowed down and pulled up to a curb.

"Are we here?" Mary Beth asked.

"We're here," Mark said.

Mary Beth looked at the club – a hole-in-the-wall tucked between a cigar shop and a café on Fremont Street – and wondered if they had come to the right place. Then she remembered something she had read in *Old Las Vegas*. Turf clubs in the 1950s were not casinos. They were low-profile businesses that operated independently from the gaming establishments and provided a service made possible by an act of Congress in 1951.

Mark turned off the ignition, set the brake, and got out of the Edsel. He stopped for a few seconds to let a taxicab pass, walked around the back of his car to the passenger side, and opened the door. He offered a hand to Mary Beth and gently helped her out of her seat.

Mary Beth appreciated the gesture. She couldn't remember the last time a man had done that. Even Jordan hadn't done that. He had opened restaurant doors and store doors for her all the time, but he had never opened her car door. This was, Mary Beth thought, a different time.

She joined Mark on the sidewalk and then took a moment to smooth the wrinkles from a jumper dress she had purchased in 2017. Even in cutting-edge, twenty-first-century Hollywood, a woman could buy something to wear in the 1950s.

Mary Beth and Piper had purchased two outfits each and planned to buy more clothes if their sojourn to the past extended beyond the weekend. Both had wanted to keep their options open.

"Are you ready?" Mark asked.

"I'm ready," Mary Beth said.

"Are you sure about the score?"

"I'm positive. Cal wins 71-70."

"Then I'll let you do the honors."

Mark retrieved his wallet, pulled out a crisp hundred-dollar bill, and handed it to the woman in the light blue dress. He had saved the bill just for this moment.

"What do I do when we go in?" Mary Beth asked.

"Just tell the clerk what *you* want to do," Mark said. "He'll take it from there."

"OK."

Mark nodded, placed a hand on Mary Beth's back, and then escorted her into a shop called the Fourth Quarter. The two walked through a narrow lobby and finally entered a main room that looked more like an 1800s saloon than a 1900s bookmaking operation.

Mary Beth smiled as she assessed the place. Sawdust and scraps of paper coated the concrete floor like snowflakes on a northern Alabama lawn. Names and numbers, representing teams and odds, covered a large blackboard bolted to a wall. The smell of stale beer, cigar smoke, and sweat assaulted Mary Beth's nostrils. She longed for the air conditioning of the car.

Mary Beth examined the blackboard, noted the betting options for the title game of the NCAA men's basketball tournament, and stepped toward a counter, where a short, plump, balding man read a newspaper and smoked a cigar. Mark followed close behind.

"Excuse me, sir," Mary Beth said. "Are you the person who handles bets?"

The man looked up and placed his cigar on a tray.

"I'm Jimmy Smith, the owner. What can I do for you?"

"I'd like to bet on the game."

"What game? Be specific."

Mary Beth looked at Mark, saw a smile, and then returned to the owner.

"I want to bet on the basketball game tonight between California and West Virginia."

Jimmy pushed the paper away.

"Do you want to pick a winner, guess the over-under, or bet on the point spread?"

Mary Beth grinned.

"I want to bet on the game. I believe Cal is going to win 71-70 and want to bet a hundred dollars on that *specific* outcome."

Mary Beth glanced again at Mark. She expected to see another supportive smile but instead saw a look of concern. Had she said something wrong? Had she overreached?

Jimmy studied Mary Beth, shook his head, and chuckled.

"Have you been drinking today?"

"No," Mary Beth said. She glared at the man. "I'm as sober as a judge."

The owner looked at Mark.

"Is she your girlfriend, mister? If she is, you might want to teach her a thing or two about beating impossible odds. She has a better chance at winning the Irish Sweepstakes than picking the exact score of tonight's game."

Mark looked at Mary Beth and then addressed the wise guy.

"I believe the lady wants to make a wager," Mark said with an edge in his voice. "Why don't you do your job and honor her request?"

Mary Beth smiled when she glanced at the man who had her back, but she frowned when she saw two others follow the exchange from the far end of the long counter. The first onlooker, a bald man who resembled the owner, smirked at Mary Beth. The second onlooker, a tall man with a badly deformed left ear, studied her quietly.

Jimmy stared at Mark and then at Mary Beth.

"OK. It's your money. If you want to throw it away, I'll accommodate you. I'll give you twenty-to-one odds on a 71-70 California victory."

"She's betting a hundred dollars on the score itself," Mark said in a testy voice. "Is twenty-to-one really the best you can do?"

"It's the best I *will* do," Jimmy said.

Mark looked at Mary Beth.

"You don't have to do this."

"I want to do it," Mary Beth said. She returned to Jimmy. "What do I have to do?"

The owner fixed his gaze on the lady.

"You have to fill out a form and give me a hundred bucks."

"I can do that."

Jimmy reached under the counter, retrieved a pad and a pen, and placed them on top of the counter. He slid both items toward the lady gambler, folded his arms, and waited.

Mary Beth peeled the top sheet from the pad, grabbed the pen, and studied the form. She realized almost immediately that she had choices to make. Did she put down her real name and address? Did she provide a telephone number that would not exist for decades?

54

Mary Beth decided to mix things up. She went with her mother's maiden name, her real home address, and a fabricated phone number. She gave the proprietor the sheet and the pen.

Jimmy looked at the slip and then at Mary Beth.

"So you're from the South?"

"Yes," Mary Beth said.

"Where are you staying in town?"

Mary Beth started to say the name of a casino that had grabbed her interest but stopped when she glanced again at the eavesdropping men. She did not want to share her travel itinerary with two unnerving strangers in a dicey gaming establishment. She turned to the owner.

"We haven't decided yet. We just got here."

"Then I need a time," Jimmy said. "I need to know when you'll collect your winnings should the gods smile on your wager."

Mary Beth appealed to Mark.

"When can we come back?"

"Let's try for noon tomorrow," Mark said.

Mary Beth returned to Jimmy.

"Will you be here at noon?"

Jimmy laughed.

"I'll be here, but I suspect *you* won't."

Mary Beth resisted the temptation to poke him in the eyes. She reached into her purse, pulled out the hundred-dollar bill, and slid it to the obnoxious owner.

"Don't count your chickens," Mary Beth said.

Jimmy took the bill and filled out another slip. He grinned as he handed the foolish woman a receipt for her foolishness.

"I will, lady. I will."

12: PIPER

Three hours after checking into a hotel, hitting a buffet, and learning that she couldn't get into any of the shows because of her age, Piper McIntire put a nickel into a slot and pulled the arm of her one-armed bandit. She knew eighteen-year-olds couldn't gamble, even in 1959, but she also knew the odds of being caught and tossed from the establishment were low.

According to Mary Beth and her impeccable source, *Old Las Vegas*, early casino operators had not vigorously enforced the age limit of twenty-one. They had not done so because they had not needed to. State regulators had not regularly punished violators with fines or suspensions.

Piper put another nickel in the hungry machine, indulged it again, and smiled when twenty coins dropped into a metal bin. She looked around for authority types, saw none, and exhaled. She knew from *Old Las Vegas* that casino employees checked for identification only when minors created a stir or won a jackpot. So far she had done nothing to invite unwanted attention.

Then she looked at the cocky boy five slots down and decided that was not entirely true. She had invited unwanted attention from Ben Ryan the moment she had arrived at the buffet in a red silk dress and matching pumps. Piper liked dressing the part of a fashionable fifties woman. She liked immersing herself in a time and a place that offered more possibilities than a twenty-first-century theme park. She did *not* know whether she wanted to make a favorable impression on an obnoxious young man who had annoyed her from the moment the time travelers had left Los Angeles. She did her best to ignore the fact he was disturbingly handsome.

Piper fed the machine again, pulled its arm, and frowned when she saw a bell, a bar, and two cherries. She started to curse when she heard a familiar voice, looked to her left, and saw a stylish couple approach. The man in the pressed gray suit and the woman in the pink dress had disappeared an hour earlier to try their luck at poker, blackjack, and craps.

"I see you found a friend," Mary Beth said. She smiled. "Are you breaking the bank?"

"I'm breaking my arm," Piper said.

Mary Beth laughed.

"Where's Ben?"

Piper pointed with her head.

"He's over there."

"Are you two getting along?" Mary Beth asked.

"No," Piper said.

Mark glanced at Ben and then at Piper.

"Do you want me to talk to him?"

Piper shook her head.

"He's having a good time. Leave him alone."

"Are you sure?" Mark asked.

"I'm positive," Piper said. "If you remind him how obnoxious and antisocial he is, then he'll just get mad and sulk the rest of the trip. I don't want that."

Mary Beth shot her sister a pointed glance.

"You haven't exactly been Miss Congeniality."

Piper sighed.

"I know."

Piper fed the bandit again and pulled his arm. She scowled when he rang his bells, spun his wheels, and absconded with her nickel.

"You should try another machine," Mark said. "That's what I do after a few unlucky pulls. I just move around until I find a slot that pays."

"I might if this continues," Piper said. "I picked this machine because I saw an old lady hit a jackpot twenty minutes ago. I think she won thirty dollars."

Mark smiled.

"That's a lot for a nickel slot."

"It is," Piper said. She looked at Mark and returned his smile. "By the way, thanks for funding my fun tonight. I'm not sure what I would have done without spending money. There is only so much a minor can do in this town without cash."

"Don't mention it," Mark said.

Mark and Mary Beth had agreed to underwrite the trip even before leaving Los Angeles. He had paid for gas, two hotel rooms, meals, souvenirs, and entertainment expenses by writing checks on his college account. She had promised to reimburse at least half of the expenses after the Boys from Berkeley delivered on a bet.

Piper looked at Mary Beth.

"Did the Bears come through for you?"

"They did!" Mary Beth said. She laughed. "Imagine that."

"That's two thousand dollars," Piper said. "That's a lot of money, Mary Beth."

"It is."

"What are we going to do with it?"

"I don't know," Mary Beth said. "I just know we have options we didn't have a few hours ago."

"What do you mean?" Piper asked.

"I mean we have *options*. I want to take a day or two to think about them and then discuss them with you, Mark, and Ben at dinner Monday."

"You're not thinking about staying longer, are you?"

"I'm thinking about a lot of things," Mary Beth said. She took a breath. "Let's just enjoy the weekend and see how things go. OK? I promise we won't do anything that you don't support a hundred percent. Is that fair?"

"That's fair."

Piper put another nickel in the machine. For the umpteenth time, she failed to get a return on her modest investment. She glanced at Mark.

"Maybe you're right. Maybe I should change machines."

Mark smiled.

"That's what I would do."

Piper looked at Mark and Mary Beth.

"So are you going to gamble some more?"

Mary Beth shook her head.

"We're going for a walk. It's beautiful out right now and a lot cooler than it was even an hour ago. I want to see more of the city."

"OK."

"What about you?" Mary Beth asked. "What are *you* going to do?"

Piper put the last of her coins in the slot and pulled the arm of the bandit one more time. She was done with this mechanical pirate.

"I think I'm going to—"

Piper stopped speaking when she saw the slot machine display a seven and then another and then another. She gasped when bells started ringing, lights started blinking, and coins started falling. She nearly fell over when the racket continued for another thirty seconds.

She shoveled hundreds of nickels into a small bucket, stepped away from the machine, and surveyed the crowded casino for potential trouble. She didn't see any men in black head her way, but she did see two casino clerks stare at her, exchange words, and walk toward a security desk.

"I think I'm going to go back to the room," Piper said. She shoveled a few more nickels into her bucket, clutched the container like a running back protecting a football, and then smiled at her sister. "I'm feeling tired all of a sudden. Good night!"

13: MARY BETH

Sunday, March 22, 1959

Jimmy Smith didn't smile when Mark and Mary Beth entered the Fourth Quarter at ten after twelve. He didn't smirk. He didn't grin. He didn't do anything to suggest that he was happy with what had transpired in the past eighteen hours.

"Hello, Mr. Smith," Mary Beth said as she approached the counter.

"Good afternoon," Jimmy replied.

"I've come to collect my winnings."

"I figured you had."

Mary Beth glanced at Mark, who stood behind her, and noted his smile. She was glad to have his strong, subtle, and unqualified support, even if she didn't require it. She smiled at Mark, returned to Jimmy, and plopped her purse on the counter.

"Do you need my receipt?" Mary Beth asked.

"No," Jimmy said. "I don't need a thing except your signature."

The turf club owner reached into the drawer under the counter, retrieved a pen and a form, and slipped both toward a woman he had clearly never expected to see again. He watched her closely as she examined the form, signed it, and pushed it back.

"Is that sufficient?" Mary Beth asked.

"That will do," Jimmy said.

The short man tossed the form into the drawer, closed it, and then retreated to a small wall safe about ten feet away. He spun a dial three times, opened the safe door, and retrieved a white envelope that looked positively pregnant. He returned to the counter a few seconds later with the envelope in one hand and his figurative hat in the other. He handed Mary Beth the cash.

"Here you go," Jimmy said. "Go ahead. Take a look."

59

Mary Beth did as requested. She opened the envelope, pulled out a wad, and placed it on the counter. Then she inventoried her winnings. She counted fifty twenty-dollar bills and eleven hundred-dollar bills, including the crisp Benjamin Franklin she had used to make the bet.

"It's all there," Mary Beth said. She looked at Jimmy. "Thank you."

Mark waited as Mary Beth shuffled the bills together, put them in the envelope, and then tucked the envelope in her purse. He smiled when she turned to face him.

"Are you ready to go?" Mark asked.

Mary Beth nodded.

"I'm ready."

Mark allowed Mary Beth to pass, put a hand on her back, and guided her toward the exit. The two took four or five steps before Jimmy called out. The couple turned around.

"Did you forget something?" Mark asked.

"Yeah," Jimmy said. "I forgot to ask your lady friend a question."

"What's that?" Mary Beth asked.

"How did you know the score? Did you fix the game or something?"

Mary Beth felt her stomach drop. She took a deep breath, pondered a reply, and finally uttered words she thought might get two time travelers out the door.

"You're an intelligent man, Mr. Smith. I'm sure you're smart enough to figure out that someone like me couldn't possibly manage something like that."

"I suppose," Jimmy said.

Mary Beth took another breath.

"Is that all?"

"No. I have one more thing."

"What's that, Mr. Smith?"

Jimmy scowled.

"Don't come back."

Mary Beth returned his stare.

"I won't."

Mary Beth turned around again and walked briskly to the exit. She placed her hand on a sticky doorknob, threw the door open, and left the building several steps ahead of Mark. He joined her on a busy sidewalk a few seconds later.

"Are you all right?" Mark asked.

"I'm fine," Mary Beth said. She shook her hand. "Do you have a handkerchief?"

"I don't. What's wrong?"

"I touched something gooey on the doorknob."

"Let me get something," Mark said.

60

"No. I'll manage. I'll just use the papers in my purse."

"OK."

Mary Beth reached into her handbag, pulled out three scraps of paper, and wiped the sticky substance off the palm of her right hand. She didn't even want to think about what it was.

A moment later, she pushed the scraps together, wadded them into a ball, and tossed them into an open trashcan a few feet away. Then she took Mark's arm and gave him a smile.

"Let's get out of here," Mary Beth said.

"You got it," Mark replied.

Mary Beth clutched her purse as she and Mark walked a block to a curbside parking spot, the Edsel, and their siblings. She could feel her anxiety decrease with each step. Though she had thoroughly enjoyed her brief time in Nevada's largest city, she was more than ready to leave.

She opened a door to the Edsel, jumped in the car, and waited for Mark to do the same. A moment later, she settled into her seat, placed her handbag on the floor, and gazed out the front window at a city on the move.

Mary Beth saw more people walk up and down Fremont than she had the previous night. She saw businessmen in suits, women in dresses, teens in shorts, and other tourists in a variety of attire walk into and out of casinos, shops, and attractions. She saw a slice of society.

Mary Beth did *not* see something else. She did not see a man with a deformed ear rise from a bench near the Fourth Quarter and pick up her trail. Nor did she see him take note of the Edsel, part of its license plate, and all of a MAULERS BOOSTER sticker affixed to its bumper.

She did not see him return to the garbage can, retrieve a wad of paper, and pull it apart. She did not see him find – and keep – a receipt showing the complete titles of three books purchased at a bookstore in Hollywood, California, on June 2, 2017. In her haste to leave Las Vegas, Nevada, on a warm and sunny Sunday afternoon, she did not see a thing.

14: MARK

Sitting at a candlelit dining table in the Painted Lady, Mark sipped some wine, dabbed his mouth with a cloth napkin, and gazed at a woman who had been on his mind for three days.

"Did you sleep well last night?"

Mary Beth smiled.

"I did not. Your mother's bed is lumpy."

Mark and Ben laughed. Each knew the claim was true. Donna Ryan slept on a mattress that was at least two years past its prime. Despite pleas from her sons to upgrade to something better, she refused to give it up. She refused to give up anything she had shared with her husband.

"How about you?" Mary Beth asked. "Did *you* sleep well?"

"I did," Mark said. He grinned. "I usually do in my own room."

Mary Beth shook her head.

"You're as bad as your brother."

Mark laughed again but did not respond. He had nothing to add and knew that he and the others had more important things to discuss than lumpy mattresses.

"What did you and Piper do today?" Mark asked.

"We walked around the neighborhood," Mary Beth said.

"Did you see anything interesting?"

Mary Beth cocked her head.

"Everything is interesting when you're stuck in the past."

"Are you stuck?" Mark asked.

Mary Beth looked at him thoughtfully.

"I don't *feel* stuck. I feel like I'm in limbo."

Mark turned to Piper.

"How about you? Do you feel the same way?"

"I do," Piper said.

"Do you want to go back to 2017?" Mark asked.

Piper took a breath.

"I haven't decided."

"I understand," Mark said.

Piper looked at her host.

"I'm glad you do. This is really hard."

"What about you, Ben?" Mary Beth asked. "You haven't said much. What do you think we should do? What do you *want* us to do?"

Ben did not answer right away. He lowered his fork to his plate, sighed, and then studied Piper for a moment, as if trying to decide whether she was worth any future aggravation.

"I don't know, Mary Beth. I don't."

"That's an honest answer," Mary Beth said. "It's not a helpful one, but it's honest. We have a lot to think about. We have a lot of options to consider."

"Do we?" Mark asked.

"Do we what?"

"*Do* we have a lot of options? It seems to me we have only three."

"Please explain," Mary Beth said.

Mark looked around the table before offering an answer. He wondered what each of the others really thought about turning a time-travel weekend into something more.

He suspected that Mary Beth wanted more. He had suspected that from the moment she had put a hand on his arm and told him that he was "nice" and "interesting." He could not believe that a woman who had had so much fun in Las Vegas was ready to walk away now.

Mark was not as sure about Piper and Ben, who sat across from each other at the table. He guessed that they wanted to do more time traveling but not necessarily with each other. They had not wanted to do much of anything with each other since Saturday morning.

Mark gazed at the frowning teens for a moment and then turned to the woman who wanted him to explain his statement. He gathered his thoughts and continued.

"I think our options are pretty clear," Mark said. "We can travel to 2017, stay here in 1959, or say goodbye and return to our respective times."

"Can't we all just come and go as we please?" Mary Beth asked.

"We can't if we want to keep our discovery to ourselves."

"What do you mean?"

"Think about it," Mark said. "Ben and I can't travel to the future without friendly assistance. We don't live in this place in 2017. We don't know Geoffrey Bell or his wife. If we traveled again to June 2, 2017, we would have to return within hours. We would have to return before your parents or the Bells came back to the house or risk losing access to the tunnel."

"What about us?" Mary Beth asked. "Couldn't Piper and I visit 1959 – and you two – as often as we wanted? I have a crystal."

"You're right. You do have a crystal. What you don't have is permanent access to the tunnel. Unless you plan to move to L.A. and bring the Bells in on our little secret, you have only a day or so to do more traveling. Didn't you say the Bells planned to return on June 3?"

"I did."

Mark frowned.

"Then there you have it."

"What if Piper and I stay here – in 1959 – for the rest of the week. We could stay here until your mom comes home on Sunday," Mary Beth said. "How does that sound?"

"That sounds nice," Mark said in a soft voice. He looked wistfully at Mary Beth. "Any option that gives me more time with you is a good one."

Mary Beth blushed and smiled.

"It appears we've found a solution."

"What if I wanted to do more?" Piper asked.

Mark looked at Piper.

"What do you mean?"

Piper took a breath.

"What if I wanted to stay longer than a week in 1959? What if I wanted to do more than take road trips to Las Vegas or go shopping or go to the beach? Could I do that?"

"I suppose you could."

"Really?"

Mark nodded.

"You would have to find another place to stay, of course. I don't think my mom would want to share her bedroom," Mark said with a laugh. "Other than that, I don't see a problem. It's not like your parents or the Bells would notice you were missing. You would be able to return to the morning of June 2, 2017, as if you had never been gone."

Mary Beth joined the conversation.

"What are you getting at, Piper? Do you want to spend a month here? I thought you didn't like the fifties and wanted to go back to the future."

"You're right," Piper said. "I *did* want to go back. Then I started thinking about the money you won in Vegas and the fun we could both have here."

Mary Beth fixed her gaze on her sister.

"Be more specific."

"I will," Piper said. "I will right after I ask Ben something."

"What's that?" Ben asked.

64

"Where do you go to school?"

"I go to Midway High in South Pasadena."

"Is it a good school?" Piper asked.

Ben leaned forward.

"It's a great school. It's just four years old."

"How do you get there?"

"I drive. It's about fifteen miles."

"So you commute?" Piper asked.

"I commute," Ben said. "Normally I take the Bird. Today I took the Edsel. Now that I have my car back from the shop, I'll drive it to school tomorrow."

"Can you take me?"

"Can I take you to *school?*"

Piper nodded.

"I want to go to your school tomorrow. Can you take me?"

Mark smiled.

"If Ben won't, I will."

"Thank you," Piper said.

Mary Beth stared at her sister.

"Why do you want to go to Ben's school?"

Mark laughed to himself. He guessed where this was going.

"I want to enroll," Piper said.

Mary Beth widened her eyes.

"You want to *enroll?* Are you crazy?"

Piper laughed.

"No. I'm as sane as I've been for days."

Mary Beth furrowed her brow.

"Then explain what this is about."

Piper sighed.

"It's about wanting to make the most of an opportunity."

"Haven't you done that already?"

"No, Mary Beth. I haven't. I went to Nevada. I rode in a car for several hours, ate cheap food, and played the slots. I didn't make the most of anything."

"So what do you want to do?" Mary Beth asked.

"I want to have an *experience*," Piper said. "I want to do the things I've done for the past four years, but in a different time. I want to take classes, make new friends, and go on dates. I want to jump into the fifties headfirst."

15: PIPER

South Pasadena, California – Tuesday, March 24, 1959

Piper pinched her side as she walked through the sunny campus. She pinched her side to remind herself that the letterman sweaters and poodle skirts she saw outside Midway High School were not costumes for a musical but rather the everyday attire of real human beings.

"Can you believe this place?" Piper asked. "It's like *Pleasantville* in color." Mary Beth laughed.

"You wanted this, remember?"

"I did. I do," Piper said. "This is so cool."

"I agree."

Piper slowed her step to take it all in. To her left, boys with crew cuts talked, laughed, and slapped backs. To her right, girls with ponytails giggled, gossiped, and clutched books. Boys gawked at girls. Girls gawked at boys. A few couples strolled the grounds hand in hand.

Piper did not see Ben. She had not come with Ben. He had left the Painted Lady that morning to attend his usual classes. Mark had volunteered to drive the girls to MHS, wait in the Edsel while they met with the principal, and then take them home. He had nothing on his afternoon slate except an engineering class that he happily skipped.

A moment later, Piper and Mary Beth approached the school entrance, opened a double door, and entered a lobby with a gleaming checkered floor. Several girls in sweaters, skirts, and saddle shoes manned tables along two walls and raised funds for a variety of causes.

Piper walked to one row of tables and saw students selling raffle tickets for the science club, the debate team, and a senior trip to San Diego. Other students collected money for Waylon West, a custodian who had broken his hip and required surgery.

Piper stepped to the last table, opened her purse, and retrieved one of twenty five-dollar bills Mary Beth had given her Monday night. She had asked for the cash after the four time travelers had made a quick trip to 2017 to collect the sisters' belongings and other essentials.

Mary Beth watched as Piper straightened the bill, smiled at the girl managing the janitor's recovery fund, and dropped the banknote in a jar. She chuckled when Piper turned around.

"That was nice of you."

Piper grinned.

"I'm feeling generous today."

Piper walked toward the opposite side of the lobby and saw even more giving opportunities. She smiled as she approached the first station and saw pictures of a boy named Tom Cain and a girl named Sue Finn. Each wore a paper crown. The couple vied against four others for prom king and queen. Students voted for couples by placing money in one of five jars.

Piper winced when she gave Sue's photo a closer inspection. Sue looked a lot like Sarah Benchley, a high school classmate who had died in a car accident in April 2017. Tom looked like a boy who needed a friend. Piper put a five-dollar bill in Tom and Sue's jar and moved down the line, a step ahead of an older sister who undoubtedly wondered what she was doing.

She left a Vegas nickel in each of the next two jars. She didn't feel a connection to the couples and figured they would do well even without her financial contribution. She put two dimes in the fourth jar to rid her purse of change and moved on to the last station.

Piper laughed when she reached the station and looked up at a photo of the man who would be king. She smiled at the picture. Ben Ryan smiled back.

Mary Beth laughed.

"It looks like Ben is a BMOC."

"It sure does," Piper said.

"That's funny," Mary Beth said. "He didn't mention that on the trip."

Piper ignored her sister's comment and gazed at the photo of Ben's running mate. Vicki Cole, queen wannabe, was a stunning blonde with a dazzling smile.

Piper scanned all five stations and noticed that students had given more pennies and nickels to Ben and Vicki than to any other couple. They had given slightly fewer to Chip Bennett and Bunny Martinez, the fourth couple and Ben and Vicki's closest competitors.

"I wonder who Vicki is," Piper said to Mary Beth. "Do you think she's Ben's girlfriend?"

"Does it matter?" Mary Beth asked.

"No. I guess not."

"Let's go. We have an appointment to keep."

"Wait," Piper said. "I'll just be a second."

Piper stepped toward the girl managing Ben and Vicki's jar.

"Excuse me. I'm new here and don't know how the prom works."

The girl smiled.

"Just ask."

"OK. I will," Piper said. "Who decides the candidates for king and queen?"

"A committee does. We pair boys and girls who look good together."

"Do the king and queen go to the dance as a couple?"

The girl nodded.

"I think it's a law or something."

Piper stifled a laugh.

"Do you think Ben and Vicki will win?"

The girl nodded again.

"The most popular students usually do."

Piper looked at Mary Beth, who pointed at her watch, and then at the young woman behind the pickle jar. She wondered how one became a money collector.

"I have just one more question," Piper said.

The girl sat up in her chair.

"OK."

"Are Chip and Bunny nice people?" Piper asked.

The girl beamed.

"They are."

Piper reached into her purse and retrieved three five-dollar bills. She walked to the fourth table, stuffed all three bills in the jar, and then returned to the girl at station five.

"Thank you," Piper said. She smiled. "I hope to see you around."

Piper glanced at the grinning girl at station four and then stepped toward her sister. She could hear Mary Beth's laugh even before she could see her smiling face.

"What was *that* all about?" Mary Beth asked.

"You heard the girl," Piper said. "Chip and Bunny are nice. They deserve to win."

Mary Beth laughed.

"Sometimes I think Mom and Dad adopted you."

"What time is it?" Piper asked.

"It's almost one. We need to go."

Piper nodded.

The sisters walked through the lobby, turned right into a long hallway, and weaved their way through a crowd of students toward the main office.

They reached their destination just as a loud bell rattled their eardrums and announced the start of the next period.

"Are you ready?" Mary Beth asked.

"I'm ready."

The sisters hesitated for only a second and then opened the door. They walked to the counter, introduced themselves to a secretary, and asked to see Principal Raines. A moment later, they followed the secretary, a friendly woman of forty, through an open work area to a sizeable office.

The secretary pointed to two chairs. Each faced a large desk.

"Take a seat, ladies. Principal Raines will see you shortly."

"Thank you," Mary Beth said.

Piper settled into her lightly upholstered chair as the secretary took her leave. She turned to face her sister when the office worker shut the door.

"Do you think he'll buy our story?" Piper asked.

"I think so," Mary Beth said. "It's pretty airtight. I also have a letter from Dad. If the principal gives me any static, I'll just tell him to take it up with the colonel."

Piper laughed.

"How did you get a 'letter' from Dad?"

"I created it," Mary Beth said. "I wrote a draft for Mark and then asked him to rewrite it in a man's handwriting. It looks pretty good. Do you want to see it?"

"Maybe later," Piper said.

"OK."

Piper took a breath and smiled at her sister. She never admired her more than when Mary Beth stepped up and helped her sibling in a big way.

"You like him, don't you?"

"Who?" Mary Beth asked. "Mark?"

"Yes, silly. Mark."

Mary Beth blushed.

"I do. I know it's crazy to like anyone in these circumstances, but I do. He's one of the nicest people I have ever met and a true gentleman."

"Don't get too attached, Mary Beth. Even if we make good friends here, we can't keep them. We can't do anything except go back to you know where."

Mary Beth smiled and put a hand on Piper's knee.

"Thanks, Mom."

Piper laughed. She started to say something about the décor in the principal's office when the interior decorator himself opened the door and walked in. He placed a folder on his desk, turned to his left, and then stepped toward his visitors.

"Good afternoon," Principal Raines said. He extended a hand as Mary Beth and Piper rose from their seats. "I'm Warren Raines."

Mary Beth shook his hand.

"It's nice to meet you. I'm Mary Beth McIntire. I've come here today to enroll my sister as a senior at Midway," Mary Beth said. She stepped back. "This is Piper."

The principal shook Piper's hand.

"It's a pleasure to meet you, young lady," Raines said. He motioned toward the chairs. "Please take a seat. This shouldn't take long."

The principal walked to the open door, gestured to a secretary as he closed it, and returned to his desk. A few seconds later, he settled into a richly upholstered chair.

"I'm sorry to keep you waiting," Raines said. "I had another matter to attend to just now."

"That's all right," Mary Beth said. "We're in no hurry."

Raines smiled at his visitors and then reached for the folder on his desk. He opened the folder wide, pulled out two forms, and gave them a quick inspection.

"I see you came here from West Germany," Raines said.

"Piper and I have lived there for the past few years," Mary Beth said. "Our father, Brody McIntire, is an Army colonel serving with the 3rd Mechanized Infantry Division."

"I see."

"Our parents are still in Germany. They plan to join us in June, after my father is discharged, and retire to the Pasadena area, where we have many friends. Piper is here now so that she can graduate from a California high school and have a California diploma when she applies for admission to one of the state universities. She has her eyes on UCLA right now."

Piper marveled at Mary Beth's ability to take a grain of truth and bake it into a seven-layer cake. She and her sister had, in fact, lived in Germany, but they had moved to the South when Mary Beth was still in preschool and Piper was still in diapers.

"Are you acting as Piper's guardian?" Raines asked.

"I am," Mary Beth said. "My father asked me to look after her even though she is already eighteen years old. He wrote a letter authorizing me to act as her representative in any legal, financial, and educational matters. Would you like to see it?"

"Yes. I would."

Mary Beth retrieved an envelope from her purse and pulled out a tri-folded letter. She straightened the letter, written on Army stationery, and handed the document to the principal.

Piper fidgeted in her chair as Raines read the letter. She wondered if he was the kind of man who would summon law enforcement if he suspected that the sisters were pulling a fast one. She relaxed when she saw the administrator smile and return the letter to Mary Beth.

70

"It looks like that part is in order," Raines said. "All I need now is proof of your residency in the school district and transcripts from Piper's high school in Germany."

"I have the first thing," Mary Beth said. She pulled a receipt from her purse and gave it to the principal. "We're staying at the Chaparral Motel on Mission Street."

Mary Beth and Piper had visited the motel earlier in the day and rented a suite with two double beds, a kitchenette, and a small dining table. They rented the room at the weekly rate of fifty dollars and paid for four weeks. Mary Beth told the manager that they intended to stay at the motel at least a month and extend their visit, if necessary, on a week-by-week basis.

"What about her transcripts?" Raines asked.

"We were unable to obtain them before we left," Mary Beth said.

"I need records, Miss McIntire. I can't graduate a student without them."

"I understand."

"Do you have the name and address of Piper's last school?"

Mary Beth nodded. She reached again into her purse and pulled out a small slip. She handed the slip to the principal. It contained more fiction than *Gone with the Wind*.

"Roger Timmons is the principal there. He can send anything you need and answer any questions you might have about Piper's coursework, marks, and conduct."

"Overseas mail moves slowly," Raines said. "This could take weeks."

Ding! Ding! Ding! Piper thought. *We have a winner!*

The principal sighed.

"I must have the records by May 15."

"That's fair," Mary Beth said.

"Then I guess that settles it," Raines said. He gave the rent receipt back to Mary Beth. "Piper may enroll."

"Thank you."

Raines turned his attention to Piper.

"I assume you have some courses in mind."

"I do," Piper said.

"Then what would you like to take, young lady?"

Piper smiled politely at the principal. She decided if he called her "young lady" one more time she would brain him with a stapler.

"I'd like to take art history, literature, civics, algebra, gym, and maybe something old school like home economics," Piper said. "I could use a cooking lesson."

Mary Beth stifled a laugh.

"I think that can be arranged," Raines said. "Do you need any specific class to graduate?"

71

"No. I completed all of my necessary coursework in Germany. I just want to enjoy a spring in California and graduate with a diploma from Midway."

"Then I'll do what I can to make it happen."

"I appreciate that, Mr. Raines."

"Do you have any questions for me?"

Piper shook her head.

"I think I'm set."

"Then I will send you to Mr. Bowers," Raines said. "He is one of our guidance counselors. He is in his office right now and can help you work out a schedule."

"Thank you," Piper said.

The principal leaned back in his chair. He studied his visitors for a moment, put a hand to his chin, and finally leaned forward.

"I do have a question for you," Raines said.

"Oh?" Piper asked.

The administrator nodded.

"I detect a southern accent. Both of you have southern accents. Surely you did not pick those up in West Germany."

"We didn't," Mary Beth said. "We picked them up in Alabama. We're Army brats."

"I figured as much."

"Is that a bad thing?"

"Oh, no," Raines said. "If anything, it's a good thing. I'm sure Piper will have no difficulty making new friends with such an interesting background."

Mary Beth and Piper exchanged knowing smiles.

"I agree, Mr. Raines," Mary Beth said.

The principal leaned back in his chair.

"Well, I guess that concludes our business," Raines said. He smiled and looked at Piper. "Welcome to Midway High School, Miss McIntire. Welcome to the Class of '59."

16: MARK

Four days after taking Mary Beth McIntire for a stroll along the Las Vegas Strip, Mark Ryan took her for a stroll along the university's most prominent thoroughfare. He conceded that the Parkway did not match the Strip's glitz, but it was familiar, inviting, and active. It was a perfect place for a walk with a woman who continued to amaze.

"Do you like what you see?" Mark asked.

"I do," Mary Beth said. "This campus is amazing."

Mark couldn't disagree. Even after four years, he never tired of the sights. He admired the broad walkways and the carefully groomed vegetation almost as much as the stately buildings that showed off the Romanesque Revival and Italian Renaissance styles.

"Is that all you like?"

"No," Mary Beth said. She offered a playful grin. "I also like the fashions. I didn't see this in Tuscaloosa. I haven't seen this anywhere."

Mark laughed.

"Well, you *are* in California – and in a different time."

Mary Beth smiled.

"I guess I am."

Mark leaned forward to get a closer look at the woman on his arm. He looked for clues that might explain her smile but found only lively eyes and the traces of another grin.

"You have something on your mind, don't you?"

"It's nothing major," Mary Beth said. "I'm just trying to make sense of all this."

"Do you mean 1959?"

"Yes, I mean 1959 – and Los Angeles and the past few days and *you*."

"Am I a mystery, Miss McIntire?"

73

Mary Beth smiled again.

"That's putting it mildly."

"Then let's unwrap the mystery," Mark said. He guided Mary Beth around a group of students who had gathered near a large bronze statue. "What do you want to know?"

"I don't know," Mary Beth said. "I guess everything. Tell me about your interests, your childhood, and your parents. Tell me why a college senior drives an Edsel bearing the bumper sticker of a high school team."

Mark laughed.

"You don't miss a thing."

"I don't miss things like that," Mary Beth said. "Did you attend Midway?"

"I didn't. I went to South," Mark said. "Ben would have too had the school district not changed its boundaries the year I graduated. My dad put the bumper sticker on the Edsel to show his support for Midway's sports teams. Ben played football at MHS and now plays tennis. He's kind of a big deal there."

"I gathered that when Piper and I visited the school. Ben and some girl named Vicki Cole are running for prom king and queen."

"Did you cast a vote?"

"No. Piper did though," Mary Beth said. She giggled. "She put fifteen dollars on some couple named Chip and Bunny."

Mark laughed.

"Don't tell Ben that. He'll go crazy. He'll consider the donation sabotage."

"I take it he wants to win."

"He wants to win everything. He's very competitive."

"Is he dating Vicki Cole?" Mary Beth asked.

Mark shook his head.

"They used to go out. They dated off and on until about a month ago. Then Ben dumped her for some girl named Brenda. I'm not sure what happened to her. Ben sees someone different every month."

"He sounds like a ladies' man."

"He is."

Mary Beth gave Mark a playful smile.

"Is his *brother* a ladies' man?"

Mark chuckled.

"No. I date every now and then and still go to fraternity dances, but I don't go out very often and haven't dated anyone seriously for more than a year."

"That surprises me," Mary Beth said. "I see a lot of pretty faces on this campus."

Mark looked at her thoughtfully.

74

"Don't get me wrong. I've had ample opportunity. I've just decided to focus on academics this year. I promised my father I would graduate with honors and get a good job out of college. I want to fulfill that promise even if he's no longer here."

"Do you think about him a lot?" Mary Beth asked.

"I think about him every day. That's why I kept his Edsel instead of trading it in and getting another car with the insurance money. I wanted to keep a reminder of him."

"That's sweet."

Mark shrugged.

"It is what it is."

"Tell me about your mother," Mary Beth said. "What kind of woman is she?"

Mark smiled.

"She's like most mothers. She fusses over her kids and volunteers for everything."

"Have you told her about your discovery?"

"Oh, no. She would drive back today if I did."

Mary Beth stopped and looked at Mark.

"So *are* you going to tell her?"

"I haven't decided," Mark said. "I'm tempted to keep it to myself. If I tell my mom, she might tell someone else and, before you know it, everyone in town will be knocking on our door."

"Are you going to tell her about Piper and me?" Mary Beth asked.

Mark sighed.

"I haven't decided that either."

"Oh."

Mark regretted his answer the second he saw Mary Beth frown. He began to wonder whether honesty was even an option in building a friendship that would someday have to end.

"Do you *want* me to tell her about you?"

Mary Beth looked at him closely.

"Yes."

"Do you want to meet her?" Mark asked.

Mary Beth nodded.

"Yes again."

Mark smiled.

"I'll see what I can do."

17: PIPER

South Pasadena, California

Piper smiled as she watched the frumpy literature teacher walk to the front of the class. With horn-rimmed glasses, a potato-sack dress, and therapeutic shoes, Evelyn Everson was as much a sign of the times as slide rules, pull-down maps, and Pee-Chee portfolios.

The time traveler braced herself for an introduction. She knew one was coming because she knew how teachers welcomed new pupils to Midway High School. They did it by making a public spectacle of the student. They had already done it to Piper five times.

"Good afternoon, class," Mrs. Everson said.

Twenty-two students sat straight in their seats.

"Good afternoon, Mrs. Everson."

"I have graded your quarterly exams and will distribute them at the end of the hour. Most of you, I am pleased to report, did quite well. I hope you keep up the good work this quarter. We will begin our final unit in a moment. In the meantime, I would like to introduce a new student," Mrs. Everson said. She looked at a girl in the back row. "Can you step forward, Piper?"

I certainly can. Whether I want to is another matter.

The teacher tilted her head.

"Come on up. Don't be shy."

Piper got up from her seat and stepped forward. When she reached the front of the room, she turned around, faced the class, and forced a smile only Leonardo da Vinci could love.

Mrs. Everson placed a hand on the newcomer's shoulder.

"I am pleased to introduce Piper McIntire to the class. Piper recently moved to Southern California from Wiesbaden, West Germany, where she has lived the past few years. She has enrolled as a senior and plans to

76

graduate in June with the rest of you. Please welcome her to the school and to the community when you have the opportunity," Mrs. Everson said. She smiled at Piper and tapped her lightly on the shoulder. "You may sit down, dear."

Piper scanned the faces of her classmates as she returned to her desk and saw a variety of expressions. Several girls smiled, two yawned, and one glared. The attractive redhead looked at Piper like she was Typhoid Mary. Every boy in class salivated.

Piper had done her best to fit in. She had donned a white blouse, a pink poodle skirt, bobby socks, and saddle shoes, tied her long brown hair in a ponytail, and worn the reddest lipstick she could find. She had even carried her books by holding them to her chest.

Still she stood out. She had expected as much. There was no hiding her wholesome good looks, her unusual first name, and an accent that screamed Talladega.

Piper took her seat, folded her hands on top of her desk, and waited for the instructor to do something besides draw attention to the new girl. She didn't have to wait long.

Less than a minute after Piper sat down, retrieved her literature text, and opened it to a random page, Mrs. Everson got up from her chair, stepped away from her desk, and walked to a door Warren Raines had quietly opened. The teacher spoke to the principal, who had paid an unexpected visit, and then returned to the front of the classroom.

"I have to leave for a few minutes," she said. "Please pull out your readers and open them to page forty-four. We will begin the works of Keats when I return."

Piper flipped to page forty-four and then looked around the classroom. Most of her peers had moved on to the lesson, daydreams, or private conversations, but a few had not. Three boys continued to stare at the new student. Two smiled. One waved.

Piper started to read a poem by John Keats but stopped when she felt the weight of a stare. She looked to her right and saw a blonde in an oversized letterman sweater look back.

The girl rested her chin on folded hands and smiled.

"Are you really from Germany?"

"Yes," Piper said.

"You don't look like a German."

"Is that so?"

The blonde nodded.

"You don't speak like a German either."

"That's because I'm from Alabama."

The girl giggled.

"You're funny."

Piper smiled.

"What's your name?"

"Sally Warner."

Piper looked at her sweater.

"What did you letter in, Sally?"

"I didn't letter in anything. My boyfriend did."

Piper laughed to herself. This really *was* a different time.

"That's nice."

"Have you made any friends?" Sally asked.

"No. I haven't – unless you count Ben Ryan."

Sally's eyes grew wide.

"You're friends with Ben Ryan?"

Piper furrowed her brow.

"I guess you could say that. He drove me to school today."

Sally smiled.

"You're definitely a friend if he drove you to school. How did you meet?"

We spent the weekend time traveling.

"We met through our siblings," Piper said. "They know each other."

"Oh," Sally said. "Has Ben asked you out yet?"

Piper sighed.

"No."

"He will," Sally said. "He doesn't give rides to just anyone."

Piper laughed.

"I'll make a note of that."

"Has your family bought a house yet?" Sally asked.

Piper shook her head.

"My parents are still in Germany. I came here early so that I could graduate from a California high school. I live with my older sister at the Chaparral Motel."

"You live in a *motel?*" Sally asked.

Piper put a finger to her lips.

"Yes."

"Oh," Sally said.

"It's just temporary."

"Can you stay out late and do what you want?"

Piper carefully considered her reply. She did not want to give anyone the impression that she lived by her own rules in a motel. Boys would love that.

"No. My sister won't allow it."

"That's too bad," Sally said.

"I know."

"Does your sister look like you?"

78

"She does," Piper said. "Why do you ask?"

"I think I saw her yesterday. I saw someone who looks like you standing near the prom tables during the lunch hour. Did she wear a yellow dress?"

Piper nodded.

"She came to school to help me enroll."

"She sounds like a mother."

"She *is* a mother, at least for now. She's even strict like a mother. She's already set down a hundred rules I have to observe."

"That figures," Sally said. She frowned. "My parents are the same way. They won't let me do anything. I think seniors should be able to break rules. We're practically adults."

"Do you *like* breaking rules?" Piper asked.

Sally blushed.

"Don't reply," Piper said. She laughed. "I have my answer."

"I just wish I didn't have a curfew. It's so unfair."

"I agree."

"What do you do for fun?" Sally asked.

I visit the fifties.

"I like to swim and dance and listen to music," Piper said. "How about you?"

Sally smiled.

"I like to *sing* and dance and listen to music."

"Then you're a well-rounded woman," Piper said.

"Maybe you can—"

Sally stopped speaking when Mrs. Everson opened the door and entered the room. She resumed speaking when the teacher walked to the blackboard, retrieved an eraser, and erased several questions and answers from an earlier class.

"Maybe you can come over to my house sometime."

"I'd like that," Piper said. "I'd like that a lot."

18: BEN

Los Angeles, California – Thursday, March 26, 1959

Ben tapped the brake pedal of his Thunderbird, slowed to forty miles per hour, and cussed silently as traffic on the Pasadena Freeway began to thicken. He hated congestion almost as much as he hated smog, but neither on this sunny afternoon bothered him as much as the silent treatment he was getting from his lone passenger.

"Do you hate me?" Ben asked. "Be honest."

"I don't hate you," Piper said. "I'm just not sure I like you."

"What's the difference?"

"Well, for one thing, if I hated you, I wouldn't get near you. I wouldn't talk to you or speak well of you – and I certainly wouldn't ride in a car with you. Thanks for giving me a ride to school, by the way."

"You're welcome," Ben said.

"Not liking you is something altogether different. It means I haven't decided whether I like you or dislike you. See the difference?"

"No."

Piper smiled.

"This is killing you, isn't it?"

Ben glanced Piper and then returned his eyes to the road.

"I don't know what you're talking about."

"Sure you do," Piper said. "I'm not fawning over you like a hundred other girls at Midway High School – and that's killing you."

Ben sighed.

"OK. It's killing me."

Piper laughed hard.

"I needed that."

"Don't gloat," Ben said. "I could still turn suicidal."

"Please don't."

"I won't if you laugh and smile more often."

Piper looked at the driver with amusement in her eyes.

"Do you like my laugh and smile, Mr. Ryan?"

"I like a lot of things."

"Then I'll laugh and smile more often."

"You do that," Ben said.

Ben smiled as he moved into and out of the left lane to pass an overloaded produce truck. He felt good about the brief exchange. He could finally talk to this difficult woman.

"What time are Mark and Mary Beth expecting us for dinner?" Piper asked.

"Five," Ben said.

"Do you think we'll get there in time?"

"I doubt it. If this traffic gets any worse, we may not get there till six. You may actually have to talk to me."

Piper smiled.

"Do I have to?"

"Yes," Ben said.

"OK. I'll talk to you. Let me ask you a question."

"Fire away."

"Do you like Vicki Cole?" Piper asked.

Ben turned his head.

"I *used* to like Vicki Cole."

"Does she like you?"

"Why wouldn't she?" Ben asked.

Piper sighed and shook her head.

"You are so full of yourself. That's why I don't like talking to you."

Ben grinned.

"Why do you want to know if Vicki likes me?"

"I'm just curious," Piper said matter-of-factly.

Ben glanced again at his passenger and saw a thoughtful look on her face. He could see that she actually cared about his answer.

"I don't know what she thinks of me, to tell you the truth," Ben said. "I haven't spoken to her much in the past month. We didn't break up on the best of terms."

"So I hear."

"Have you been checking me out?"

"I have," Piper said. "I hear you're quite the player."

"What's a player?"

"It's a guy who plays the field. It's someone who collects girls like coins and throws them out when they have outlived their usefulness."

"Who told you I was a 'player'?" Ben asked. "You're making that up."

"No, I'm not."

"It's all a lie. I'm as humble and chaste as a monk."

Piper laughed.

"I'll believe that when I see it."

Ben paused to consider that comment. It was as loaded as a hunting rifle.

"You don't think I can be a gentleman?"

"No," Piper said.

"Then let me prove it to you."

"I don't like where this is going."

"The Spring Fling is coming up," Ben said.

"What's the Spring Fling?"

"It's a hop."

"Do you mean a dance?" Piper asked.

"I mean a dance," Ben said. He looked at his passenger and smiled. "What are you doing Saturday night?"

19: MARY BETH

Laguna Beach, California – Friday, March 27, 1959

Mary Beth ran out of the surf like she was fleeing a shark. She liked swimming and loved the ocean, but she did not like or love bathing in water that was at least twenty degrees cooler than the Gulf of Mexico. "The water is freezing," Mary Beth said.

Mark laughed as he handed her a dry towel.

"I take it you're used to something warmer."

"I'm used to something *much* warmer."

"Then next time I'll take you to San Diego."

"You do that."

Mary Beth toweled off her cold, wet, shivering body and then placed her towel next to Mark's on a boulder. She didn't know if the waters off San Diego were any warmer than the ones off Laguna Beach, but she was more than ready to give them a try.

"Do you want to go for a walk?" Mark asked.

Mary Beth nodded.

Mark placed his arm around Mary Beth as they started to walk, but he pulled it back a minute later and let it drop to his side. Despite his obvious interest in the time traveler from Huntsville, Alabama, he was not yet comfortable demonstrating that interest in an affectionate way.

"Thanks for bringing me here," Mary Beth said. "This is really nice."

"Don't mention it," Mark replied.

"I still can't believe you skipped two classes. For someone who wants to 'focus on academics' and 'graduate with honors,' you sure play hooky a lot."

Mark smiled.

"I'm not missing anything important. I brought you here today because I knew we would have the beach mostly to ourselves. That wouldn't be the case tomorrow or Sunday. This place is packed on weekends."

"I believe it," Mary Beth said.

She smiled at the engineering student at her side and then turned her attention to the rock outcroppings that punctuated the beach. She decided she could live in a place like this.

The two walked in blissful silence for another five minutes and took in the sights. A surfer on a large wooden board navigated small waves. Seagulls fought over what looked like the carcass of a fish. An elderly man picked up shells and placed them in a bag.

Mark finally broke the silence with a question that took Mary Beth by surprise. "Who is Jordan?"

Mary Beth slowly met his gaze.

"He was my fiancé."

"Did you say *was*?" Mark asked.

Mary Beth nodded.

"He died eight months ago – or at least eight months ago as I measure time. He was shot in a holdup at a convenience store."

Mark stopped.

"I'm so sorry. I can't imagine getting news like that."

"I didn't get *any* news," Mary Beth said. "I was there."

"You saw him get shot?"

She nodded.

"He died in my arms."

Mark sighed.

"I feel stupid now."

"Don't feel stupid," Mary Beth said. "You asked an honest question."

Mark looked at her.

"I still feel stupid."

Mary Beth did not respond to the statement. She instead shifted her focus to a slightly different matter as the two resumed their stroll down the sandy beach. "How did you learn about Jordan?"

"Piper mentioned him in passing the other day," Mark said. "I didn't press her for more information, but I figured he was someone important."

"He was," Mary Beth said.

"What was he like?"

Mary Beth took a deep breath. What a question, she thought. How did one describe Jordan Taylor in a nutshell? How did *she* describe him to someone she wanted to impress?

"He was a lot like you," Mary Beth said. "He was smart, thoughtful, and kind, the type of person most people want in their lives."

"Did he have any interests?" Mark asked.

Mary Beth laughed.

"It's funny you ask."

"Why is that?"

"Jordan was really into the 1950s," Mary Beth said. "He loved this era. He loved the movies, the music, the TV shows, and especially the cars. He was in the process of restoring a '57 Chevy when he died. I think he would have loved talking to Ben."

"I'm sure he would have," Mark said. "Did you share his interest?"

"I didn't at first. I thought his obsession was nutty. Then I started checking out some of the things he liked. I began watching a lot of movies that were set in the late fifties or early sixties. I must have seen *Grease*, *Pleasantville*, and *American Graffiti* at least a dozen times."

"That's commitment."

Mary Beth chuckled.

"That was just the beginning. I also went to fifties functions and fundraisers and listened to a *lot* of old music. Within a few months, I was as into this time as he was. I even insisted on having a fifties-themed reception at our wedding."

"That's funny," Mark said.

Mary Beth smiled as she considered the irony of befriending a man who actually *was* from the 1950s. She wondered how Jordan would have spent a day in 1959, if given the chance.

She also wondered what she could do with a friendship that was doomed to end and feelings that would not go away. As much as she wanted to enjoy Mark's company indefinitely, she knew she could not. Her sojourn to the fifties was as temporary as a sand castle.

Mary Beth pondered the coming weeks as she and Mark approached a cluster of rocks that essentially cut the beach in half. She felt a twinge of sadness and then a spark of electricity when Mark took her hand and led her through the rocks and back onto the beach.

"Do you mind if I hold your hand?" Mark asked.

"No," Mary Beth said. She giggled. "I don't mind at all."

She smiled again as she pondered his question. What kind of man asked a woman if he could hold her hand? What kind of man opened car doors? A gentleman, she thought. They walked another hundred yards in silence until they approached a bevy of boulders. The rocky obstruction marked the turnaround point in their mile-long stroll.

Mary Beth released Mark's hand and walked about twenty feet to the largest boulder. A moment later, she sat on top of the rock, patted the space next to her, and smiled.

"Sit!"

Mark laughed.

"Someone's feeling assertive today."

85

Mary Beth grinned.

"I'm a fan of succinct commands."

"Giving them or taking them?"

"Sit!"

Mark laughed again and did as commanded. He climbed up on the massive rock, sat next to Mary Beth, and threw his arm around her.

"Is this better?"

"Yes."

Mary Beth said no more for the next several minutes. She leaned into Mark's side and stared blankly at an ocean that had grown more restless during their walk.

"You seem deep in thought," Mark said.

"I am."

"What are you thinking about?"

"I'm thinking about a lot of things," Mary Beth said.

"The plot thickens."

Mary Beth took a breath.

"Do you ever think about the craziness of all this?"

"I do," Mark said. "I do all the time."

"I'm looking at a world that my parents never saw and a lot of older people from my time can't remember. I'm still trying to wrap my head around that."

Mark tightened his hold.

"Do you like the fifties?"

Mary Beth nodded.

"I know many in 2017 don't share my view. They see how we treated black people, women, and others and wonder how anyone could view this time with anything but scorn, but I think they miss the point. People here seem happier. They talk. They play. They enjoy life. Too many from my time isolate themselves from others and stare at plastic screens."

"Surely you miss some things," Mark said.

"I do. I even miss some of the gadgets with plastic screens, but I don't miss everything. I like it here. I like the people," Mary Beth said. She paused. "I like *you*."

Mark lessened his hold on Mary Beth, leaned forward, and looked at his new friend like someone he had just discovered. He placed his free hand on her face, turned it toward his, and gave her a long, soft kiss. Mary Beth sighed and burrowed into Mark's side. Then she smiled and looked again at the surging sea. In just a few seconds, her troubled life had taken a turn for the better. It had also, she realized, become infinitely more complicated.

20: PIPER

Piper tapped her right foot in front of her left, brought it back, and tapped it again as she slowly worked her way toward the front of a conga line. She didn't need to remember to step, cross, and step. She had learned "The Stroll" in a dance class and knew the steps by heart.

So, apparently, did Ben. He tapped, stepped, and crossed with precision in the same position in the facing queue. Like most of his classmates, no doubt, he had done this before.

Piper smiled at Ben when he smiled at her. She didn't trust him. She still wasn't sure she even liked him, but for the first time since he had asked her to the Spring Fling, she conceded that he was probably a decent guy. He certainly knew how to surprise a girl.

Tap. Tap. Tap. Step. Cross. Step.

Piper watched with interest as another boy and another girl stepped forward at the head of the lines, met in the middle, and strolled to the other end. She loved "The Stroll" and the song of the same name, which an Anaheim band named Otis and the Operators covered to perfection.

Piper smiled again at Ben and then turned to other things. No matter where she looked, she saw something new, iconic, or interesting. Blue and white crepe streamers hung from the rafters of the gym. Tables of refreshments lined the walls. Boys in button-down shirts and cuffed slacks and girls in crisp blouses and knee-length skirts filled every section of the floor.

The time traveler saw pompadours and ponytails, wingtips and saddle shoes, and enough bobby socks to fill fifty chests. When she took in the trappings of the Spring Fling, she saw more than two hundred students enjoy themselves on a Saturday night. She saw the fifties on parade.

Tap. Tap. Tap. Step. Cross. Step.

87

Piper looked at Ben as they reached the head of their respective lines and noticed that his silly grin had morphed into something resembling a thoughtful smile. Was this a sign of humility? She hoped so. She returned his smile, took a breath, and stepped forward.

Piper laughed when she met Ben in the middle. She had no idea how he wanted to proceed between the rows. Couples at this point did their own thing. She guessed from watching others that Ben might go with the standard step. She guessed right.

The pair joined hands, came together, turned away, and then turned back as they began their slow journey between two rows of smiling schoolmates. The journey was electric.

Piper drew energy from every touch and turn. She gained confidence with every step. She could not imagine a more exhilarating public experience. This was what she had wanted when she had thrown caution to the wind. *This* was her fifties experience.

A dozen touches and turns later, Piper and Ben reached the end of the aisle, separated, and headed for the back of the gym. They finally met up at a table bearing large bowls of punch.

"Well, that was fun!" Piper said.

Ben grinned.

"I see you've done this before."

"I learned 'The Stroll' in a dance class. But trust me when I say I've never performed it with a cocky ladies' man in 1959," Piper said. She laughed. "That part is new."

Ben chuckled.

"You're not going to let that go, are you?"

Piper grinned.

"Nope."

Ben smiled and then looked at Piper thoughtfully.

"Do you want some punch?"

She shook her head.

"No, thanks. I just want to stand here a minute and take it all in."

"OK."

As the band finished "The Stroll," Piper scanned the gym and looked for familiar faces. She saw more than a few. Tina Green, a girl in her literature class, snuggled up to her boyfriend. Peggy Henderson, a fellow student in civics, straightened her date's collar. Two girls from gym class spoke to each other in an animated fashion. Chip Bennett, prom king candidate, shared a laugh with another boy. Bunny Martinez, his would-be queen, had apparently hopped away.

Piper gazed at the scene for another minute as the band started playing "Blue Moon." Then she turned to the boy who had picked her up in a red Thunderbird and brought her to the dance.

"Thanks for bringing me."

Ben grinned.

"Are you having fun?"

Piper laughed.

"You know the answer to that question."

Piper started to say something else but stopped when she saw a bubbly blonde, her first girlfriend in the Age of Eisenhower, approach the punch table. She laughed as Sally Warner, dressed in pink, pulled her hunky date across the floor like he was a little red wagon.

"You two are hilarious," Piper said.

"There you are," Sally said. "I've been looking for you all night. Where have you been?"

Piper pointed at Ben with her head.

"I've been dancing with this guy. Believe it or not, he knows how to dance."

Sally laughed. She turned to her date.

"I told you she was funny."

"Is this your letterman?" Piper asked.

"He is. This is my boyfriend, Wayne Bridges," Sally said. She turned to her male companion. "Wayne, this is my friend Piper McIntire. We met in our literature class. She says she's an Army brat from Germany, but she's really a redneck from Alabama."

Ben and Piper laughed.

"It's nice to meet you," Wayne said.

"You too," Piper replied.

"Have you been here all night?" Sally asked.

Piper shook her head.

"We arrived about an hour ago. Mr. Ryan insisted on taking me to dinner and cruising Colorado Avenue before coming here. I think he wanted to show me off."

Ben smiled and nodded.

"I would show you off too if I were a boy," Sally said. "I love your dress."

"Thanks," Piper said. "My sister picked it out."

Piper smiled as she revisited the start of her day. She had spent three hours shopping for a dress and two more looking for shoes at some of Pasadena's finest stores. She finally settled on a floral swing dress and a pair of snazzy white flats.

"Are you having a good time?" Sally asked.

"I'm having a *great* time," Piper said. "I never thought a dance could be so much fun."

"This is nothing. Wait until you go to the prom."

Piper nodded but did not reply. She did not know what to say about a dance that was still four weeks away, an event she might never see. Since enrolling at Midway High School, she had thought of the prom as little more than a coronation for a king and a queen. Now she thought of it as something she might actually attend and perhaps enjoy.

She gazed again at the masses in the middle of the gym and this time saw something that did *not* bring a smile to her face. She braced herself for trouble as Vicki Cole, the blond, blue-eyed queen wannabe, pulled Bill Corning, her reluctant date, toward the party of four.

"Hi, Ben," Vicki said a moment later. "I didn't see you arrive. Who is this?"

"This is Piper McIntire," Ben said. "She just moved here."

"So I hear."

"Piper, this is Vicki Cole."

"Hi, Vicki," Piper said with little enthusiasm.

"Hello."

"Piper is from—"

"I know all about your friend, Ben," Vicki said. She raised a brow. "She's the girl who stuffs five-dollar bills into the jars of our competitors."

Piper smiled.

"I think Chip and Bunny make a great team."

"Ben and I make a great team too. In fact, we made a great team for several months," Vicki said. She smiled at her former beau. "Isn't that right?"

Ben squirmed.

"Let's talk about something else."

Vicki smirked.

"Let's do. Let's talk about your friend," Vicki said. She looked at Piper. "I hear that you live in a motel with your sister. Is that true?"

Piper felt her anger rise.

"It is."

"That's awfully convenient."

"I don't know what you mean."

"Of course you do," Vicki said. "Unlike every other girl in this school, you can do what you please, when you please, and with *whom* you please."

Each person present reacted to the comment differently. Ben glared at Vicki. The other boys looked away. Sally turned white and stepped back. She clearly wanted no part of this.

"You're right, Vicki. I can do all of those things and more," Piper said. She took Ben's arm and smiled. "I can – and I do."

Vicki fumed.

"Let's go, Bill. I need some air."

Vicki seized Bill's hand and led him away from Ben, Wayne, Sally, and the promiscuous girl from Germany. The two marched toward an exit and disappeared though a door.

"I'm sorry about that," Ben said. "She's still sore about our breakup."

Piper sighed.

"I never would have guessed."

Sally stepped forward and put a hand on Piper's arm.

"I didn't tell her a thing. I mean it."

"I know," Piper said. "You're not the kind to gossip."

"Just ignore her," Ben said.

"I will. I won't give her a second thought."

Piper knew that was not true. She would think about Vicki Cole the rest of the weekend. She had needlessly provoked a powerful enemy and would have to live with the fallout.

"Are you all right?" Ben asked.

"I'm all right," Piper said.

She looked at Ben thoughtfully, turned away, and once again surveyed her surroundings. She glanced at the stage just as the band, dressed in white blazers, started a new set by playing "At the Hop." Within seconds, dozens of couples put down their punch cups, returned to the front of the gym, and started moving and swinging to a song made popular by Danny and the Juniors.

"What do you want to do now?" Ben asked.

The new girl smiled.

"I want to do what we came here to do," Piper said. She took Ben's hand. "I want to dance."

21: MARK

Mark filled two ceramic mugs with steaming coffee from the percolator, stared out the kitchen window, and returned to the small dining table a few feet away. He offered Ben a mug.

"Here you go," Mark said.

Ben accepted the offering.

"Thanks."

Mark pulled out a chair, took a seat, and pushed the morning paper aside. He took a sip of the strong brew, sighed, and looked across the table.

"You got in late last night."

Ben returned his brother's gaze.

"My date didn't have a curfew."

"Does that mean you had a good time?" Mark asked.

"*I* had a good time," Ben said. "I'm not sure Piper did."

"What do you mean?"

"I mean when I kissed her good night, she just sat there. She just sat in the front seat of the car and didn't move. It was awkward, to say the least."

"Maybe she's old-fashioned. Maybe she doesn't like to kiss on the first date. Maybe she just wants to be friends," Mark said. He smiled. "Not everyone succumbs to your charms."

Ben laughed.

"I guess not."

"Did she even talk to you?" Mark asked.

"Oh, she did. She did a lot. That's the thing," Ben said. "She sent me positive signals all night – or at least until I took her back to the motel. I don't know what to make of her."

Mark took a breath and sipped his coffee. He could relate to dating mysterious women. He had dated one for a week and didn't really know her any better than the day they had met.

"It doesn't matter," Mark said.

"Why do you say that?" Ben asked.

"I say it because Piper's a short-timer here. So is Mary Beth. None of this is real, Ben. In a few weeks, maybe sooner, the girls will go back to their time, we'll stay in ours, and we'll go back to doing the things we've always done."

"I suppose you're right."

"I know I'm right," Mark said. "I've thought of little else for days. The fun can't last."

Ben sipped his brew.

"You sound depressed."

Mark smiled sadly.

"I am. I really like Mary Beth. I've never met anyone like her."

"I feel the same about Piper," Ben said. "I'm smitten."

Mark laughed softly.

"I've never heard you say that about anyone."

"Well, there's a first time for everything."

"I guess."

Ben looked at his brother.

"Mom is coming home today."

"I know," Mark said.

"What are you going to tell her?"

"What do you *think* I'm going to tell her?"

Ben laughed.

"I guess honesty is not always the best policy."

"It's not in this case," Mark said. "I don't know what I'm going to tell her. I just know I can't tell her the truth. She would have us both committed."

Ben smiled.

"She wouldn't do that. She would miss us too much."

Mark didn't doubt that. Donna Ryan lived for her sons. She would walk through a river of lava before committing them to an institution or sending them away.

Mark sipped more coffee and gazed at Ben. He noted his brother's quiet demeanor and wondered what was going through his mind.

"What do you plan to do today?"

"I'll probably wash the car and sleep," Ben said. "What about you?"

"I'm going to study," Mark said. "I skipped three classes last week and have some work to make up. Believe it or not, I still want to graduate."

Ben laughed.

"Imagine that."

Mark started to speak but stopped when he heard the front door open. He turned to his right and saw Donna step into the house, lower a small suitcase to the floor of the entry, and proceed down the hallway toward the kitchen.

Mark got out of his chair, a second ahead of Ben, and met his mother as she reached the doorway that connected the hallway to the kitchen. He gave her a hug.

"You're early," Mark said.

"That's because I left early," Donna said.

Ben hugged his mother.

"Hi, Mom."

"Good morning," Donna said. She stepped back and looked at her sons. "Have you had breakfast yet? I can make some if you haven't."

"I had some cereal an hour ago," Mark said.

Donna turned to Ben.

"How about you?"

"I'm not hungry," Ben said.

"Suit yourself," Donna said matter-of-factly. She looked around the spotless room. "Which one of you boys cleaned the kitchen?"

"Ben did," Mark said.

Mark laughed to himself. He had cleaned the kitchen on Saturday, shortly before taking Mary Beth to a movie, but he thought his slightly spurned brother needed a break.

"Well, I appreciate it," Donna said to Ben. "It's nice to come home to a clean house."

"Did you leave any bags in the car?" Mark asked.

Donna shook her head.

"I traveled light this time."

"OK."

Donna studied Mark for a moment and then put a hand on his cheek.

"You look kind of sad. Are you all right?"

"I'm OK, Mom," Mark said.

"I hope so," Donna said. "I worry about you two when I leave you alone."

"You didn't have to worry. We managed just fine."

Donna smiled.

"That's good. Did you do anything interesting while I was gone?"

Mark looked at Ben and returned a knowing smile.

"No," Mark said. "We just studied and fended for ourselves in the kitchen. This was one of the most uneventful weeks of our lives."

22: BEN

South Pasadena, California – Monday, March 30, 1959

B en Ryan smiled as he approached the girl at the reference desk of the Midway High School library. He had not seen the striking blonde since Saturday night and wanted talk to her before moving on to the girl who did not care for good-night kisses.

"Hi, Sally," Ben said.

Sally Warner looked up from a stack of papers she was sorting.

"Hi, Ben."

"Can you talk?"

Sally, a student assistant, did not answer right away. She instead glanced at Delores Grant, the school librarian, and watched her for a moment as she checked in books at the other end of the long desk. She returned to Ben when a freshman girl approached the desk and asked Mrs. Grant for help.

"I can talk if we keep our voices down," Sally said.

"OK," Ben said.

"What do you want to talk about?"

"I think you know."

"Is this about Piper?" Sally asked.

"Yes, it's about Piper. I want to know if she said anything when you went to the girls' room Saturday night. I think she might be mad at me."

"She's not mad at you."

Ben glanced at Mrs. Grant and saw that she had finished helping the freshman. He returned to Sally when the librarian went back to her books.

"How do you know she's not mad?" Ben asked.

"I just know. Girls don't say nice things about boys when they are mad at them."

"She said nice things about me?"

Sally nodded.

"She said *several* nice things. She said she misjudged you."

Ben took a moment to process the information. If nothing else, he was happy to learn that Piper McIntire, the girl who kept him awake at night, didn't think he was a bore or a jerk.

"That's good to hear," Ben said.

Sally returned to her papers.

"Why are you worried? I thought you two had a nice time."

"I thought so too," Ben said. "It's just that our date ended on a sour note."

"Oh?" Sally asked. "How so?"

"I don't know. She just—"

Ben stopped when a tall person entered his field of vision. He turned his head and watched with interest as the person, a well-dressed middle-aged man with a deformed ear, carried a short stack of yearbooks to the reference desk and handed them to the librarian.

"Did you find what you're looking for?" Mrs. Grant asked.

The man shook his head.

"I didn't. Do you have more yearbooks?"

"No. That's it," Mrs. Grant said. "This school is just four years old."

"I see."

"Are you looking for a person, Agent Richards?"

Agent Richards?

The man nodded.

"I'm looking for a young woman."

"What's her name?" Mrs. Grant asked. "Perhaps I can help."

The man hesitated.

"I believe her name is Colleen Finley, but I don't know for sure. I know only that she visited Las Vegas two weekends ago with a male of similar age and left town in an Edsel bearing California plates and a MAULERS BOOSTER bumper sticker."

Ben gave the man his full attention. He had no doubt that the woman he sought was the woman he knew as Mary Beth McIntire.

"What does she look like?" Mrs. Grant asked.

The agent paused again before answering.

"The man she victimized described her as a slim, pretty brunette of medium height. He guessed her age to be twenty to twenty-two. That's why I wanted to see your yearbooks. We believe she or her male companion graduated from this school a few years ago."

The librarian rubbed her chin. "I don't know what to tell you. Dozens of former students fit that description. Can you offer more details?"

Agent Richards nodded.

"There is one more thing."

"What's that?"

"Miss Finley spoke with a southern accent and may have come to this area from Huntsville, Alabama. Can you think of a girl who came here from the South?"

Mrs. Grant shook her head.

"I remember some students from Nevada, Arizona, and even two from New York, but I don't recall any from the South. The only new student this year is a girl from Germany."

The man frowned.

"I see."

Ben felt his stomach twist when Mrs. Grant looked around the mostly empty room. He felt it drop when the librarian turned to her right and zeroed in on the students at the end of the desk.

"Perhaps one of you can help," Mrs. Grant said. "Ben and Sally, this is Special Agent Trent Richards of the FBI. He's trying to find a slim brunette who committed a crime in Las Vegas this month. He believes the woman attended Midway a few years ago and may have come here from Huntsville, Alabama. Can either of you think of a person who fits that description."

Sally looked at Ben, sighed, and then returned to her supervisor.

"I can't think of anyone in particular, but then I'm probably not the best person to ask. I didn't know many juniors and seniors as an underclassman."

"How about you, Ben?"

"I'm the same way, Mrs. Grant. I'm drawing a blank."

The librarian frowned.

"Well, thank you, anyway."

Ben nodded. He relaxed when Mrs. Grant turned away and grimaced when Agent Richards studied him closely. He did not care for the intense scrutiny.

The librarian resumed her conversation with the visitor.

"Have you met with Principal Raines?"

"I have," Agent Richards said. "He sent me here."

"Then I'm afraid I can't help you more," Mrs. Grant said. "I'm sorry."

The lawman smiled.

"That's all right, ma'am. You've been very helpful. I'll show myself out."

Ben watched the FBI agent walk across the room and disappear through a door. He did not know what to make of the odd exchange, but he did know one thing. The authorities wanted Mary Beth and maybe Mark for reasons that were as clear as a desert sky.

Ben wanted to speak to Sally and clarify a few things, but he knew he couldn't say a word with others around. So he waited for a break. He got that break a few minutes later when the librarian stamped the last of her books, put them on a cart, and turned to her student assistant.

"I have to leave for a minute," Mrs. Grant said. "Can you watch the desk?"

Sally nodded.

"I can handle things."

"Thank you."

Ben watched Mrs. Grant closely as she turned around, pushed her cart against the wall, and headed for the door. He waited until she exited the room and then returned his attention to Sally. When he did, he saw a classmate with a pale face and troubled eyes.

"I know what you're thinking," Ben said. "You're thinking that Piper lived in Huntsville and has an older sister who looks just like her. You're thinking that one or both of them might be criminals. Well, I can tell you, unequivocally, they are not. Mark and I spent that entire weekend with them. They even have a different last name. The Alabama connection is nothing more than a crazy coincidence."

Sally sighed.

"That's a relief. That's a *big* relief."

"Don't tell anyone about this," Ben said. "I don't want Piper to hear a rumor that the FBI is looking for someone from the South. She'll just worry over nothing."

"I won't say a thing," Sally said.

"Thanks."

Ben took a deep breath and relaxed. He finally had time to digest the past ten minutes. He had time to think about what he would say to Mark, Mary Beth, and Piper.

The peaceful moment did not last long. Five minutes after Mrs. Grant put away her books, asked Sally to watch the desk, and left the room, she returned. She reentered the library with Principal Warren Raines, Vice Principal Dale Thompson, and a look of panic on her face.

"He stood right there," Mrs. Grant said. "We spoke for several minutes. Ben and Sally saw him too. They can probably give you an accurate description."

The principal stepped toward Ben and Sally. "Is that true?" Raines asked. "Did you see the man who spoke to Mrs. Grant?"

Sally nodded nervously.

"Ben?"

"I saw him," Ben said. "What's going on, Mr. Raines? The FBI agent said he met with you. He said you sent him to the library to talk to Mrs. Grant."

The principal sighed. "I didn't meet anyone, Ben. I didn't send anyone to the library," Raines said. "The man you saw was not an agent. The man you saw was an imposter."

23: MARY BETH

Mary Beth stared at Ben and repeated the question.

"Are you sure? Are you sure about his ear?"

"I'm positive," Ben said. "It looked like a stub."

Mary Beth closed her eyes and slumped in her bright red booth seat. She could no longer deny the obvious. Someone in Southern California wanted to find her and perhaps harm her.

"I feel sick."

Mark reached across the table for four, one of a dozen in Dino's Diner, and took Mary Beth's hands. He held them until she finally met his gaze.

"What do you want to do?" Mark asked.

"I don't know," Mary Beth said. "I need time to think."

"Why would he look for you?" Piper asked. "Even if he found you, he couldn't prove you did anything but make a legal bet. You didn't bribe a player to miss a shot. You put money on a game two thousand miles away. He can't prove you cheated."

Mark tapped his fingers on the table.

"Maybe that's not what he wants to do."

"What do you mean?" Ben asked.

"I mean the 'FBI agent' is not the man we cheated," Mark said. "He's not the man who paid us two thousand dollars. He was a bystander."

"What are you getting at?"

"I think he wants the book. That's the only thing that makes sense. He's not after two thousand. He's after two million. He wants a sports guide that's potentially priceless."

Mary Beth took a breath.

"I think you're right."

"Do you still have the book?" Mark asked.

Mary Beth nodded.

"It's back at the motel."

"How could he possibly know about the book?" Piper asked. "You didn't take it into the club. You left it in the car. I remember seeing it both times."

Ben looked at Mary Beth.

"Did you mention the book to anyone? Did you *say* something?"

Mary Beth closed her eyes, pressed her temples, and searched her mind for answers. She needed only a minute to identify her mistake.

"I didn't say something," Mary Beth said. "I *did* something. I discarded a receipt."

"You what?" Ben asked.

"I threw out the receipt for the book. I tossed it in a garbage can when Mark and I walked from the club to the car. I gave a stranger the title of a book that won't be published for nearly sixty years. He knows I have the book and knows I'm from the future."

Piper looked at her sister.

"Did the man see you leave the club? Did he follow you out?"

"I don't think so," Mary Beth said. "He wasn't even there on Sunday."

"Then I think it's unlikely he has your receipt."

"He has *something*, Piper!"

"You're right. He does," Piper said. "He has instructions from the club owner to find you, watch you, and wait for you to make a mistake. As long as you don't say or do anything that suggests you swindled a bookie out of two thousand dollars, you'll be fine. *We'll* be fine."

Mary Beth conceded Piper's theory had merit. She did *not* concede the danger had passed. She did not have enough information to cross that bridge. She thought about the matter for another minute and turned to the young man who had called the gathering.

"Tell me more about yesterday, Ben. Who knows about the man? Who knows about *us*?"

Ben leaned forward.

"The whole school knows about the man. The principal made an announcement this morning. He advised us to watch out for a guy pretending to be an FBI agent."

"What did you tell the principal?" Mary Beth asked.

"I told him what I told the police," Ben said. "I told him I saw a man approach Mrs. Grant, the school librarian, and ask questions about a woman named Colleen Finley."

"What else did you say?"

"I said the 'FBI agent' thought Miss Finley was from Huntsville, Alabama, and had attended Midway a few years ago."

Mary Beth sighed.

100

"Do the authorities think the woman is me?"

Ben shook his head.

"I don't think so. They didn't ask about you. I'm pretty sure the police think the fake agent is just a pervert who likes looking at yearbook pictures of high school girls."

Mary Beth frowned. She could believe that.

"What about Sally? What does she think?"

"She suspects something," Ben said. "She knows you're from Alabama and knows that you fit Colleen Finley's description, but I don't think she'll be a problem."

"Why do you say that?"

Ben smiled.

"I told her that you and Piper spent the weekend in question with Mark and me in L.A."

"You vouched for us?"

"I did. I would do it again too."

"Thank you," Mary Beth said.

"Did Sally talk to the police?" Piper asked.

Ben nodded.

"She gave a brief statement and left. She wanted no part of it."

Mary Beth looked at Ben with new admiration. He was more than just a cocky high school senior who collected girlfriends like trading cards. He was a stand-up guy.

"Did you say the fake agent looked at yearbooks?" Mary Beth asked.

"That's what he did first," Ben said. "He apparently looked at every one."

Mary Beth turned to Mark.

"It's a good thing you didn't attend Midway High School. The man would have needed only minutes to find your class picture and learn your identity."

"You're right," Mark said.

Mary Beth returned to Ben.

"Did the man get a good look at you?"

Ben nodded.

"He did. He even looked at me funny."

"Weren't you scared?" Mary Beth asked.

"I was at first," Ben said. "Then I remembered he wanted a woman in her early twenties and her male companion. Sally and I didn't look like Bonnie and Clyde."

Mary Beth laughed.

"Oh, Ben, that is just what I needed. I feel better already."

Mark looked at Mary Beth.

"We still need to figure out what to do next."

101

Mary Beth nodded.

"I know."

"Let's at least get rid of the book," Ben said. "If we ditch the book, then the man won't bother us. He won't have a *reason* to bother us."

"That's not necessarily true," Mark said.

"You think we should keep it?" Mary Beth asked.

"I do."

"Why?"

"I can think of two reasons," Mark said.

"Oh?"

"The first should be obvious. If we tell the man we discarded the book, he'll just think we're lying. He'll have a powerful incentive to 'convince' us to tell him where it is."

"What's the other reason?" Mary Beth asked.

Mark looked at each of the others.

"That should be even more obvious. If we hold on to the book, we'll have a bargaining chip. We'll have something we can give him if we find ourselves in a spot."

Piper leaned forward.

"You're still assuming that this man knows about the book."

"I am," Mark said. "I am for the sake of argument."

"So what should we do?" Mary Beth asked.

Mark looked at her thoughtfully.

"You should do what's best for you. If you think it's too dangerous to stay in 1959, then you should go back to 2017. I'll understand. So will Ben."

Mary Beth appealed to Piper.

"What do you want to do?"

Piper glanced at each of the others and then gazed out a plate-glass window at cars zipping down a busy street. She needed only a moment to produce an answer.

"I want to stay," Piper said. "There's still more I want to do here."

"What about the stalker?" Mary Beth asked.

"I know things could still get dicey, but I want to stay. We will never again have the chance to time travel. I don't want to go back until we absolutely have to."

"I feel the same way."

"That's good," Piper said.

"I have one request though."

"What's that?"

"I want to make a quick trip to 2017," Mary Beth said. She took a breath. "I want to check in on Mom and Dad."

24: MARK

Beverly Hills, California – Friday, June 2, 2017

Several hours and fifty-eight years after setting aside one problem at a table for four, Mark, Ben, Mary Beth, and Piper rushed into another at a table for six. Each found it easier to elude the grasp of a Las Vegas stalker than the scrutiny of two Alabama parents.

Mark handed his menu to a waiter, sipped his water, and smiled at the couple sitting across from him. He had smiled a lot at Brody and Colleen McIntire since they had invited him to lunch. Smiling beat answering pointed questions seven days a week.

"Thanks for letting us join you," Mark said. "It's not every day that Ben and I have the opportunity to meet people from the South. This is a real treat."

"It is for us as well," Brody said. "It is not every day we have the chance to meet two young men from Los Angeles. This city has changed a lot in the last thirty years."

You have no idea.

"It has."

"Mary Beth tells us you're a college senior."

"I am," Mark said. "I'm currently working toward a degree in engineering."

"What do you want to do after graduation?" Brody asked.

"I want to build rockets and missiles."

Brody smiled.

"Then you should come to the Rocket City. Huntsville is a hub for rocket and missile development. I know. I've worked on NASA's Space Launch System since 2012."

Mark glanced at Mary Beth, who sat to his left, and noticed a playful grin. If she was sweating through this hastily arranged gathering, she had a funny way of showing it.

"I've read about that program, Colonel. I plan to look into it."

"I hope you do, Mark. I hope you do."

Mark took a breath when it appeared he had weathered the storm. He didn't mind talking to parents, but he did mind running a gauntlet of endless questions. He knew it was only a matter of time before he said something stupid. Encounters like this were risky.

Mark had already taken his share of risks in the preceding hours. He and Ben had smuggled Mary Beth and Piper into the Painted Lady while Donna Ryan slept, woken them before Donna got up, and led them through the time tunnel and into the drizzle of June 2, 2017.

Mary Beth and Piper rewarded Mark and Ben by inviting them to lunch. They told their parents they had met some boys on a morning walk and wanted to liven up a family meal by bringing them along. Neither parent objected.

Mark sipped his water again and looked around the table. He wanted to assess the faces in his party before jumping into another conversation. He saw both safety and danger.

Mary Beth and Piper grinned. They had arranged the unlikely gathering and no doubt felt they were getting a good return on their investment. Nothing beat watching confident young men from 1959 interact with a perceptive fiftyish couple from 2017.

Ben maintained a poker face and kept to himself. He had objected to meeting Brody and Colleen for reasons that now seemed obvious. He was even more afraid than his brother of saying something that might trigger a barrage of questions.

Brody smiled politely and divided his attention between the people at the table and an investment brochure next to his plate. He obviously had better things to do than interrogate two men he would almost certainly never see again.

Colleen apparently did not. She had asked several questions of Mark and Ben and continued to study them like curiosities in a traveling circus. She sipped her iced tea and smiled at Mark when he looked across the table and returned her gaze.

"I like your attire, Mark. Most college students prefer T-shirts and shorts over nice shirts and slacks," Colleen said. "I admire people who make an effort to look their best."

"Thank you," Mark said.

"Mark is very old school, Mom," Mary Beth said. "He told me this morning that nothing is more important than making a good first impression."

Colleen smiled.

"I like that. I believed the same thing when I was your age."

Mark nodded. He considered letting the matter drop but decided to keep it going. He wanted to move the conversation onto safer ground and perhaps spare Ben unwanted scrutiny.

"Did you grow up in Alabama, Mrs. McIntire?"

Colleen nodded.

"I was born and raised in Huntsville. So was Brody. We consider it home even though we have spent much of our lives living in other places."

"So I hear," Mark said. "Mary Beth said you spent several years in Germany."

Mark looked at Mary Beth and saw her grin vanish. He had control of the narrative now and planned to drive it in a new direction. Turnabout, he thought, was fair play.

"I don't know if 'several' is the right word," Colleen said. "We spent a few years there when the girls were very young."

"So Mary Beth and Piper did not attend school in Germany?"

"Oh, heavens no. We left Europe when Mary Beth was five."

"That's funny. I'm sure she said she attended school in Germany," Mark said. He rubbed his chin. "I guess I misunderstood what she said."

Mark laughed to himself when he saw Mary Beth throw daggers with her eyes. For the first time since stepping foot into Barton's of Beverly Hills, he was enjoying himself.

"That's easy to do," Colleen said. "I misunderstand people all the time when they talk about their backgrounds. I think it is human nature to hear only what we want to hear."

"I agree," Mark said.

Mark relaxed and enjoyed the rest of the meal. For the next fifty minutes, he engaged in light conversation with Brody, his inquisitive wife, and their suddenly reticent daughters. He covered for Ben when he could, changed the subject when he had to, and gently needled Mary Beth every chance he got. He found the experience much to his liking.

Mark was grateful that Mary Beth had asked him to lunch and just as grateful he did not have to pick up the tab. He could not believe that the cost of one entrée exceeded what he had made in a week as a soda jerk in high school. He smiled kindly at Brody when he placed several large bills on the table and the others rose from their upholstered seats.

"Thank you for lunch, Colonel," Mark said.

"Thank you," Ben added.

"You're welcome, gentlemen. It's been a pleasure."

Brody helped Colleen out of her chair and guided her around the large table. He stopped when they reached the young adults on the other side. He looked at his oldest daughter.

105

"Are you going back to the house?" Brody asked.

Mary Beth shook her head.

"We're going to hang out with these two for a while. We want to spend some more time with them before dropping them off."

"Where do you boys reside?" Colleen asked.

"We live in West Adams," Mark said. "We live with our mother in a turn-of-the-century mansion. It's not far from where we met Mary Beth and Piper."

Colleen cocked her head.

"What a coincidence. We've stayed in a turn-of-the-century mansion in the same area all week. I didn't realize Los Angeles had so many old homes."

Mark smiled.

"This town has a lot of things."

"I guess so," Colleen said.

Brody looked at Mary Beth and Mark.

"You four should check out the Farmers Market. I understand it's quite a place."

"It is," Mark said.

"I imagine you've been there," Brody said.

"I have. It's nice."

The colonel turned to Mary Beth.

"There's always the tar pits too."

Mary Beth smiled.

"Thanks for the suggestions, Dad, but I think we have it covered."

"Are you sure?" Brody asked.

"I'm sure," Mary Beth said. She smiled. "We might even investigate more of the mansions. You never know what one can find in old houses."

25: MARY BETH

Los Angeles, California – Wednesday, April 1, 1959

I f there was one thing Mary Beth did not like about time traveling, it was that it killed any chance to rest. Since leaving South Pasadena around nine thirty Tuesday night, she had tossed and turned on a guest bed, spent half a day in 2017, and then returned to 1959 in the wee hours of the morning. If she did nothing else on this day of fools, she would sleep for eighteen hours.

"Are you sure your mom is not awake?" Mary Beth asked.

Mark nodded.

"I'm pretty sure. She rarely rises before seven."

Mary Beth sighed. She hoped that was true. She did not want to meet Donna Ryan for the first time while sneaking out of her house under the cover of darkness.

She leaned against the wall of the time tunnel as blue and white crystals flickered above. She never tired of the pretty lights that signified something both beautiful and mysterious.

"Do you have a plan for the day?" Mary Beth asked.

Mark smiled.

"I have a plan for the *week*."

Mary Beth raised a brow.

"What's that supposed to mean?"

Mark grinned.

"It means I'm taking you to a fraternity formal on Friday."

"What if I don't want to go?" Mary Beth asked.

"Then I'll take Piper," Mark said. "I hear she likes dances."

The others laughed heartily.

Mary Beth liked seeing her sister laugh. She had not seen Piper laugh more than once or twice since she had returned from the Spring Fling

Saturday night. She wondered if Piper and Ben still got along. She wondered if they even liked each other. Sixty seconds after leading three people into the time tunnel, Mark led them out. Then he walked to a switch, flipped on the lights, and stepped to the center of the dingy basement. Mary Beth, Piper, and Ben joined him a moment later.

"What do we do now?" Mary Beth asked.

"We walk up the stairs quietly," Mark said. "When we get to the door, I'll pop it open, check for signs of life, and let you pass if the coast is clear. I don't think Mom is awake, but I don't know for sure. There's a first time for everything."

"Then what?"

"Then Ben will drive you back to the motel."

"Won't your mother suspect something?" Mary Beth asked.

"No. She'll just think he left early for school," Mark said. He looked at Ben. "You have a test today, don't you?"

Ben nodded.

"I have two."

"There you go," Mark said.

"What about you?" Mary Beth asked.

Mark looked at his questioner.

"I'll leave for school at ten like I normally do. If Mom asks why I have bags under my eyes, I'll just tell her I hung out with a wild crowd Tuesday night. She'll believe me."

Mary Beth smiled and shook her head.

"You're something."

Mark laughed.

"I try."

Mary Beth looked at the group leader more thoughtfully.

"I still want to meet her."

"Who?" Mark asked. "My mom?"

"Yes. I want to meet her."

Mark sighed.

"You will. I just need to think of a way to introduce you and Piper. Unlike your folks, my mother won't believe we all met on a morning walk."

"Are you saying my parents are gullible, Mr. Ryan?"

Mark chuckled.

"No. I'm saying *my* parent can tell when I'm lying. I'll have to come up with a story she'll believe. I don't think she'll buy the time-travel thing."

Mary Beth giggled.

"I don't either."

Mark looked at the group.

"Is everyone ready?"

Three people nodded.

108

"Then let's go," Mark said.

The engineering student led the others through the basement and up the stone steps. When he reached the door, he opened it slowly, stuck his head through the gap, and then pulled his head back. He turned to the group, smiled, and held up a thumb.

Mary Beth stifled a laugh when she saw Mark give the OK. She felt like a sixth-grader sneaking out of a slumber party. She hadn't had this much fun in years. A moment later, the time travelers entered the mansion's living quarters, walked through a dark hallway with a squeaky floor, and gathered near the front door. They managed to do so without rousing anything more than a fluffy gray cat. The Himalayan walked over to Mary Beth, looked up at her, and then nuzzled against her leg.

Mark smiled.

"Meet Charlotte."

Mary Beth waved at the cat.

"Hi, Charlotte."

Ben quietly opened the front door, motioned to Piper, and then stepped back as she exited the residence and walked into the cool morning air. He turned to face Mary Beth.

"We'll be in the car."

"I'll just be a minute," Mary Beth said.

Ben glanced at Mark.

"Tell Mom I'll mow the lawn after school."

"OK," Mark said.

Ben gave his brother a half-hearted salute and walked out the door.

"What's the matter with Ben?" Mary Beth asked. "He doesn't seem happy."

"He's not," Mark said. "He's been that way since Saturday night. I don't think his date with Piper ended on a high note."

"She's acting funny too."

Mark chuckled. "People do that in high school."

Mary Beth took Mark's hands and met his gaze.

"Thank you for meeting my parents. I think they like you."

Mark smiled sadly.

"I like them too."

Mary Beth leaned forward and kissed him softly on the lips.

"Call me this afternoon if you can't stop by."

Mark nodded.

"I will."

Mary Beth released his hands and stepped to the door that Ben had left ajar. She opened the door wide, turned to face Mark, and offered a sweet smile. "I'm looking forward to Friday."

26: PIPER

South Pasadena, California – Thursday, April 2, 1959

S itting on a hot bleacher that only a diehard fan could love, Piper stared at an asphalt court and watched a fuzzy ball go back and forth. She didn't care much for tennis – or most sports, for that matter – but she watched anyway. She wanted to show some school spirit and at least passively support one of the best high school players in the area.

"Ben's good," Piper said.

Sally Warner smiled.

"That's putting it mildly."

"What do you mean?"

"I mean he's the defending league champ."

Piper nodded.

"That's impressive."

Sally looked at her friend.

"You don't sound impressed."

"I'm impressed," Piper said. "I'm just not very happy."

"What's wrong?"

"It's complicated."

Sally smiled.

"Nothing can be *that* complicated. You just got here."

Piper laughed.

"You should bottle that optimism."

Sally studied Piper's face.

"Does this have anything to do with Ben?"

"Yes," Piper said.

"I don't understand. I thought you liked him."

"I do. I like him a lot. *That's* the problem."

Sally tilted her head.

"Now I'm really confused."

Piper turned to face Sally.

"Then let me un-confuse you. I'm leaving school in a few weeks."

"I know," Sally said. "We all are. We're graduating!"

"You don't understand. I'm leaving California and never coming back," Piper said. "So I don't want to start something I can't finish."

"Are you going back to Germany?"

"No. I'm going farther."

Piper laughed to herself as her new BFF frowned and furrowed her brow. She wasn't sure which was more painful to watch: Sally frowning over the loss of a new friend or Sally trying to figure out which countries were farther away than Germany.

"That stinks," Sally said. "We just met."

Piper sighed.

"I know."

"Will you at least stay until graduation?"

"I'll try."

"I hope so," Sally said. "I like you."

"I like you too."

Piper smiled at Sally. She wondered if all blue-eyed blondes had sunny dispositions. Then she saw her least favorite person approach and remembered they did not.

"I see Ben's backers are here today," Vicki Cole said.

Piper braced for battle.

"Hello, Vicki."

The not-so-sunny blonde led a friend up the mostly empty bleachers. She stopped about halfway up, looked around for a suitable place to sit, and then continued toward the top. She finally settled on a seat about eight feet to Piper's right. No one sat between them.

"I hear you've been stuffing ballot boxes again," Vicki said. "Where on earth do you get all that money?"

Piper lifted her nose.

"I'm a successful entrepreneur."

"I believe it. You're young and pretty and live in a motel," Vicki said. She grinned. "I'm sure you do quite well."

Piper turned away and fumed. She berated herself for carelessness. Instead of shutting down the ice queen with a clever comment, she had stepped in a pile the size of Mount Whitney.

"Just ignore her," Sally said.

Piper frowned.

"I'm trying."

Piper smoothed the wrinkles from her plaid skirt and returned her attention to the match. She gave Ben a subtle wave when he looked her way.

"I don't know why you bother," Vicki said to Piper. "He's not going to acknowledge you. He wouldn't acknowledge you if you stripped naked in front of the net."

"Don't respond," Sally said.

Piper tapped her fingers on the wooden bench as she pondered the consequences of scratching Vicki's eyes out. She took a breath and turned toward her antagonist.

"Do you really believe that?" Piper asked. "Do you really believe he wouldn't acknowledge me?"

"Yes. I do," Vicki said matter-of-factly. "You're simply not that distracting."

Piper hardened her stare.

"I'm more distracting than you."

"I don't think so," Vicki said.

"Let's put it to a test then," Piper said. She scanned the vicinity for eavesdroppers and then returned to Vicki. "I'll bet you five dollars I can get Ben to miss a serve before you can."

Vicki smiled smugly.

"You're on."

Sally put a hand on Piper's knee.

"I don't think this is a good idea."

Vicki laughed.

"You should listen to your friend."

"I probably should," Piper said. "I should probably walk away and let you wallow in your arrogance, but I'm not. I would much rather rub your nose in it."

Vicki smirked.

"Let's get on with it then."

"Let's do. You can even go first."

"OK."

Vicki turned toward the court and awaited the start of a new game. She called out to her would-be prom king when he bounced the ball and prepared to serve.

"Let's go, Ben! You can do it!"

Ben looked at Vicki and smiled. Then he threw the ball in the air, struck it with a wooden racket, and fired it past his Burbank opponent.

Piper smiled.

"I guess he's focused today."

Vicki huffed.

"I'm just getting started."

112

Piper laughed.

"Sure you are."

Piper turned away from Vicki, looked at Ben, and considered her first move. She pondered a few creative options but ultimately settled on something simple. She whistled loudly when Ben tossed the second ball skyward. He answered her interruption with an ace and a glare.

Vicki laughed.

"That's precious. You inspired him *and* made him mad."

Piper stared at the blonde.

"Shut up."

Vicki laughed again. She laughed loudly and heartily until Ben retrieved both balls, walked up to the end line, and prepared to serve.

Vicki raised her game the second time around. She called out to Ben, fluffed her thick platinum hair, and batted her lashes.

Ben responded in predictable fashion. He hit a pathetic serve that his opponent returned easily and forcefully. He lost the point after a short volley.

"You're getting better," Piper said. "I guess it's time to get serious."

Vicki raised a brow.

"I guess it is."

Piper turned to Sally.

"What's the score?"

"Ben's up thirty to fifteen," Sally said. "Don't make him lose."

"I won't," Piper said. She giggled. "I'm not that mean."

Piper considered her next move as Ben returned to the service line and bounced a ball. She decided to answer Vicki's creativity with fresh audacity.

"Come on, Ben. Do it for us," Piper said. "Do it for *me*."

Ben again eyed his cheering section.

Piper again tried to distract him. She gazed at Ben seductively, blew him a kiss, and watched with amusement as he served a ball that barely cleared the net.

Piper smiled at Vicki.

"I'm getting closer."

"Zip it!" Vicki snapped. "You're starting to annoy me."

Piper laughed.

"I'm sorry."

Vicki returned to the action. She focused again on Ben but this time did nothing to irritate or distract him. She watched in silence as he aced a serve to take a forty-to-thirty lead.

Vicki did not stay silent for long. She resumed the fight after Ben collected a loose ball, walked toward the line, and glanced at the bleachers.

"Finish him off, Ben," Vicki said. "If you do, I'll bake you something special."

113

She touched the buttons on her blouse.

Ben apparently liked baked goods. He fired a rocket that raced over the net. The serve put his opponent on the defensive, but it did not put him away. Nor did an equally brutal second shot. The Burbank player regrouped, turned the tables, and rallied to force a tie.

"I like your style," Piper said to Vicki. She smiled. "You're good."

"You can't do this all day," Sally said. "It's not fair to Ben."

Piper pondered the comment and nodded.

"You're right. It's not."

Vicki raised a brow.

"Does that mean you're conceding?"

"No," Piper said. "It means I'm going to show some class. I'm not going to let this escalate into something ridiculous."

Vicki sang a taunting song.

"Someone's backing out. Someone's backing out."

Piper ignored the dig and focused on Ben. She watched him closely as he walked to a corner of the court, collected a ball, and slowly returned to the line.

"Come on, Ben!" Piper said. "You can do it."

Ben responded positively to the positive reinforcement. He tossed the ball in the air, brought his racket forward, and fired a blistering serve past his opponent.

Piper shouted her approval and then shouted it again. She shouted until she forgot all about her pity party with Sally Warner and her silly bet with Vicki Cole.

She smiled at Ben when he dropped to tie a shoe. She still didn't know what she would do with him, but she *did* know she could no longer ignore him. He was as much a part of her fifties experience as the Painted Lady, Midway High School, and poodle skirts.

Piper cheered Ben again when he finished tying his shoe and picked up his racket.

"Come on, Ben. End this *now*," Piper said. "If you do, I'll take you to dinner."

Ben looked at Piper, laughed, and gave her a thumbs up. Then he retrieved a tennis ball from his pocket, threw it in the air, and hit it into the net.

Piper and Sally laughed hard.

"Let me guess," Sally said. "That's not what you had in mind."

Piper smiled and shook her head.

"No. I forgot about the bet."

"Sure you did," Vicki said.

Piper grinned.

"Believe what you want. You owe me five dollars."

Vicki frowned.

"I don't have five dollars."

Piper looked at her disgruntled rival.

"Then get five dollars from you parents," Piper said. "Bring it to school tomorrow and donate it to Mr. West's surgery fund. Or give it to my favorite charity."

"What's that?"

Piper smiled.

"I think you know. Just look for the jar with the fives."

27: MARY BETH

Los Angeles, California – Friday, April 3, 1959

Mary Beth settled into her chair at her round candlelit table for eight and took a moment to simply breathe. She had found it difficult to breathe since walking into the Ambassador Hotel, a six-story Mediterranean Revival colossus on Wilshire Boulevard.

She gazed at the front of the Embassy Ballroom and tried to imagine Robert Kennedy speaking to supporters in the very same room. She could picture the noisy rally following Kennedy's victory in the California primary on June 4, 1968. She could not picture the chaos following the successful attempt on his life a few hours later.

Then Mary Beth reminded herself that much of the history of the hotel and the world at large had not yet been written. Bobby Kennedy was still alive and well. So were many of the artists who had performed and still would perform in the hotel's famous Cocoanut Grove lounge.

"Are you all right?" Mark asked.

"I'm fine," Mary Beth said. "I'm just a little overwhelmed. I've never been in a place like this. I've never been in a place even remotely like this."

Mark took her hand.

"That's why I asked you to the dance. I knew you would appreciate it."

Mary Beth smiled.

"You asked me to the dance because you needed a *date.*"

Six others laughed.

"She has a point, Mark. You didn't give the dance a moment's notice until Wednesday," Margaret Pringle said. She laughed. "You're lucky you found such a nice girl on short notice."

"I can't argue with that," Mark said.

Margaret sipped a martini and then turned toward the woman Mark had introduced as Mary Beth McIntire, a recent graduate of the University

116

of Alabama who had come to Southern California to enroll her younger sister in a local high school. The redheaded English major had already asked many questions about the slim brunette with the southern twang.

"I understand you graduated with a degree in biology," Margaret said. "Is that right?"

Mary Beth nodded.

"I earned a Bachelor of Science degree last semester."

"Are you going into teaching?"

"No," Mary Beth said. "I'm going into medicine. I hope to become a surgeon."

Margaret smiled.

"That's ambitious."

Mary Beth resisted the temptation to say something snotty. She suspected that Margaret meant no offense. She also remembered that most women in 1959 went from diplomas to diapers and rarely ventured beyond the fields of nursing, education, and librarianship.

"I know I'll face obstacles, but I still want to take that path," Mary Beth said. "I want to work in a large hospital and save lives."

"Have you applied to any medical schools?" Margaret asked.

Mary Beth paused before answering. She wanted to tell the truth but did not want to paint herself into a corner. She had no idea which medical schools operated in 1959. She did not know which ones admitted women. So she went with something safe.

"I've applied to several schools in the South. I hope to hear from at least one of them by the end of the month and go from there."

"Have you considered schools in California?" Margaret asked.

"No."

"You should. There are four in Los Angeles alone."

"I didn't know that," Mary Beth said.

"I know it because this big lug applied to them all," Margaret said. She took the hand of the blond man to her left. "Dennis starts classes in Loma Linda this fall."

Mary Beth addressed the lug.

"Have you decided on a specialty?"

"No," Dennis Green said. "I want to consider my options for at least a year before committing to anything."

"That's smart," Mary Beth said. "It's a big decision."

"I think so."

Mary Beth smiled at Dennis, Mark's best friend and Zeta Alpha Rho roommate, and then looked around the linen-covered table. She saw Jack Prince, a tall water polo player; Joyce Gaines, a gymnast with a lovely smile; Carter Williams, the suave rush chairman; and Anita Hutchinson, a bubbly cheerleader who attended the university on a full-ride scholarship.

117

"Are all of you seniors?" Mary Beth asked.

"I'm not," Joyce said. "Neither is Anita. We're juniors."

Mary Beth nodded.

"What about the rest of you?"

"We're seniors," Jack said.

"What do you plan to do after graduation?" Mary Beth asked.

Jack sipped his drink, a whiskey sour, and looked across the table.

"I intend to enlist in the Navy."

Joyce cleared her throat.

"Excuse me," Jack said. He smiled. "I intend to marry Joyce and *then* enlist in the Navy."

Mary Beth laughed.

"I see you have your priorities in order."

"I do *now*," Jack said.

The others laughed.

"What do you plan to do in the Navy?" Mary Beth asked.

"I hope to fly jets," Jack said. "I'd like to learn a thing or two on Uncle Sam's dime and then try my hand at commercial aviation. I think it has a bright future."

Mary Beth laughed to herself. She wondered what Jack Prince would think of Boeing 747s, Concorde SSTs, and Airbus A380s. She knew what Mark thought of them. He had gushed about modern aircraft and spacecraft several times since learning about them through magazines.

Mary Beth squeezed Mark's hand, gave him a warm smile, and then turned to the rush chairman. She noticed that he seemed in tune with the ongoing conversation.

"What about you, Carter?" Mary Beth asked. "What's next for you?"

"Senator Kennedy is next," Carter said with a distinctive Boston accent. He pulled his arm from Anita's shoulders and looked at Mary Beth. "I start work in his D.C. office in June."

"You know John F. Kennedy?"

Carter nodded.

"I've known him for years. Our families are close."

Mary Beth smiled.

"I'm impressed."

"You shouldn't be," Carter said. "He's just a senator."

Mary Beth grinned.

"I think he's more than that. He's a man with serious potential."

Carter laughed.

"You ought to sit down with my father. He is convinced that Kennedy is going to run for president next year."

"You don't think he will?" Mary Beth asked.

Carter shook his head.

118

"He'll wait until sixty-four or sixty-eight. I'm sure of it."

Mary Beth glanced at Mark and saw a subtle smile form on his face. She did not know how much he had read or heard about John F. Kennedy, but she suspected that he had read or heard enough to know that the senator would not sit out the 1960 election.

"I guess we'll see," Mary Beth said.

Carter smiled.

"I guess we will."

Mary Beth nodded and sighed as Carter, Anita, and the others started private conversations. As much as she wanted to tell them about things to come, she knew she could not. She had an obligation to keep her knowledge to herself and let history play out. She pondered the coming year and the coming decade until her date brought her back to the here and now.

"Are you thinking about something interesting?" Mark asked.

Mary Beth smiled.

"Aren't I always?"

"I don't know. I'm not privy to your thoughts."

Mary Beth laughed.

"I guess you're not."

Mark smiled.

"Perhaps we can change that."

"Perhaps we can."

"Are you having a good time?"

"I'm having a great time," Mary Beth said. She paused for a moment as two waiters brought salads and breadsticks to the table. "Thanks for inviting me. I don't think I've ever been to a nicer dinner. In fact, I know I haven't."

Mark chuckled.

"You're saying that to make me feel good."

"I'm saying it because it's *true*," Mary Beth said. "I went to a few nice dinners in high school and college but never one in a five-star hotel swarming with celebrities."

"That surprises me," Mark said.

"It shouldn't. I'm pretty down-to-earth. Piper is the one who likes glitz."

"What's she doing tonight?"

"You mean you don't know?" Mary Beth asked.

"No."

"She's out with Ben."

"She's with Ben?" Mark asked.

Mary Beth nodded.

"She promised to buy him a dinner if he won his tennis match yesterday."

"That's funny," Mark said. "He didn't say a thing to me."

"Don't feel bad. The only reason I know is because Piper asked for money."

"I thought you gave her money the other day."

"I did," Mary Beth said. "She spent it all on clothes and charities."

"Charities?"

"She's still donating generously to Chip and Bunny."

Mark laughed.

"I think someone doesn't want someone to go to the prom with Vicki Cole."

"It appears so," Mary Beth said.

"Are Ben and Piper getting along now?"

"I think so. She doesn't tell me much."

"He's pretty secretive too," Mark said.

Mary Beth gazed at her date.

"Are you?"

"Am I what?" Mark asked.

"Are *you* secretive?"

"I not sure what you're getting at."

"Then let me be clear," Mary Beth said. "Have you told your mom about me?"

Mark nodded.

"In fact, I've done more than that."

"Is that so?" Mary Beth asked.

"That's so."

"Please elaborate."

Mark beamed.

"I told her that Ben and I picked up some girls on Hollywood Boulevard."

"You didn't," Mary Beth said.

Mark laughed.

"I did."

"Mark Ryan!"

"Don't worry. Mom is pretty open-minded about these things. Just wear a nice dress and bring an appetite Sunday afternoon," Mark said. He smiled. "Dinner is at two."

28: PIPER

Piper sucked on the plastic straw three times, smiled seductively at the young man sharing her chocolate milkshake, and raised a brow. For five minutes, she had attempted to get him to laugh and smile. For five minutes, she had succeeded. He, in turn, had done the same.

"Do you like making me laugh?" Ben asked.

Piper smiled.

"I like making you *blush*."

Sally Warner shook her head.

"You two are beginning to worry me."

Wayne Bridges laughed.

"Are they always like this?"

"No," Sally said. "They didn't even like each other until Thursday."

Piper giggled.

"That's not true. I liked him. I just didn't know what to *do* with him," Piper said. She gazed at Ben and smiled. "I *still* don't."

Sally stared at Piper.

"Your milkshake begs to differ."

Piper, Ben, and Wayne laughed loudly. They had laughed several times since crowding into a padded booth at Patty's Drive-In, a teen hotspot on the west side of town.

Piper lifted her nose.

"I'm just getting to know him better."

"That's great," Sally said. "Can you do it without a prop?"

Piper laughed and looked at Ben.

"I think it's time we behaved ourselves."

Ben chuckled.

"I guess."

Sally smiled at Piper and Ben and then settled into her seat at the closed end of the booth. She sipped a strawberry shake she shared with Wayne, grabbed a French fry from a basket in the middle of the table, and then looked thoughtfully at her boyfriend of two years.

"I'd like some music, Wayne."

Piper giggled as she watched Wayne reach into his pocket, pull out a quarter, and hand the coin to Sally. She had no doubt who wore the pants in this relationship.

"I should try that," Piper said.

Sally beamed.

"You should. Boys are easily trained."

Sally winked at Ben and then turned to the tabletop jukebox that stood between a stainless steel napkin dispenser and two condiment bottles. She popped the quarter into a slot and pushed a series of buttons. Within seconds, the first song, "Blueberry Hill" by Fats Domino, streamed out of the musical toaster.

"I like this song," Piper said. "It reminds me of dinner last night."

"Oh?" Sally asked.

Piper nodded.

"I ordered blueberry pie for dessert."

Ben laughed.

"Did you two have a good time?" Sally asked.

"We did. I did anyway," Piper said. She looked at Ben. "It was nice."

Sally looked at Wayne.

"Piper took Ben to dinner last night. She rewarded him for winning his singles match on Thursday even though he took six extra serves to do it."

Piper grinned.

"I believe in rewarding effort."

Sally stared at Piper.

"You *believe* in sticking it to Vicki Cole."

Piper laughed.

"OK. There's that too."

"Where did you go?" Sally asked.

"We went to the El Camino in Alhambra," Piper said. "Mr. Ryan insisted on steak."

Wayne looked at his date.

"Something is wrong here. I've won almost as many matches as Ben. I even beat a guy he lost to last year. How come you never take *me* to dinner?"

Sally smiled and batted her lashes.

"I don't take you, sweetie, because I don't have any money."

Piper giggled.

"She's got you there, Wayne."

122

Wayne huffed.

"It doesn't seem right."

Ben put his arm around Wayne and slapped his shoulder. He grinned as Elvis Presley's "Don't Be Cruel" took its turn on the jukebox.

"You just have to find yourself a rich girl, buddy. It shouldn't be too hard," Ben said. He smiled at Piper. "Rich girls are as common in California as southern belles and fräuleins."

Sally looked at Ben and then at Piper.

"How do you put up with him?"

"I exercise patience," Piper said. "I view Ben like I view the weather in Alabama. If I don't like what I see, I just wait a few minutes for him to improve. He usually does."

"I take it he was better last night," Sally said.

Piper nodded.

"He was a lot better. He was a nice guy – too nice, in fact."

Ben pulled his arm from around Wayne's shoulders.

"What's that supposed to mean?"

Piper looked across the table.

"It means I've seen only a few sides of you. I keep hearing about this wild man who regularly sets the world on fire, but so far all I've seen is a cocky boy who backs up his mouth maybe thirty percent of the time."

Sally smiled.

"Those are fighting words."

Ben stared at Piper.

"I thought you liked me."

"I *do* like you," Piper said. "I think you're cute, smart, and even funny."

"That's better," Ben said.

Piper met his gaze.

"I also think you're overrated. I don't think you're wild at all. When you get right down to it, Ben Ryan, you're kind of boring."

Wayne and Sally grinned.

"You think I'm boring?" Ben asked.

Piper reached across the table and touched Ben's arm.

"Yes. I do."

Ben turned to his best friend.

"Did you hear that, Wayne? Piper thinks I'm boring. Am I boring?"

Wayne shook his head.

"You're obnoxious, but you're not boring."

Ben nodded.

"What do you think, Sally?"

Sally stared at Ben.

"I think you should drop it. Piper obviously misspoke."

Piper snorted.

"No, I didn't. I meant every word. Ben is boring."

Ben grinned at Wayne.

"I think someone needs a demonstration."

Sally turned to her left.

"Say you're sorry, Piper."

"I'm not saying sorry to anyone," Piper said.

Ben looked at Wayne.

"You pick the spot."

"Let's go to the lot," Wayne said.

"The lot it is," Ben said. "The last one there pays for the movie."

"Where is *there*?" Piper asked.

Ben jumped out of his seat. He took Piper's hand.

"Let's go."

"Ben, what's 'the lot'?"

Ben pulled Piper out of the booth.

"It's a magical place."

Wayne and Sally quickly joined them in the aisle.

"Sally, what's going on?" Piper asked.

Sally smiled sheepishly.

"Remember when we talked about breaking rules?"

"Yes."

"Well, we're about to break some."

"Are you ready?" Ben asked Wayne.

Wayne grinned.

"Let's go."

Ben tightened his hold on Piper's hand and led her toward the exit. He looked over his shoulder and smiled at the others when he reached the door.

"See you at the Rose Bowl."

"The what?" Piper asked.

She didn't have a chance to say another word. Before she could say, "Ben is boring," not-so-boring Ben led her to the parking lot and his shiny Thunderbird.

"Get in and buckle up!" Ben said.

Piper did as requested. She opened the passenger door of the T-Bird, plopped onto the leather bucket seat, and fastened her seat belt. For the first time since walking through the time tunnel of the Painted Lady, she regretted opening her mouth.

Ben jumped into the driver's seat of the uncovered convertible, started the ignition, and backed out of his parking space like a robber leaving a bank. He sped through the lot, turned onto Monterey Street, and raced west a few blocks to an intersection and a red light.

He waited only for one car to pass. When Wayne and Sally, who had taken a different route, blew through the intersection from the south in a black 1957 Chevrolet, Ben turned north onto Arroyo Boulevard, stomped on the gas, and began a hot pursuit.

Piper's eyes grew wide.

"Ben?"

"Yeah?"

"I don't think this is a good idea."

Ben laughed.

"You're right. It's not. Hold on!"

Piper looked around.

"Hold on to what?"

Ben smiled but did not reply. He instead leaned toward the radio, punched a button on the dash, and settled into his seat as the T-Bird hit fifty miles per hour. Seconds later, "Whole Lotta Shakin' Goin' On" by Jerry Lee Lewis streamed through the speakers.

"Ben?"

"Yeah?"

"Pasadena has a speed limit."

"I know," Ben said. He grinned. "Yee-haw!"

With that declaration of reckless enthusiasm, Ben Ryan, tennis player, time traveler, and sometime companion of Piper McIntire, stepped up his game. He pressed on the accelerator and continued a mad dash that stretched from South Pasadena to the mother of all stadiums.

Ben needed only a minute to catch up to Wayne. He pulled behind the Chevy as the cars reached a bend in the road and passed it when they entered a straight stretch.

Piper watched in horror as two fuzzy dice, which hung from the rear-view mirror, began to bounce like ping-pong balls in a lottery machine. She gulped when she saw oncoming lights.

"We're in the wrong lane, Ben."

"I know. Isn't it great?"

"No. It's not!"

Ben moved into the right lane when a small truck approached. He returned to the left lane, passed a car in the dwindling light, and smiled at his passenger.

"Are we having fun?"

"No!" Piper said. "You've made your point. Now slow down!"

Ben did not slow down. He sped up to pass another car and then sped up again after Wayne caught him on a stretch, blew past him at seventy miles per hour, and began to pull away.

"I'm not kidding, Ben. This thing doesn't have airbags!"

Piper put her hands on the glove box door, pushed back, and dreamed of outcomes that didn't involve broken bones, severed limbs, or body bags. She vowed never again to feed the brain of a boy whose ego was apparently as fragile as an eggshell.

Ben caught up to Wayne a second time as the cars finally emerged from the hilly Arroyo Seco district and entered an open stretch that led directly to the Rose Bowl. He passed Wayne as the two zipped through a busy intersection and then raced toward the legendary stadium.

"Stop, Ben!" Piper shrieked. "Stop this thing now!"

Ben grinned but did not respond. He instead turned into a spacious parking lot, raced toward a spot in the middle, and finally spun, squealed, and slid to an unsettling stop.

"I hate you!" Piper said. "I really, really *hate* you."

Ben unfastened his seat belt and turned toward Piper. He smiled as Wayne and Sally honked and came to a sliding halt about fifty feet away.

"I know you hate me," Ben said in a mellow voice. "But do you think I'm boring?"

Piper stared at him defiantly.

"Yes!"

Ben softened his gaze.

"Piper?"

"What?"

Ben cocked his head.

"Do you think I'm boring?"

Piper pouted.

"Maybe."

Ben smiled softly.

"Piper?"

"What now?"

"Do you—?"

"Oh, shut up and kiss me."

29: DONNA

Los Angeles, California – Sunday, April 5, 1959

Thirty minutes into the most interesting dinner of her life, Donna Ryan concluded two things. The first was that Mary Beth and Piper McIntire possessed more secrets than a CIA agent. The second was that Mark and Ben did too.

Donna helped herself to more ham and potatoes, sipped some water, and then resumed what she had done for most of the meal. She quietly observed the two delightful young women who sat to her left at the long rectangular table. Each wore a white floral dress, a ponytail, and a captivating smile. Both were slim, pretty, and as southern as fried okra.

Donna studied Mary Beth as she ate her dinner and exchanged playful glances with Mark. She liked this girl. She liked her a lot. Whether she trusted her was another matter.

"Mark tells me you want to be a doctor," Donna said. "Is that true?"

Mary Beth nodded.

"I've applied for admission to several medical schools and hope to hear from at least one by the end of the month. I want to be a trauma surgeon someday."

"Your parents must be proud," Donna said.

"They are."

Donna turned to Piper.

"How about you, young lady? Do you have grand plans as well?"

Piper nodded.

"I do. I hope to pass algebra."

Ben laughed.

"I told you she was funny, Mom."

Donna smiled.

"Yes, you did."

Piper looked at her hostess.

"I didn't mean to sound flippant, Mrs. Ryan. I'm just not as focused as my sister. Assuming I pass my math test on Thursday and graduate from Midway, I intend to study art history and dance at one of the state universities. I'm looking hard at UCLA right now."

"That's wonderful," Donna said. "I wish you the best."

"Thank you," Piper said.

Donna smiled as she processed the girls' comments and the story they had peddled shortly after arriving at twenty past one. She had no difficulty believing that two bright women had set their sights on college and careers. She had great difficulty believing they had come to California from West Germany and had stumbled into Mark and Ben outside a Pasadena movie theater on March 21. She suspected the truth was far more complicated.

She also suspected that Mary Beth and Piper had visited at least once before. Each knew where to find the bathroom. Both wandered through the Painted Lady like it was a second home. And Mary Beth spoke like a woman who had conversed with Mark in the wee hours of April 1.

Donna frowned as she recalled the morning she had risen early, walked down the stairs, and stopped when she had heard footsteps and whispers. She had listened long enough to hear two male voices she knew and one female voice she did not.

Donna suspected the obvious when she walked through the mansion later that morning and found a freshly made bed in the guest room. She was certain that at least one of her sons had engaged in premarital activity in a bedroom only fifteen feet from her own.

Then she pondered the matter and concluded her theory had holes. Mark and Ben had cars, their own money, and independence. They already had the means to fool around. They were also not the kind of young men to act so brazenly. Both loved and respected their mother. They would sooner walk through a hail of bullets than embarrass or disappoint her.

So Donna said nothing to her sons. She kept to herself and went about her daily routine. She was confident that the truth, whatever it was, would announce itself in due course.

Donna gave the matter another moment and then turned to more pressing questions. Who were these girls? Why had they come to Southern California? Where were they from? What spell had they cast on her sons? She laughed silently and looked at Mary Beth.

"Did you enjoy the formal?" Donna asked.

"I did," Mary Beth said. "I enjoyed every minute."

"Did you see much of the hotel?"

"I saw enough. I could spend a week there."

"I feel the same way. I remember my first visit. Ted took me there for our seventh anniversary, a few weeks before Pearl Harbor. I had never been to a hotel that large or fancy," Donna said. She took a breath. "Did you go to the Cocoanut Grove?"

Mary Beth nodded.

"We went there after the dance."

She smiled.

"I could spend a week there too."

Everyone laughed.

"I'm glad you had fun," Donna said. "I think it's important for people to get out and enjoy life while they can. You never know what tomorrow will bring."

"I agree," Mary Beth said.

Donna turned to Piper.

"I take it you're enjoying California as well."

"I am," Piper said. "Thanks to Ben, I am."

"I'm afraid to ask what that means," Donna said.

Piper giggled.

"It's nothing bad. Ben just knows how to show a girl a good time. Your son is a lot of things, Mrs. Ryan, but he's definitely not boring."

Donna stared at Ben.

"Have you been racing?"

Ben blushed.

"He didn't race," Piper said. "He just showed me what his car could do."

Donna sighed.

"I hope so. I don't want to get another call in the middle of the night."

"You won't," Ben said.

Donna looked at her son with skeptical eyes but let the matter drop. She knew there was only so much she could do to prevent an eighteen-year-old from acting his age. She stared at Ben for a few more seconds and then returned her attention to the table at large.

"So what is everyone doing this week?" Donna asked.

"I've got classes and tests," Mark said. "You know that."

"How about you, Mary Beth?"

"I'm going to go to a campus lecture."

"Is that so?"

Mary Beth nodded.

"A science fiction author is giving a lecture on time travel on Thursday."

"I think that's a fascinating topic."

Mary Beth smiled at Mark and then at Donna.

"So do I. That's why I talked Mark into going."

"You'll have fun," Donna said.

"I'm sure we will."

129

Donna looked at Ben.

"What's on your plate this week?"

Ben sipped some water.

"I have some tests and a match on Thursday."

"Is it a home match?" Donna asked.

Ben shook his head.

"It's in San Bernardino."

"Darn it," Donna said. "I was hoping to see you play."

"You can a week from Tuesday. We host John Muir."

"OK."

Donna looked at Piper.

"Are you doing anything special?"

"I am, actually," Piper said.

"Oh?"

Piper nodded.

"I'm going out with Ben, Mark, and Mary Beth tomorrow night."

"This sounds interesting," Donna said. "What are you going to do?"

"I'm going to do something I've wanted to do since coming to Los Angeles."

"Oh? What's that?"

Piper smiled.

"I'm going to watch the stars come out."

30: MARY BETH

Hollywood, California – Monday, April 6, 1959

She saw the glitter before she saw the gold. Sitting next to Mark in the back seat of Ben's open convertible, Mary Beth watched with awe and interest as the four time travelers drove west down Hollywood Boulevard and approached the historic Pantages Theater.

Nearly three thousand fans lined both sides of the street and cheered loudly as limousines and taxicabs brought actors, directors, producers, and others to the 31st Annual Academy Awards. Those who could not sit in bleachers stood on sidewalks or drove past in cars or motorcycles.

"OK. Color me impressed," Mary Beth said. "Thank you."

"Don't thank me," Mark said. "Thank Ben. He's the one who thought driving in circles for an hour would a great way to spend a Monday night."

Mary Beth laughed.

"Thank you, Ben."

The driver looked over his shoulder.

"You're welcome."

Mary Beth burrowed into Mark's side when he threw his arm over her shoulder and laughed to herself when Piper tried to do the same with Ben. Unlike Mary Beth, who shared a bench seat with Mark, Piper had to deal with a wide center console. The obstacle separated the high school daters as effectively as an eighteenth-century bundling board.

Mary Beth thought about the two as Ben turned right on Whitley Avenue and started another spin around Hollywood's most famous blocks. She knew that their off-and-on relationship had once again taken flight, but she didn't know why. She knew only that Piper had smiled almost nonstop since returning to the Chaparral Motel Saturday night.

She watched Ben fiddle with the radio. When "All I Have to Do Is Dream" streamed through the speakers, she placed her head on Mark's shoulder, took a breath, and relaxed.

"Are you having fun?" Mary Beth asked.

"I'm having fun," Mark said with little enthusiasm.

Mary Beth lifted her head.

"You don't *sound* like you're having fun."

"I am," Mark said. "That's the problem."

"I don't understand."

"I'm having *too* much fun. I'm dreading the day this will end."

Mary Beth frowned.

"I know. I'm dreading it too."

Mark chuckled.

"It's all your fault."

Mary Beth raised a brow.

"Is that so?"

Mark nodded.

"It is. If I had run into anyone else outside that basement door two weeks ago, I wouldn't be here now. I sure as hell wouldn't be cruising Hollywood Boulevard with my brother."

Mary Beth giggled.

"I've never looked at it that way."

Piper looked over her shoulder and smiled.

"There's nothing wrong with cruising."

Mary Beth stared at her sibling.

"Mind your own business."

Piper stuck out her tongue and then did as instructed. She scooted closer to Ben and pressed a few buttons when the Everly Brothers gave way to an advertisement. A moment later, "Donna," a ballad by the late Ritchie Valens, filled the air and made private conversations possible.

"I like this song," Mary Beth said. "I like it even though it makes me sad."

"Why does it make you sad?" Mark asked.

Mary Beth looked at her date.

"It makes me sad, Mr. Ryan, because it's a love song. It's a love song that the artist will never again be able to sing to the girl he loves."

Mark nodded. Like everyone else under thirty or in tune with popular music, he did not need to be reminded of that fact. Valens, Buddy Holly, and J.P. "The Big Bopper" Richardson had died just nine weeks earlier when their small plane crashed in an Iowa field.

Mary Beth smiled.

"This song also reminds me of your mother."

Mark chuckled.

132

"Is that a good thing or a bad thing?"

"It's a good thing, silly. I like your mom," Mary Beth said. "I like her even though she asked a lot of questions and stared at me all through dinner."

"She just likes you."

"It's more than that. I don't think she believes our story."

"Sure she does," Mark said. "She would have said something if she didn't."

Mary Beth laughed.

"You obviously don't know women. We keep things to ourselves."

Piper looked over her shoulder.

"Speak for yourself."

Mark chuckled.

"I'm not getting in the middle of this."

Mary Beth considered a reply but let the matter drop. She had better things to do than debate whether women regularly kept to themselves. She sat up and again looked at the sights as Ben turned off Gower Street and onto Hollywood Boulevard.

Mary Beth noticed changes as the four approached the Pantages. More people crowded the sidewalks and more cars crowded the street. Cabbies honked horns and competed with each other for curb space. Pedestrians ventured onto the street and crossed when they could.

Attendants in white jackets and black pants assisted those who could not reach the curb. They rushed to the taxis and limos and escorted academy members to the front of the theater.

Mary Beth smiled as Ben drove past a particularly active group. Dozens of fans chanted, "We want Ingrid! We want Ingrid!" A few held up signs and openly professed their love. All clamored to see Ingrid Bergman, who had returned to Hollywood after a ten-year absence.

Mary Beth looked hard for a legendary Swedish actress but saw nothing of the kind. She saw only attendants, policemen, and boisterous fans.

"Does anyone see a star?" Piper asked.

"I do," Mark said. He grinned and pointed. "I see two."

Mary Beth shot up in her seat like toast from a toaster and stared at two people making their way through the throng toward the theater. Eddie Fisher and Elizabeth Taylor had arrived to cheers and jeers – and without Debbie Reynolds, the other member of a highly publicized marital triangle.

"Do you see her?" Piper asked. "Do you see her?"

"I do," Mary Beth said. "This is amazing. This is so worth it."

Ben held out his right hand.

"I accept gratuities."

Mary Beth laughed.

"I'll pay you when you drop us off. How's that?"

133

"That works for me," Ben said.

Mark grinned.

"I think you've made his day."

"I hope so," Mary Beth said. "He's made mine."

Piper looked over her shoulder.

"Did you see her gown?"

Mary Beth smiled.

"Yes, I did."

"Elizabeth Taylor is gorgeous," Piper said.

Mary Beth laughed.

"Yes, she is."

Mary Beth settled back into her seat and pondered the insanity of it all. She had seen a storied actress in her prime, a woman who had been nominated for an Oscar before even Brody and Colleen McIntire had been born. She could get used to time travel.

"Are any more stars coming?" Piper asked.

Ben looked at his watch.

"I don't know. Do you want to go around again?"

"Yes!" Piper said.

Mary Beth laughed. She loved seeing her sister like this. She loved seeing a smile on the face of a girl who had frowned much too often in the past fifteen days. She tapped Piper's shoulder.

"Are you enjoying yourself?"

"I am," Piper said. "This is so much fun."

"I'm glad to hear that," Mary Beth said.

Piper again looked over her shoulder.

"I would so love to meet a celebrity in person."

"So would I."

"Do you think we will?"

"I wouldn't rule it out," Mary Beth said. She smiled. "This *is* Hollywood, after all."

31: MARK

Los Angeles, California – Thursday, April 9, 1959

Mark knew he was in trouble the second he saw her hand go up. He had expected Mary Beth to follow the lecture closely. He had *not* expected her to participate in the question-and-answer session that followed. He braced himself for the worst when Professor Austin Ballinger, author of six time-travel novels, called on the pretty brunette in the second row.

"First of all, thank you for coming to campus," Mary Beth said. "It's not every day I have the chance to hear someone speak on a topic as exotic as time travel. This has been fun."

Ballinger reached for a glass of water on his lectern, took a sip, and then returned his attention to the complimentary young woman. He folded his hands and smiled.

"I'm glad I met your expectations. Do you have a question?"

"I do," Mary Beth said. "You said a minute ago that time travel is still a product of science fiction and will remain so until science catches up to fiction. Is that correct?"

"That is correct," Ballinger said. "I think we will eventually develop the means to send people forward in time, but I believe that moment is decades, if not centuries, away."

"Do you believe in other possibilities?"

"What do you mean?"

Mark looked around the small lecture hall and saw that Mary Beth had grabbed not only the professor's attention but also that of a hundred other people. He wondered whether she had been this inquisitive in her classes at the University of Alabama.

135

"I mean supernatural possibilities," Mary Beth said. "I mean time portals and time tunnels and other things that exist outside the boundaries of science. Do you believe in *them?*"

Ballinger grinned.

"As a writer of science fiction, I believe in many things. I am a man who is open to nearly every idea and possibility. As a professor with advanced degrees in engineering, physics, and mathematics, I am from the Show Me State. I am a man who believes what he can see or smell or hear or touch. I am a skeptic of the first order."

"I see," Mary Beth said.

"You seem disappointed."

Several in the audience laughed.

"I guess I am," Mary Beth said. "I was hoping you could comment on other possibilities. I would like to believe that time travel is not something that only our descendants will see."

Mark smiled and shook his head. He wondered how long Mary Beth would toy with an expert who clearly had no clue. He now hoped she would do it all day.

"I would like to believe that too," Ballinger said. "I would like to believe we will someday stumble upon something magical, but I don't think that will happen anytime soon. If a time portal or a time tunnel or something similar existed today, we would surely know about it."

Mary Beth sighed.

"I'm sure we would. Thank you for taking my question."

Ballinger nodded at Mary Beth and then scanned the audience for more raised hands. Failing to see any, he took another sip of water, shuffled his papers together, and smiled.

"Thank you for inviting me to speak today. I hope to do this again."

Faculty, students, staff, and members of the public rose to their feet and applauded as Ballinger smiled, waved, and then put his papers in a leather portfolio. When the speaker took his leave a moment later, the attendees stepped toward the aisles and slowly filed out of the hall.

Mark laughed.

"You sure know how to keep a guy on his toes."

Mary Beth grinned.

"Did I make you a wee bit nervous?"

Mark nodded.

"You did at first."

"I just thought I'd spice things up," Mary Beth said. "I don't have much use for people with little imagination. He's an author, for crying out loud."

Mark chuckled.

"He is. He's an author who will probably have a time portal or a time tunnel in his next book. I suspect you've convinced him that time machines are passé."

Mary Beth offered a warm smile.

"Thanks for telling me about this lecture. This was a nice change of pace from shopping in Pasadena and watching soap operas at the motel."

"Then maybe I should take you to my engineering classes."

"Maybe you should."

Mark nodded, put a hand on Mary Beth's back, and guided her toward the center aisle. He started to ask her a question but stopped when he saw a man and a woman approach the passage from the other side. Both fixed their eyes on the twenty-two-year-olds.

The thirtyish couple reached the aisle a few seconds later, stopped, and waited for Mark and Mary Beth. They smiled when the two finally joined them in the aisle. The man spoke to Mark.

"Excuse me. I'm sorry for the intrusion, but I wonder if I could trouble you for a moment. I would like to ask your lady friend about something she said to the lecturer."

Mark turned to Mary Beth.

"Do you have a minute?"

"Unless you're taking me to lunch right now, I have all day," Mary Beth said. She gave Mark a playful glance and then turned to the man. "How can I help you, Mr.—?"

The man offered his greetings.

"I'm Joshua Bell."

Mary Beth shook his hand.

"I'm Mary Beth McIntire. Do you have a question for me?"

"I do," Joshua said. "When you spoke to Professor Ballinger, you asked about the 'supernatural possibilities' of time travel. Is that an interest of yours?"

"It is."

"How did that interest come about?"

Mary Beth smiled at Mark and then answered the question.

"It came about through reading. I read a lot of fantasy novels. I find magic portals far more interesting than time machines and would like to believe they are real."

"I see."

"I also like learning about things science can't explain or rule out."

"I'm the same way. So is my wife," Joshua said. He stepped back and looked at the attractive flaxen-haired woman behind him. "This is Julia."

"It's nice to meet you," Mary Beth said. She turned slightly. "This is my friend Mark Ryan."

The couples exchanged greetings.

137

"Are you students here?" Joshua asked.

"Mark is. He's still a student," Mary Beth said. She grinned at the undergraduate and then turned to Joshua. "I graduated from the University of Alabama last semester."

"I thought I detected an accent."

Mary Beth laughed.

"It's pretty hard to hide around here."

"I believe it," Joshua said.

"How about you?" Mary Beth asked. "Are you affiliated with the university? Are you a student or a professor?"

Joshua shook his head.

"I'm afraid I'm none of the above. I'm an attorney."

"There's nothing wrong with that," Mary Beth said. "You don't have to be a student or a professor to have an interest in time travel. I assume that's why you're here."

"It is," Joshua said. "I came here to see Professor Ballinger speak because I wanted to learn as much as I could about the subject. I have sort of a personal interest in it."

"Oh?"

Joshua nodded.

"My grandfather believed in time travel. He wrote about it extensively in a diary and in private letters to his brother and his wife. He wrote about time tunnels and portals and many other things that make no sense to me."

Mark looked at Mary Beth and saw uncertainty in her eyes. He could see that she had made the same connection and did not know how to proceed.

"Tell me about your grandfather," Mark said. "Did you know him well?"

"I didn't know him at all," Joshua said. "He died when my father was a child. I know only that he was a professor at this university and once lived in a mansion in West Adams."

"Have you shown his papers to others?" Mary Beth asked.

"Oh, no. People might think me mad if I did that. It's one thing to peddle time travel as science fiction. It's another to suggest, even through old letters, that it has already been done."

Mark took a breath.

"So what do you plan to do with your grandfather's writings?"

"I plan to keep them," Joshua said. "I plan to keep them to myself, learn what I can about this strange and mysterious subject, and perhaps decide on a course at a later time."

"I think that's a wise decision," Mark said.

Joshua looked at Mary Beth.

"What about you? Do *you* think that's a wise decision?"

138

Mary Beth smiled.

"I do, Mr. Bell. I think the best way to preserve your grandfather's legacy and reputation is to protect his papers and proceed slowly."

"That's what I think too," Julia said.

Mary Beth laughed.

"Then there you have it."

"I suppose you're right," Joshua said.

"I know I am."

Joshua smiled and sighed.

"I'm sorry to take up your time. You've both been very helpful."

Joshua shook two hands and then guided his wife forward. He disappeared with her through a nearby exit a moment later.

Mark looked at Mary Beth and saw the traces of a grin.

"What are you thinking?"

Mary Beth chuckled.

"I'm thinking that Percival Bell was quite a man."

"What do you mean?"

"I mean he mastered something that experts deny is real. He left behind papers and mysteries his own family can't decipher," Mary Beth said. She smiled. "He also brought four strangers together, including two standing right here. That's the best thing of all."

Mark couldn't deny that.

Percival Bell had started a story that was still being written. He had laid the groundwork for fantastic possibilities. He had made it possible for two lonely souls to find each other and their siblings to find common ground. He had changed lives.

Mark smiled at Mary Beth, took her hand, and led her to the exit. As he did, he left the lecture hall, time travel, and Percival Bell behind. He did not care about the possibilities of tunnels and portals. He did not care about letters. He cared only about the person at his side.

32: BEN

Pasadena, California – Saturday, April 11, 1959

The journey from the front seats to the back was seamless and swift. Two people locked in a passionate embrace slid into the larger, softer, more comfortable part of a covered 1959 Ford Thunderbird convertible like honeymooners transitioning from a doorway to a bed.

For the next forty minutes, Ben Ryan and Piper McIntire kissed, wrestled, and explored with reckless abandon as dozens of their Midway High School peers did the same. Most had come to the Rose City Drive-In to experience exhilarating freedom and escape the prying eyes of their parents. Few had come to see *Up Periscope* or *Rally Round the Flag, Boys!*

Ben and Piper had pushed the boundaries of passion three times since concluding that Ben was not boring. They had put aside doubts, fears, and the realities of time travel and simply enjoyed each other like two people on the cusp of adulthood.

Ben shifted his weight from his right to his left as he tried to get comfortable on a bench seat designed to accommodate vertical and not horizontal passengers. He succeeded only in pinching the side of a young woman pinned between his six-foot frame and an uneven seat.

"Ouch!" Piper said.

"Did I hurt you?" Ben asked.

Piper nodded and then scolded him with a smile.

"You broke my rib and probably a few other things."

Ben chuckled.

"I won't ask."

"Don't," Piper said.

"I'll try to be more careful."

"Do."

Ben smiled and then dropped his head to kiss the sassy brunette in the white blouse and the rumpled blue skirt. He had smiled a lot since joining Piper in the back seat. He had found her petulance and sense of humor as intoxicating as her pert nose and deep blue eyes.

He brushed back her hair, kissed her soft lips again, and tried to get comfortable when he heard someone pound repeatedly on the foggy driver's side window. Slowly, reluctantly, and with some irritation, he sat up, reached for the handle, and rolled down the window. He needed only a second to identify the awful people who had interrupted a beautiful moment.

"Hello," Sally Warner said. She stepped in front of Wayne Bridges, stuck her head through the open window, and grinned. "We're just checking to make sure everything is OK."

Ben stared at Sally.

"Everything is OK."

"That's good. We heard that some lecherous seniors were in the area and wanted to make sure that none had troubled my good friend," Sally said. She glanced at Piper and widened her grin. "Has anyone troubled my good friend?"

Piper sat up, looked at Sally, and raised a brow.

"You mean in the last thirty seconds?"

Sally laughed.

"Yes!"

"Then I can safely say that someone has," Piper said.

"I'm sorry if we interrupted anything," Sally said. She smiled. "We just couldn't pass up the opportunity to say hello and tell you that we were going to the concession stand."

"I'm so glad you did," Piper said.

Ben looked at Wayne and saw him shrug. He didn't have to guess who was behind the couple's decidedly untimely visit.

"Can we get you anything?" Sally asked.

"Yes," Piper said. "Get me some privacy. It's on the candy shelf."

Sally grinned.

"I'll look for it. I hear it's hard to find, but I'll look for it."

Piper laughed.

"You do that."

"I will," Sally said. She waved. "Toodle-oo, you two."

Ben rolled up the window as Sally and Wayne left the scene and walked toward a gray cinder-block building about fifty yards away. A moment later, he returned to his seat, his date, and a situation that had once seemed so promising. He smiled at the lovely disheveled woman at his side.

"You and Sally have at least one thing in common," Ben said.

"What's that?" Piper asked.

141

"You're impetuous."

Piper offered a seductive grin.

"There's nothing wrong with that."

Ben pondered the comment for a moment and then turned his attention to a speaker that hung from the top of the passenger's side window. James Garner, playing U.S. Navy Lieutenant Kenneth Braden in *Up Periscope*, barked an order to a subordinate.

"Do you want to listen to the movie?" Ben asked.

Piper laughed.

"We haven't yet. Why start now?"

Ben chuckled and shook his head. He wondered if it were even possible to tire of her wit. He moved toward the passenger door, rolled down the window about a third of the way, and pushed the bulky gray speaker out of the car. He looked back at Piper.

"Do you want some music?"

Piper nodded.

Ben rolled up the window, leaned toward the dash, and turned on the radio. He punched a few buttons and fiddled with a knob until he settled on an AM station playing "The Book of Love," a recent top-five hit by a doo-wop group called the Monotones.

"Is this better?" Ben asked.

"It's much better," Piper said.

Ben returned to the back seat, put his hands around Piper's face, and gently kissed her lips. A moment later, he kissed her a second time, brushed back her hair, and met her gaze.

"I'm nuts about you."

"Are you nuts about me or just nuts?" Piper asked.

Ben smiled.

"Both."

Piper giggled.

Ben took a deep breath, kissed her again, and then lowered her onto a back seat that had lost none of its warmth. This, he thought, was heaven.

For the next fifteen minutes, Ben and Piper made heaven a little warmer. They twisted and turned on the narrow seat, changed places as frequently as the songs on the radio, and explored each other's mouths and bodies until they approached the point of no return.

Ben unbuttoned Piper's ruffled blouse, unhooked her bra, and moved his hands in places they didn't belong. He moved freely and recklessly for several more minutes until Piper stiffened a bit and offered resistance for the first time.

"Maybe we should slow down," Piper said.

"I don't know if I can," Ben said.

Piper sighed.

142

"You can."

The two continued grappling on the seat. They continued eagerly and enthusiastically until Piper again took a breath and tapped the brakes.

"Ben?"

"Don't you want to?"

"I want to," Piper said in a whisper.

"Then let's—"

"Not here, Ben. Not now."

"Come on."

"No, Ben. Not now."

"Come on, Vick."

Piper shot up from the seat.

"*What* did you say?"

"What?" Ben asked.

"You just called me Vick."

Ben sat up and looked at Piper with bewildered eyes. He could see he had stepped in it even before she refastened her bra and started buttoning her blouse.

"I didn't call you anything."

"Yes, you did."

"Piper, don't—"

"Don't what, Ben? Don't stop? Be more like Vicki Cole?"

"That's not what I meant."

"Then what *did* you mean?" Piper asked.

"I don't know. Just calm down a minute."

Piper glared at Ben.

"I *am* calm. I'm so calm I'm going to calmly step out for some air."

Piper pushed the driver's seat forward, reached for the door handle, and pulled. She pushed the door open, slid past the seat, and quickly moved out of the vehicle.

"Piper?"

"Stay put, Ben. Don't follow me."

Piper slammed the door and walked to the back of the T-Bird. She paused for a moment, as if considering her options, and then marched toward a building that contained the concessions and the restrooms. The structure was the only indoor facility at the outdoor theater.

Ben tucked his shirt in his slacks, tightened his belt, and slid toward a door that Piper had inconveniently locked. Angry, frustrated, and more than a little flustered, he unlocked the door, exited the vehicle, and ran to the open space between rows one and two. He glanced at the building just as an angry woman turned left and stepped through a door.

"Piper!"

143

Ben asked himself several questions as he walked toward the building. Why had he felt the need to push things? Why had he opened his mouth? Why had Piper not given him a chance to explain or apologize or even talk? Had he somehow botched things for good?

He did not know. He knew only that he had to catch Piper and at least try to make amends before a wonderful evening turned into a disaster.

Several peers called out as Ben strode toward the building. Some offered condolences. Two offered a beer. At least one jeered and laughed. All seemed to take great interest in watching a big man on campus struggle with a conspicuous setback and potential humiliation.

Ben reached the building a few seconds later. He stepped inside, scanned about forty faces in the dining area, and zeroed in on a group by the far wall. He walked briskly toward Wayne, Sally, Piper, and several other members of the Class of '59.

"Don't come near me," Piper said as Ben approached. "I've had enough for tonight."

"Look," Ben said. "I'm sorry. I don't know what came over me."

"It doesn't matter. I want to go home."

"Then let me take you home."

"No. I'm going with Wayne and Sally."

Ben looked at Wayne and saw indecision. Then he looked at Sally and saw judgment. He knew in two glances he would not win this battle publicly.

"Can we at least talk before you go?" Ben asked.

"No," Piper said. "I just want to leave."

Ben looked again at the assembled masses and saw everything from sympathy to glee. He wondered what he had done to deserve any of the judgment. Then he glanced at the faces of a few former girlfriends and answered his own question.

He stared at Piper and tried to find meaning in her suddenly hostile eyes. He could not believe the evening had deteriorated so rapidly.

"Please, Piper. Let's just talk."

"No, Ben. We're done talking."

Ben started to offer one last plea but stopped when he saw a familiar blonde approach from the side. He knew what she was going to say even before she opened her mouth.

"What seems to be the problem?" Vicki Cole asked.

"It's nothing," Ben said.

"It doesn't look like nothing."

Ben turned his head.

"Can we talk about this later, Vicki?"

"We can. Or we can talk about it now."

Ben returned to Piper.

144

"Let's just go for a walk. That's all I'm asking."

Piper stiffened.

"I don't want to walk. I don't want to talk. I just want to *go*."

Ben huffed.

"Then go. Leave. Run off. Just don't come knocking on my door again."

Piper stared at him with sad eyes.

"I won't."

Ben turned to Vicki and grabbed her hand.

"Let's go."

Vicki did not reply. She just held on to Ben's hand, gave Piper an I-told-you-so grin, and followed her old boyfriend out the door before forty jaws could drop.

33: MARY BETH

South Pasadena, California – Sunday, April 12, 1959

Mary Beth counted the socks and shook her head. She had put five pairs in the dryer at nine o'clock and pulled out two at ten. Someone in need of footwear had helped herself to plenty in the laundry room of the Chaparral Motel.

She folded her remaining laundry on a table, loaded it into a basket, and then carried it through a door, down a narrow hallway, and up some steps. As she ascended the stairs and worked her way toward Room 212, she pondered the coming week, her feelings toward Mark, and her brief but unsettling encounter with her sister Saturday night.

Piper had come home at ten, crawled into bed, and quietly cried herself to sleep. She did not explain her early return from her date with Ben or the reason for her unhappiness. She said only that she wanted to sleep and would say more the next day.

Mary Beth did not anticipate a morning discussion. She had found Piper's bed made and unoccupied when she had risen at eight. She assumed her sister had gone for a morning walk.

Mary Beth reached Room 212 a minute later, lowered her basket to the floor, and pulled out her key. She listened for signs of Piper's presence as she put the key in the door and turned the knob, but she heard nothing new. No television. No radio. No anything.

She pushed the door open, peeked inside the dimly lit room, and frowned when she saw closed drapes and two unoccupied beds. Piper, she concluded, was still out and about.

Mary Beth returned to the empty hallway, picked up the basket with both hands, and laughed when she looked at the laundry. Who would steal six socks and leave four? Who would spare her *newest* pairs? She wondered if the thoughtful thief was still in the building.

146

Mary Beth turned around, walked through the door, and pondered where to put the basket. She didn't ponder for long. She knew the second the door closed and someone grabbed her from behind that she had far more pressing matters to consider.

"Don't scream," a man said.

Mary Beth froze.

"I won't. Please don't hurt me."

The man chuckled as he brought a knife to her neck.

"I'll do my best. I would hate to cut such a lovely throat."

Mary Beth closed her eyes when the man tightened his hold on her and nudged her to the middle of the room. She opened them when he lowered the knife.

"What do you want?" Mary Beth asked.

The man spoke into her ear.

"I think you know what I want."

"Do you want money? I can give you money."

"I don't want your money. I want something far more valuable."

"What?" Mary Beth asked. "What do you want?"

"I want the book. I want the special book you used to make a special bet."

Mary Beth felt her stomach drop.

"I don't have it here. I put it in a safe-deposit box."

The man sneered.

"I don't believe you."

"Just give me a day," Mary Beth said. "I can get it tomorrow."

"Tomorrow is too late."

"No. It's not. I can get it. Please don't—"

Mary Beth stopped when she heard someone stick a key in the door and panicked when that someone turned the knob and opened the door. She turned around and screamed when she saw Piper stand in the doorway with her mouth agape and her eyes open wide.

"Run, Piper! Run!"

Piper did not run. She did not hide. She instead entered the room and joined the fight. She charged the assailant with the fury of a linebacker pursing a quarterback.

The man released Mary Beth, pushed her aside, and then turned to face the new threat. He stepped toward Piper and raised his knife. Mary Beth screamed when he brought it down.

"Mary Beth?" Piper asked. "Mary Beth? Are you all right?"

Mary Beth shot up, opened her eyes, and turned toward the sound of the voice. She saw Piper sitting on the edge of her bed.

"What?"

"I asked if you were all right," Piper said.

147

Mary Beth looked around the room and sighed as the truth set in. She was still alive. So was her sister. The man was gone. The threat was gone. She had survived a dream.

"I think I had a nightmare," Mary Beth said.

Piper tilted her head.

"You screamed my name. You told me to run."

"I had a nightmare," Mary Beth said. "I dreamed of the man with the deformed ear. He had a knife. He wanted the book. You came in the room."

"It's OK. I'm here. We're both here," Piper said. "We're both all right."

Mary Beth smiled faintly.

"I guess we are."

"Can I get you anything?" Piper asked.

Mary Beth shook her head.

"No. Just stay here. Stay here and talk to me."

Piper nodded. She climbed into the bed, fluffed a pillow, and scooted up next to her sister. Like Mary Beth, she wore the pajamas she had slept in. She had not gone for a morning walk.

"What do you want to talk about?" Piper asked.

Mary Beth smiled.

"How about something light and pleasant?"

Piper offered a sad laugh.

"I'll do what I can."

Mary Beth turned to face Piper. She saw a girl with heavy eyes, a frown, and obviously a lot on her mind. She patted her sister's hand.

"What's the matter? You don't look happy."

"I'm not," Piper said.

"What happened last night? Did you and Ben quarrel?"

"You might say that."

Mary Beth fixed her gaze on her sister.

"Care to elaborate?"

"No," Piper said. "It doesn't matter anyway."

"What do you mean it doesn't matter?"

"I mean it doesn't *matter*. Ben and I are done."

"Don't you like him?" Mary Beth asked.

"Of course I like him."

"I don't understand. If you still like Ben, then why are you 'done'?"

Piper stared at her sister.

"We're done because we can't possibly go any further. We can't possibly make a relationship work. Don't you understand? None of this is real, Mary Beth. We're just visitors here."

148

"I know," Mary Beth said. She looked away for a moment. "I think the same thing whenever I'm with Mark. I guess I'm just better at putting off the inevitable."

Piper sighed.

"I almost made a mistake last night. Ben and I got a little crazy in his car – and I almost gave in. I *wanted* to give in. I wanted to show him how much I like him. Then he said something that snapped me out of a daze. He reminded me that he has a life here – and a past and a future. I don't. I'm just a time traveler who is quickly getting in over her head. You are too."

Mary Beth frowned.

"Do you want to leave? Do you want to return to 2017?"

"Yes," Piper said. "I think we should go back before we do something stupid. I know you like Mark. I know you want to stay. I know you want to enjoy all this as long as you can, but I think we should leave. We don't belong here."

Mary Beth took a deep breath.

"Can you give it another week?"

"I'm not sure what that would accomplish," Piper said. "What do you want to do that we haven't already done?"

Mary Beth smiled.

"There are several things I want to do, including something I want to do for you. Just give it a few more days, Piper. If you still want to leave on Saturday, then we'll leave. We'll pack our bags, say our goodbyes, and leave. Can you give it one more week?"

Piper nodded.

"I can do that."

"Thanks," Mary Beth said. She threw an arm around her sister, pulled her close, and kissed the top of her head. "Now let's talk about something else and get some breakfast. I'm hungry."

34: PIPER

Tuesday, April 14, 1959

Twelve days after watching Ben play tennis for the first time, Piper prepared to watch him for the last. She settled into her bleacher seat, eyed the senior with the nasty serve, and waited for him to score an ace. This time she did not intend to distract him.

Piper watched Ben and Wayne win a point in their doubles match with John Muir's best and then turned her attention to the people around her. Donna clapped her hands and cheered every time Ben touched the ball. Sally did the same for Wayne. Mary Beth alternated between cheering for the Maulers and cheering up her sister. She had done a lot of that since Sunday.

"Where did Mark go?" Piper asked.

"He went to get me a drink," Mary Beth said. "He'll be back in a minute."

"Are you two going out tonight?"

"I think so. He mentioned something about a movie."

"Have fun," Piper said.

"Do you want to come along?" Mary Beth asked. "I'm sure Mark wouldn't mind. I know *I* wouldn't mind. I would much rather have you come with us than mope at the motel."

"I'll be fine."

"Are you sure?"

"I'm sure."

Piper laughed to herself. She wasn't sure about anything. She had found more misery than contentment since Saturday night and had approached each new day with dread. She counted the hours until she could return to the predictable but happy life she had left behind on June 2, 2017.

Piper watched more of the match and then again turned her attention to something closer to home. This time she gazed at an unhappy blonde at the end of her bench.

She did not need to ask Vicki Cole why *she* wore a frown. She already knew the reason. The students of Midway High School had denied her a crown and maybe a date by electing Chip Bennett and Bunny Martinez as their prom king and queen.

Piper resisted the temptation to gloat. She knew what it was like to lose something she wanted and, for that reason alone, wished Vicki the best. Schadenfreude was for losers. She thought about misery, company, and loss until she saw a man approach the bleachers.

"Here's your drink," Mark said a moment later.

He handed a bottle of Royal Crown Cola to his leading lady.

"Thanks," Mary Beth said.

"Did anything bad happen while I was gone?"

"No. Ben and Wayne haven't lost a point."

"I figured as much," Mark said.

Mary Beth patted the wooden bleacher.

"Come sit with me."

"I'd rather go for a walk," Mark said.

"You want to go for a walk *now*?"

"I do. I want to go for a walk – with Piper."

Piper turned her head.

"Surely you mean my sister."

"No," Mark said. He smiled. "I mean you. Can you spare a few minutes?"

Piper glanced at Mary Beth.

"Do you mind?"

"I don't mind at all," Mary Beth said. She smiled. "I would much rather lose Mark to my darling sister than some sorority hussy."

Donna and Sally laughed.

"OK then," Piper said. "I'll go."

Piper stood up, stepped toward the middle aisle, and descended the bleachers. She joined Mark just as he finished a quiet conversation with Mary Beth.

"We won't be long," Mark said.

"Take your time," Mary Beth said.

Piper looked at Mark.

"What do you want to do?"

"Let's take a stroll around the school."

"OK."

Mark waved to Mary Beth and Donna and then guided Piper toward a sidewalk that encircled the campus. He spoke when they reached the walk.

151

"I hope you don't mind the intrusion."

"I don't," Piper said. "What do you want to talk about?"

Mark smiled.

"Let's start with your travel plans."

Piper sighed.

"I see my sister has filled you in."

"She's told me a few things," Mark said.

"Don't blame Mary Beth. I'm the one who wants to go."

"I'm not blaming anyone. I know this can't last forever. I just want to know why you want to leave so soon. There's really no need to rush."

"I know," Piper said.

"Is this about your fight with Ben?" Mark asked.

Piper shook her head.

"It's bigger than that. It's about facing reality. Every day I stay here, I find it harder to walk away from Ben and Sally and others I've met. If I don't break these attachments now, I may not be able to break them at all."

"I understand," Mark said.

"I still have a family in the future, Mark. I have parents, grandparents, cousins, friends, and people I want to see again."

"Mary Beth does too."

"She does," Piper said. "The difference is that she's fallen for you. She's fallen so hard I don't think she can act without help."

Mark frowned.

"That surprises me. She's known me for only three and a half weeks."

"You obviously don't know my sister."

"What do you mean?"

"Mary Beth is a person who trusts her instincts," Piper said. "If she likes you after five minutes, she will probably like you for life. In your case, it's more than that."

Mark did not reply. He kept to himself as a group of students approached and passed. He resumed the conversation a moment later.

"Have you two always been close?"

Piper looked at Mark.

"We have since grade school."

"You weren't before that?" Mark asked.

Piper shook her head.

"Mary Beth didn't even acknowledge me until she reached the sixth grade. She was too caught up in her own life. Then one day she decided to be a big sister."

"I don't understand," Mark said.

"She stood up to kids who bullied me."

"You were bullied?"

Piper nodded.

152

"I had a big mouth in the second grade. Hard to believe, I know."

Mark chuckled.

"So what did she do? Beat the kids up?"

"No. She threatened them. She said, 'If you don't leave my sister alone, I'll have you all spayed and neutered.' Mary Beth didn't even know what the words meant. She heard them on a TV commercial. But her warning worked. The bullies never bothered me again."

Mark laughed hard.

"That is funny."

"I've worshipped her ever since," Piper said. "She's the best sister a girl could have."

"That's beautiful."

"Are you and Ben close?"

"We are, for the most part," Mark said. "We've definitely become closer since Dad died. We depend on each other more and do more together."

"Did you ever have a bonding moment?"

"If you're asking whether I ever spayed or neutered his friends, the answer is no," Mark said. He laughed. "If you want to know whether we've had important moments as brothers, the answer is yes. We've had several."

Piper smiled.

"Give me one."

"OK," Mark said. "One of the best was just three years ago."

"What happened?"

"Ben asked me for dating advice."

Piper widened her eyes.

"Ben asked for *dating* advice?"

Mark nodded.

"He needed it too."

"I can't imagine that," Piper said.

"That's because you didn't know Ben his freshman year," Mark said. "Back then he wasn't a big man on campus. He was a relatively shy guy with a squeaky voice and pimples."

"So why did he need advice?"

"He needed it because he wanted to take a gorgeous junior to the winter formal."

"What did you tell him?" Piper asked.

"I told him what others told him," Mark said. "I told him he should give up and pursue girls his own age. Then I remembered something a friend had told *me* in high school. She said that girls like poetry and that the surest way to win them over was to write a poem."

Piper smiled.

"She's right."

"I thought so too," Mark said. "So I told Ben to write the girl a poem every day for a week, slip the poems in her locker, and then ask her out at the end of the week."

"Let me guess," Piper said. "She went out with him."

Mark met her gaze.

"She went out with him for six months."

Piper smiled again.

"I'm impressed. You did a good thing."

"You could say that," Mark said. "Most say I created a monster."

Piper laughed hard. She loved the story. She loved hearing about a future Lothario's humble start. She loved hearing that Ben Ryan was *human*.

Then she felt a twinge of sadness as she and Mark turned a corner and headed back toward the tennis courts. She realized how much she liked Mark and Ben and their mother. She liked them a lot. It was one of the reasons she had to walk away and do so sooner rather than later.

"So when do you think you'll leave?" Mark asked.

"I don't know," Piper said. "Mary Beth has given me until Saturday to make the call."

Mark forced a smile.

"I understand."

Piper looked closely at Mark's face and saw the sadness in his eyes. She could see that Mary Beth was not the only one to fall hard in three and a half weeks.

"Mark?"

"Yeah?"

"I want you to know something."

"What's that?" Mark asked.

Piper placed her hand on his arm and stopped walking.

"I want you to know that you've done more than show my sister a good time. You've put a spark in her eyes and a smile on her face," Piper said. "Be happy with that."

154

35: MARY BETH

Barry's Bistro exuded more character than glitz. A hole-in-the-wall tucked between a bank and a boutique, it offered just twelve tables, a limited menu, and a noisy swamp cooler. It was the kind of place people avoided unless they wanted to hide from the world. Mary Beth didn't mind. She had come to Barry's to meet an individual and not enjoy comfort, cool air, or chili that was said to be the best in Los Angeles.

She entered the bistro at half past ten, spoke briefly to a waitress, and then led Piper through the restaurant proper to a small, sunny, unoccupied patio in back. A moment later, she settled into a seat with a good view of the door, sipped a glass of water, and gazed across her table.

"Are you hungry?" Mary Beth asked.

"No," Piper said. "I am curious though. I want to know why I had to skip school and take a sweaty bus across Los Angeles to a diner I've never heard of."

Mary Beth smiled.

"Must you know everything?"

Piper laughed.

"Yes!"

"You'll find out soon enough," Mary Beth said. "In the meantime, I want to talk to you about this weekend. Do you still want to leave early?"

Piper nodded.

"I think so. I just don't see a reason to stay."

"What about the prom?" Mary Beth asked.

"What *about* the prom? No one is going to ask me. I humiliated one of the most popular boys in school. I doubt even a pimply freshman would ask me now."

"What?"

155

"Never mind," Piper said. "I'm just feeling sorry for myself."

Mary Beth paused when the waitress approached the table. She gave the server her order, waited for Piper to do the same, and then resumed the conversation.

"What did you and Mark talk about on Tuesday?"

"Didn't he tell you?" Piper asked.

"No. He didn't tell me a thing."

"Then maybe I should take the Fifth."

"Just tell me," Mary Beth said.

Piper sat up in her chair.

"We just swapped anecdotes about you and Ben and talked about the weekend. He doesn't want us to leave, of course. He wants us to wait until at least the end of April."

Mary Beth sighed.

"I know."

"You have to break it off, Mary Beth. You have to end things now. It's not right to give Mark false hope. He's in love with someone he can't have."

"I know."

"It's mutual, too, isn't it?" Piper asked. "You're in love with him."

Mary Beth nodded.

"I know it's crazy."

"It's not crazy. It's normal. People fall in love every day," Piper said. "They just don't do it in different time zones."

Mary Beth laughed.

"How did you get to be so wise?"

Piper smiled.

"I had a good teacher."

Mary Beth reached across the table and touched Piper's arm. She wanted to show her sister that she appreciated her love and support, if not her pointed advice.

She pondered that advice when the waitress brought out two sandwiches and considered her options when the server took her leave. She knew Piper was right. She didn't have a choice in the matter. She had to break things off with Mark and do so at the earliest opportunity.

Mary Beth started to say something about Piper's order but stopped when she saw a woman step onto the patio. She smiled when the woman sat at a table about ten feet away.

In some respects, the new arrival, a lady in her early thirties, was no different than a thousand other women in Los Angeles. She was roughly five-foot-five and 120 pounds with a round face and a curvy figure. She wore sunglasses and a silk scarf over her platinum hair.

In other respects, she was night-and-day different. With twenty-six film credits, a Golden Globe nomination, and a fan base that numbered in the tens of millions, she was arguably the most famous and popular woman on the planet.

Mary Beth watched closely as the woman in the blue blouse and the white Capri pants pulled a pen and a few sheets of stationery out of her purse, placed the paper on her table, and scribbled a few notes. She didn't need to guess what the lady was doing. She already knew.

Marilyn Monroe was keeping track of her day. She was completing a log that would someday occupy page forty-two of *Marilyn: Her Life in Letters*.

For the next ten minutes, Mary Beth ate her sandwich, sipped her water, and considered the ways she could add her oblivious sister to the mix. She glanced at Marilyn frequently, held the gazes as long as she could, and turned away when she sensed she had looked too long.

Mary Beth halted her surveillance when the waitress entered the patio, pulled out a pad, and took the celebrity's order. She resumed her watch after the server brought the star some iced tea, wiped her table, and walked away. She continued the game of visual cat and mouse until the mouse removed her sunglasses, looked at the cat, and raised a brow.

"Hello," Marilyn said.

Mary Beth offered a feeble wave.

"Hi."

Piper looked at Mary Beth with puzzled eyes, peered over her shoulder, and stared at her sister's new acquaintance. She needed only five seconds to realize that the woman at the nearby table was no ordinary diner. She dropped her peanut butter sandwich on the patio.

"You're … you're *her*," Piper said. She snapped back to Mary Beth. "It's her. You knew. You knew she would be here today. That's why we came."

Mary Beth smiled.

"Aren't you glad you skipped school?"

Piper looked over her shoulder again.

"Hi."

Marilyn smiled.

"Hello."

Piper returned to her sister.

"We have to talk to her. What do we say?"

Mary Beth shrugged.

"You can say whatever you want," Marilyn said in a voice that carried.

Piper looked over her shoulder a third time.

"Really?"

Marilyn smiled and nodded.

"I won't bite."

Piper grinned at her sister.

"She won't bite."

Mary Beth laughed.

"Then I think you should talk to her."

Piper turned her chair to face the blonde.

"Do you mind if I talk to you?"

"You already are," Marilyn said. "Why don't you join me? I could use a diversion."

Piper and Mary Beth did not wait for another invitation. They got out of their chairs, stepped across the patio, and sat at the other table as Marilyn put away her pen and papers.

"I'm sorry for staring at you," Mary Beth said. "I'm sure you get that a lot."

Marilyn sipped her tea.

"I do. But I don't mind."

"That's good," Mary Beth said. "I feel better already."

"You girls are southern," Marilyn said. "I don't meet southerners very often."

"We're visiting from Alabama."

"I see."

"I looked for you at the Oscars," Piper said. "Were you there?"

Marilyn shook her head.

"I was in New York with my husband."

"Oh."

Marilyn looked at Mary Beth.

"Have you enjoyed your visit to California?"

"We have," Mary Beth said. "We've had a blast."

"How long do you plan to stay?"

Mary Beth looked at Piper and then at Marilyn.

"We haven't decided. We're kind of on an extended vacation. I want to extend it. My sister does not. We'll probably meet somewhere in the middle."

Marilyn turned to Piper.

"Why do you want to leave?"

Piper hesitated before producing an answer.

"I'm homesick."

"You're homesick for *Alabama*?" Marilyn asked.

"She's homesick for a boy, Miss Monroe," Mary Beth said. She smiled at her clearly relieved sister. "She has a smoking-hot boyfriend back home and is starting to miss him."

Marilyn laughed.

"I should have suspected."

"He's only mildly hot," Piper said.

Marilyn smiled.

"There's nothing wrong with that. I'm sure he's very nice."

Piper smiled.

158

"He is."

"Speaking of 'hot,' I saw your latest movie on Tuesday," Mary Beth said. She referred to the recently released *Some Like It Hot.* "I enjoyed it."

"I'm glad you did," Marilyn said. "I enjoyed making it."

Mary Beth doubted that was true. She knew from a book she had read in 2015 that the making of the film was a hellish experience for all involved. Marilyn could not memorize many of her lines and needed as many as forty-seven takes to get some of them down. Her acting coach and husband tried to influence the production. Director Billy Wilder joked that his doctor and psychiatrist told him that he was "too old and too rich" to do another movie with the actress.

"Do you like making movies?" Mary Beth asked. "It seems like a lot of work."

"It is," Marilyn said. "There are a lot of rules to follow."

"That's how we feel about school."

"What grades are you in?"

"Piper, my sister, just graduated. She's headed off to college. I graduated from college a few weeks ago. I'm on my way to medical school. I'm Mary Beth McIntire, by the way."

Marilyn smiled.

"It's a pleasure to meet you – both of you."

"The pleasure is ours," Mary Beth said. "Believe me."

"I confess I'm a bit envious," Marilyn said. "I never finished high school."

Mary Beth took a moment to ponder the admission. She had not known that. She suddenly felt great sympathy for a woman who had everything except a high school diploma.

"You read though, right? I've heard you like to read."

"I do. I love reading," Marilyn said. She sighed. "It's one of the ways I stay sane. That can be hard to do in this town."

Mary Beth looked again at Marilyn. This time she didn't see a glamorous movie star. She saw a fragile, tired, and somewhat sad woman who did what she could to get through each day.

A moment later, the waitress, carrying her pad, stepped onto the patio. She paused to assess the new seating situation, glared at Mary Beth, and then spoke to Marilyn.

"Are they bothering you, Miss Monroe?"

"No," Marilyn said. She smiled. "These ladies are making my day."

"OK. Let me know if that changes."

"I will."

The waitress turned toward the girls, frowned, and then did what she had come to do. She tore a sheet from her pad, handed a bill to Mary Beth, and left the scene.

159

Mary Beth laughed.

"I think that's our cue to leave. We've taken up enough of your time."

"I don't mind," Marilyn said. "I like talking to real people."

"I still think we should go."

"Do as you wish."

Mary Beth got up from her chair, pushed it in, and then motioned to Piper to do the same. A moment later, she looked at Marilyn, took a deep breath, and offered her hand.

"Thanks for putting up with two bumpkins."

Marilyn smiled as she shook Mary Beth's hand.

"Let's do it again."

"Let's do," Mary Beth said.

She laughed to herself as she considered the likelihood of a second encounter. She was more likely to win a multi-state lottery than to share a table with Marilyn Monroe again. Mary Beth gestured to Piper to lead the way and then followed her sister toward the door. She made it about halfway when she heard a voice and stopped.

"Girls?" Marilyn asked.

Mary Beth turned around.

"Yes?"

Marilyn smiled warmly.

"Don't you want an autograph?"

Mary Beth shook her head.

"I think we're OK."

Marilyn chuckled.

"Are you sure?"

Mary Beth appealed to Piper for a second opinion and got one in the form of a hard stare. She laughed and looked again at Marilyn.

"I believe Piper would like an autograph."

"I thought so," Marilyn said. "Most people do."

The actress retrieved her pen and a piece of stationery and scribbled a few lines. Then she got out of her chair, stepped toward the girls, and handed the note to Piper.

"Enjoy college, dear."

Piper beamed.

"I will. Thank you, Miss Monroe."

Marilyn looked at Mary Beth.

"Are you sure you don't want anything?"

The older sister nodded. "I'm sure," Mary Beth said. She placed her hand on Piper's shoulder and smiled. "I have a wonderful memory. That's more than enough for me."

36: PIPER

On the morning of her last day as a member of the Class of 1959, Piper McIntire exited the Chaparral Motel, stepped toward a red Thunderbird, and smiled at its driver. She did not know what she would say to him or what he would say to her. She knew only that she had to set things straight before she left this time for her own.

"Good morning," Piper said.

Ben offered a wistful smile as he stood next to his car.

"Good morning."

He opened the passenger door.

"Thank you," Piper said. "What a gentleman."

Ben nodded but did not reply. He shut the door, walked around the vehicle, and entered it from the other side. He did not speak again until after he had driven the T-Bird out of the lot, turned onto the street, and pointed the car toward Midway High School.

"How are you doing?" Ben asked.

"I'm doing fine," Piper said. She paused. "How about you?"

"I'm miserable."

Piper did not need to ask why. She knew Ben had been miserable since Saturday, when she had left him at the drive-in, and especially miserable since Thursday, when she had informed him that she intended to leave the past for good on April 18.

"Don't be miserable. Be happy," Piper said. She looked at the driver. "We had some good times, Ben. We had some really good times. Let's remember those and not the rest."

Ben sighed, glanced at Piper, and nodded. Then he returned his attention to a road filled with cars, motorcycles, trucks, and buses headed to the east side of the city and points beyond.

"Have you told Wayne and Sally you're not coming back?" Ben asked.

"No," Piper said. "I'm going to do that today."

Piper berated herself for not saying something sooner. She could have at least hinted at a possible departure when Wayne and Sally had taken her to school on Monday, Tuesday, and Wednesday, but she had not. She had saved almost everything for her final day.

Ben stopped for a red light. As he waited for the light to change, he sat up in his seat, tapped the steering wheel with his fingers, and stared blankly at the car ahead.

"Piper?"

"Yes, Ben?"

"I'm sorry."

"There is no need to apologize," Piper said. "You did nothing wrong."

"Yes, I did. I took you for granted. I treated you poorly and compounded my mistakes with more mistakes. I screwed up."

"Ben?"

"Yeah?"

"Who brainwashed my friend and is forcing him to say kind and thoughtful things to me on my last day of school?"

Ben laughed.

"No one brainwashed me. I came to my senses on my own."

"Has Mark said anything to you?" Piper asked.

"No," Ben said. "Was he supposed to?"

"No."

"I heard you two went for a walk on Tuesday."

"We did," Piper said.

"What did you talk about?"

"We talked mostly about our difficult siblings."

Ben chuckled.

"Did he approach you?"

"As a matter of fact, he did. He approached me during your doubles match and pulled me away from the action," Piper said. "I'm glad he did though. We had one of the best conversations I've had in a long time."

"Is that so?"

"It is. Your brother is a nice guy."

Ben nodded.

"Did he delve into my sordid past?"

"No. He did just the opposite," Piper said. "He told me about your 'innocent' youth. He told me about the poems you wrote as a freshman."

Ben laughed.

"That was a long time ago."

Piper gazed at Ben.

"It wasn't that long."

"I suppose not," Ben said. "What else did he tell you?"

"He said the two of you have grown closer since your dad died."

"That's true. Did you talk about anything else?"

"Yes," Piper said. "We talked a little about this weekend."

Ben started to say something but stopped when they approached the school. He pulled the signal lever, turned into a parking lot, and drove halfway through the lot to his favorite space. A moment later, he turned off the ignition, set the brake, and pivoted to face his passenger.

"We're here," Ben said.

Piper gazed at the driver.

"Yes, we are. Thanks for the ride, Ben. Thanks for all the rides. Thanks for everything you've done to make my time here enjoyable."

Ben nodded.

"You're welcome."

Piper grabbed a door handle.

"We should go."

"Piper?" Ben asked.

"Yes?"

"Can I ask you one more question?"

"Of course."

Ben turned away for a moment and took a deep breath. When he looked again at Piper, he did so with eyes that reflected anxiety, sorrow, and humility.

"Will you go to the prom with me?"

Piper sank in her seat. She hadn't seen that coming. For the first time since jumping into Ben's car at seven thirty, she didn't know what to say to him.

"Aren't you taking Vicki?" Piper asked.

"No," Ben said.

"Can't you take someone else?"

"I don't want to take someone else. I want to take *you*."

Piper sighed.

"I don't know, Ben. This is awfully late. If I say yes, I'll have to stay here an extra week. I'm not sure I want to do that."

Ben dropped his head and stared at his feet. He did so for what seemed like an eternity before lifting his head, looking at Piper, and making his final pitch.

"I know it's late. I know I could take someone else. I know I could have a good time with someone else, but I don't want to do that. I don't want to settle. I want to take the girl who has been in my head for nearly a month. I want to give you the experience you came for."

Piper pondered the matter as a bell rang and students ran toward the school. She weighed the pros and cons, considered Mary Beth, and came

163

away as undecided as ever. Then she looked at Ben, saw the sincerity in his eyes, and decided that a week, in the great cosmic scheme of things, was still just seven days.

"I'll need a dress," Piper said.

Ben perked up.

"My mom is a dressmaker."

Piper smiled.

"I'll need shoes too."

Ben chuckled.

"Pasadena has stores."

"Can I pick the restaurant?" Piper asked.

Ben grinned.

"You can pick anything you want."

Piper looked at Ben warily.

"Will you behave yourself?"

"I'll be as good as the pope."

Piper giggled.

"I suppose that's good."

"It is," Ben said.

"In that case, Mr. Ryan, I accept your offer," Piper said. She leaned to her left and kissed him on the cheek. "You have a date."

37: MARK

Los Angeles, California – Saturday, April 18, 1959

Mark watched his mother with admiration, interest, and concern as she reached for the bottle of whiskey in the middle of the table and filled her glass for the fourth time. She continued to inspire him even as she continued to worry him.

"Are you all right, Mom?" Mark asked.

"I'm fine, honey," Donna said. "I'm just feeling a little sentimental. I've found that whiskey and sentiment go hand in hand."

Mark laughed. He couldn't argue with that. He had spent the last two hours drinking whiskey and getting sentimental as he and his mother remembered Theodore Henry Ryan on what would have been his fiftieth birthday. He allowed his mind to drift to pleasant places from his past until a woman with a pleasant voice brought him back to the present.

"Thank you for dinner, Mrs. Ryan," Mary Beth said.

"You're welcome," Donna replied.

"Thanks as well for including me in your day. I know how hard it is to be around strangers when mourning the loss of a loved one. It's an honor to be here."

Donna sipped her spirit and gazed at the woman to her left. She looked at Mary Beth like the daughter she never had or perhaps the woman she used to be.

"I appreciate your presence," Donna said. "I know young people have better things to do on a Saturday night than help an old woman reminisce."

Mark shook his head.

"You're not old, Mom. You're forty-eight."

Donna laughed.

"I am. But I feel *ninety*-eight."

Mary Beth smiled.

"You don't look a day over thirty to me."

Donna looked at Mark.

"She's a charmer, son. Don't let her go."

Mark gave Mary Beth a wistful smile.

"Trust me, Mom. I don't want to."

Mark didn't either. He didn't want to let her go. He didn't want to say goodbye. He wanted to hold on to Mary Beth McIntire for as long as he could.

Mark felt fortunate to have her at all. Until Ben had come home from school on Friday and announced he was taking Piper to the prom, he had expected to spend the weekend alone, directionless, and in a perpetual state of misery. He had expected to watch Mary Beth and her sister step into the tunnel and vanish forever.

Now he did not know what to expect. He knew only that he had another week to enjoy a woman who mesmerized him on a daily basis. He gazed at Mary Beth for a moment and then turned his attention to the other important woman in his life.

"What are you doing tomorrow?" Mark asked.

Donna looked at her son.

"I'm going to the cemetery to put flowers on your father's grave."

"I thought you did that today."

"I had planned to."

"So why didn't you?" Mark asked.

"I went shopping instead," Donna said.

"You went shopping?"

"Yes. I went shopping. I went shopping with two charming girls."

Mark looked to Mary Beth for a clue and found one in the form of a wide grin. He could see she was part of a conspiracy to keep him in the dark.

"What's going on?"

Mary Beth laughed.

"We scoured the earth for rayon."

"You're not helping," Mark said.

Donna finally came to the rescue.

"We went shopping for fabric today. I'm making Piper a prom dress, Mark. She wanted a certain fabric. I agreed to help her find it."

Mark looked at Mary Beth.

"Is that why you passed up the game?"

"It's one reason," Mary Beth said. She smiled. "I also wanted a manicure."

Donna laughed.

"I'm so glad I'm not a girl," Mark said.

"I am too," Donna said.

166

Mary Beth giggled.

"That makes three of us."

Mark laughed to himself as he remembered how the day had begun. He and Ben had called the Chaparral Motel at nine, asked Mary Beth and Piper to a baseball game, and frowned when told that the sisters needed time together to do something important. He could not have known that Donna was already on her way to South Pasadena or that shopping and manicures held more weight than the Dodgers and the Cubs in the minds of two time travelers.

Mark and Ben drove to the motel after the game, blissfully unaware of the shopping spree. They picked up their dates at six, took them back to the Painted Lady, and enjoyed a beef stroganoff dinner that Donna had prepared.

Ben and Piper had stayed only for dinner and dessert. Five minutes after eating pie in honor of a terrific husband and father, they walked out the front door, jumped into the T-Bird, and drove directly to the Rose City Drive-In. Both had told their siblings that they wanted to exorcise the demons of the previous weekend by revisiting the haunted house.

Mark smiled at their bold and creative decision and also at his good fortune. Ben and Piper had done more than bury the hatchet. They had given their siblings an extra week to make sense of a situation that became more complicated by the day.

Mark gazed at Mary Beth as she carried out a light conversation with Donna and noticed that she wore the turquoise earrings she had purchased in Las Vegas. He had not noticed them until now and wondered if there were other things about her that he had not picked up. It was easy to miss details when one focused on a pleasant voice and a pretty face.

He thought briefly about the weekend in Nevada, which seemed a lifetime ago, and the man who had apparently followed the time travelers to Los Angeles. Though he no longer worried about the man with the deformed ear, he could not entirely forget him. He wondered whether a man in pursuit of a potential fortune would ever give up his search. He thought not.

Mark gave the matter another moment and then turned his attention to Donna and Mary Beth. He smiled at both, joined their conversation, and resumed a most enjoyable evening.

38: MARK

Two hours later, after Donna had retired and a waxing moon had risen above the San Gabriel Mountains, Mark helped Mary Beth wash the dishes and then led her from the kitchen to a living room that all but announced its budding promise. The room featured a large sofa, a recliner, a jukebox, and a freestanding television set with "wrap-around" sound. A black rotary telephone, much like the one in the kitchen, sat on one table. A 1930s cathedral radio rose from another.

"This is my favorite room in the house," Mark said.

"I can see why," Mary Beth said. "It's filled with gadgets."

Mark smiled.

"Do you want to sit?"

Mary Beth nodded.

"I do."

Mark waited for Mary Beth to take a seat, plopped down next to her, and then threw his arm over her shoulders. He could literally feel her relax as she burrowed into his side.

"Did you enjoy dinner?" Mark asked.

"I did," Mary Beth said. "I enjoyed the whole day."

"My mother adores you."

"I like her too."

Mark pulled her closer.

"Was she helpful on your little shopping spree today?"

"She was more than helpful. She paid for everything," Mary Beth said. "She said Piper and I were the daughters she had always wanted to spoil. The comment made me cry."

"Why would it make you cry?"

Mary Beth lifted her head and stared at Mark.

"You really *are* a guy."

Mark laughed.

"I confess."

Mary Beth sighed.

"Your mom's comment made me cry because it reminded me that we don't always get the things we want in life. She'll never have daughters to spoil or even a husband to enjoy in old age. She'll be mired in memories and laments for the rest of her days."

"She'll be fine," Mark said. "She has Ben and me."

Mary Beth nodded.

"That's a lot. I just hope it's enough. Your mother has so much to give. It's a shame to see her call it quits before she's even fifty. It's just plain sad."

"I suppose it is," Mark said. "We've all had to make adjustments since last fall. Dad was a pretty big part of our lives. I still think of him every day. I think of him every time I walk into this room. He purchased every one of the 'gadgets' you see."

Mary Beth sat up, leaned forward, and gazed at the appliances in the room as if looking at relics in the Smithsonian Institution. She focused on the large machine in a distant corner.

"Tell me about the jukebox."

"What do you want to know?" Mark asked.

"I don't know. I guess everything. How did your dad get it? How much is it worth? How does it work? Is it loaded with records?" Mary Beth asked. "I've never seen anything like it."

Mark smiled.

"I keep forgetting that you're used to better things."

Mary Beth gave him a pointed glance.

"I'm used to *different* things, Mark. Not all are better."

Mark chuckled.

"I can't argue with that. I've seen the future."

Mary Beth raised a brow.

"Can you answer my questions, please?"

"OK. I'll try," Mark said. "The jukebox is a Wurlitzer 1015. Dad bought it six years ago for cost from a man in San Diego. I honestly don't know how much it's worth today, but I suspect it's worth a lot. It's still in mint condition and fully functional."

"How does it work?"

"You press a few buttons and wait for the music."

"You don't need coins?" Mary Beth asked.

Mark shook his head.

"That was an option Dad passed up. He refused to pay for his own music."

Mary Beth scolded him with a smile.

"You're a smart aleck. Do you know that?"

Mark laughed.

169

"I'm sorry. I couldn't resist."

Mary Beth sighed.

"Can we play something?"

Mark nodded.

"Come on. I'll show you what it can do."

Mark helped Mary Beth from the sofa and escorted her to the corner of the room and an appliance he knew well but rarely used. He flipped on a power switch in back and waited for the device – a flourish of bright lights, wood cabinetry, and chrome trim – to come to life.

Mary Beth placed her hands on the see-through dome as a kaleidoscope of lights flickered and the dormant music machine began to hum and click. She peeked through the small windows in front, frowned, and then looked at Mark.

"There's nothing printed on the title strips."

"I know."

"That makes no sense," Mary Beth said.

Mark chuckled.

"It does in this house."

"I don't understand."

"We never bothered to write the titles on the cards. Dad knew which buttons to push for his songs. Mom and Ben know which buttons to push for theirs. We all do."

"What do your guests do?" Mary Beth asked.

"They fend for themselves."

"That's not very hospitable."

"No," Mark said. He smiled. "It's not."

"Can you play something now?" Mary Beth asked.

Mark nodded.

"What would you like?"

Mary Beth looked at Mark.

"Play a slow song. I'd like to dance."

"You've got it."

Mark stepped toward the jukebox, pressed five buttons, and waited patiently as the machine selected the first vinyl disc. A moment later, he took Mary Beth in his arms, guided her to an open space, and started dancing to "Smoke Gets in Your Eyes."

"Do you like the Platters?" Mark asked.

Mary Beth nodded.

"I have an album of their greatest hits. Jordan gave it to me one Christmas. He said my life wouldn't be complete unless I listened to all the fifties classics at least once."

Mark laughed to himself at the reference to "classics." He had never thought of fifties music as classic because, to him, it was cutting edge and

170

fresh. He could not imagine what it would be like to go *back* in time and view the world as it was.

Mark pondered the comment for a moment and then turned his attention to the woman in his arms. He pulled Mary Beth close as they moved slowly, smoothly, and effortlessly across a squeaky hardwood floor. He wondered what it would be like to dance with her every night.

"What are you thinking?" Mark asked.

Mary Beth took a breath.

"I'm thinking about how much I'm going to miss you."

"We don't need to talk about that now."

"You're right. We don't."

Mark acknowledged the statement with a nod and gave the impression he had moved on to another subject, but he had not. Like Mary Beth, Ben, and Piper, he could not set aside the painful separation to come. He had allowed himself to hope that this magical experience could continue when he knew as well as anyone it could not.

"I wonder how our siblings are doing tonight," Mark said. He slowed the pace as the Platters gave way to Little Anthony and the Imperials. "I didn't see their reconcilement coming."

"I didn't either," Mary Beth said. "I guess Piper really wanted to go to the prom. Or maybe she likes Ben more than she let on. She hasn't told me much."

Mark smiled.

"I'm in the dark too. The only thing I know for sure is that my brother is a different person. He told me something today that he's never told me before."

"What's that?"

"He said he's caught the love bug."

"I'm not surprised," Mary Beth said. She gave Mark a sad smile. "It's going around."

Mark nodded.

"It is."

Mark resisted the temptation to elaborate. He wanted to say more. He wanted to *do* more. He wanted to act on feelings he had harbored for weeks, but he knew he could not. He had to man up and face the world as it was and not as he wished it to be.

So he focused on the music, the dancing, and the moment. He held Mary Beth close and moved in tight circles across the floor as "Tears on My Pillow" turned into "Since I Don't Have You" and "When I Fall in Love."

Mark did not look at Mary Beth's face during the last song. Nor did he look at it when the Wurlitzer traded Nat King Cole for Jo Stafford and "You Belong to Me." He did not want to see a smile or a frown or a glance that might somehow take away from the moment.

171

He could not maintain the posture for long. As Stafford began to sing about pyramids, sunsets, and marketplaces in old Algiers, Mark sensed a change – an unpleasant change. He felt Mary Beth slow her step and relax her hold. He heard her sniff. He saw her wipe away a tear.

"What's wrong?" Mark asked.

"It's nothing," Mary Beth said.

"People don't cry over nothing, Mary Beth. What's wrong?"

Mary Beth smiled through her tears.

"It's just this song."

Mark slowed the pace even more.

"Don't you like it?"

"I love it. It's my favorite," Mary Beth said. She wiped away another tear. "I was going to play it at my reception."

Mark stopped the dance.

"I'm sorry. I didn't know. Do you want me to change it?"

Mary Beth shook her head.

"No."

Mark put his hands to her face.

"Are you sure?"

"I'm positive," Mary Beth said. She sighed. "Just hold me."

39: PIPER

South Pasadena, California – Monday, April 20, 1959

Piper glanced at the girl with the grin and then at the woman with the smile and tried to decide which deserved her attention. She went with the former. Even in an interesting art history class, Sally Warner beat the *Mona Lisa* seven days a week.

Piper waited patiently as Sam Ginsberg, her goateed instructor, adjusted an easel supporting an oversized print of Leonardo da Vinci's masterpiece. When he turned his back and stepped toward the blackboard, she texted her BFF fifties style by passing her a folded note.

Ginsberg scribbled a few words on the board, turned around, and walked to a stool that stood next to the easel. He scanned the faces in his class of thirty and then plunged into the lesson, one of six on famous Renaissance paintings and the last before a midweek exam.

"Why is this woman smiling?" Ginsberg asked.

Piper saw a hand go up in the front row. Even from the back row she could tell the hand belonged to Bunny Martinez. The bubbly senior and recently elected prom queen never went anywhere without pink plastic bracelets on each wrist.

Ginsberg acknowledged the student.

"Bunny?"

"She's keeping a secret," Bunny said. "She knows something the artist doesn't and is having a laugh at his expense."

The teacher chuckled.

"She may be," Ginsberg said. "Da Vinci didn't leave us a lot of clues. Much of what we know about this painting comes from others. Does anyone else want to hazard a guess?"

Another hand shot up.

173

"*Mona Lisa* is smiling because she's thinking of killing someone," Tom Cline said. "Look at her eyes. She doesn't look happy."

Piper laughed with several other students. She knew Tom wasn't trying to be funny, but she thought he was funny nonetheless. If there was one thing she enjoyed about attending school in the 1950s, it was that no one checked their opinions at the door. They said what they thought and thought what they said. Piper glanced again at Sally when Ginsberg got up, returned to the board, and wrote down two dates. She knew even before Sally dropped a hand to her side that she had a note ready.

The southerner reached to her right, took the note, and unfolded it on her desk. She scanned the vicinity for nosy neighbors. Seeing none, she read the message, let it sink in, and smiled.

"So what happened Saturday night? It's killing me not to know!"

Piper pondered the question, picked up her pencil, and scribbled a short reply.

"We kissed and made up!"

Piper passed the note to Sally and laughed when she started to read it. She knew her suggestive, detail-free reply would probably cause her friend to bust a vein. She returned her attention to Ginsberg when the oblivious instructor walked back to his stool.

"Can anyone tell me why the years 1503 and 1506 are important?" Ginsberg asked.

A cheerful junior raised her hand.

"It's when *Mona Lisa* was born," Sandy Perkins said.

Piper covered her mouth and bit her lip. It was all she could do to stifle a laugh. She would miss classes like this. She would miss it all.

The instructor smiled.

"You're close, Sandy. Though Lisa del Giocondo, the real *Mona Lisa*, was born in 1479, the painting that bears her likeness was 'born' between 1503 and 1506. Da Vinci did not just throw paint on a canvas and call it a day. He took three years to create the painting and during that time added numerous elements, including, some believe, *Mona Lisa's* iconic smile."

Sandy beamed.

"This brings me back to my original question," Ginsberg said. "If *Mona Lisa* is smiling, then *why* is she smiling?"

Ginsberg pointed to a boy in back.

"Randy?"

"She's smiling because she's plotting something," Randy Thompson said in a serious voice. "She's plotting something big."

174

"Is that so?" Ginsberg asked.

Randy nodded.

"She's going to put a frog in da Vinci's soup. She's mad at him for making her sit in a chair for three years and wants to put a croaker in his minestrone. It's the only thing that makes sense."

The class erupted in laughter.

"I like your interpretation," Ginsberg said. "I'm not sure many art historians would support it, but I admit it's the most creative I've ever heard."

Piper smiled when Randy acknowledged new laughs by standing up and bowing. One more student of art history had claimed his fifteen seconds of fame. Ginsberg let his students enjoy the light moment until the talking and laughing subsided. Then he reclaimed control of the class and returned to the matter at hand.

"Can anyone offer a more grounded interpretation?" Ginsberg said. "Why is the *Mona Lisa* smiling instead of frowning? What is this young Renaissance woman trying to tell us?"

Piper looked at Sally as she scribbled furiously on a sheet of notebook paper. She didn't need to see more to know that her friend was not pleased with her five-word reply. Piper prepared to receive the long message but withdrew her hand when Ginsberg rephrased his question and called on another boy. She leaned forward as the senior, who sat next to Wayne Bridges in the front row, started to speak.

"I don't think *Mona Lisa* wants to kill anyone or put a frog in his soup," Ben Ryan said. "I think she's doing what a lot of women did back then. She's sending a message to men."

The teacher put a hand to his chin.

"What message is that, Ben?"

"I think she's telling every guy who's ever messed up that there's always a chance he can make things right," Ben said. He turned his head, gazed at Piper with thoughtful eyes, and then returned to the instructor. "She's sending a message of hope and forgiveness."

Ginsberg scratched his chin.

"You got all that from a smile?"

"I did, Mr. Ginsberg. I do."

Piper did not gauge Sally's reaction. Nor did she acknowledge the snickers and grins. She simply gazed at the youth in the pressed white shirt and lost herself in the moment. She was no longer a time traveler having an adventure or a high school student having some fun. She was a girl seeing a boy as she had never seen him before. She was a woman in love.

40: MARY BETH

Los Angeles, California – Friday, April 24, 1959

M ary Beth heard the sounds before she saw the sources. Along with eighty others, she heard the grunts, chants, and calls of ten "Tahitian warriors" before they carried a sacred roasted pig into the courtyard of Zeta Alpha Rho and placed it on an altar.

"I take it the PC police are off today," Mary Beth said.

"What do you mean?" Mark asked.

"I mean times have changed."

"I imagine they have."

Mary Beth watched with amusement as the warriors – college boys with painted faces, nose rings, and wild hair – turned to face the diners and pounded their bare chests. She laughed when they raised their hands and danced in place to the beat of distant drums.

"How come you're not up there?" Mary Beth asked.

"I'm not because I'm a senior," Mark said. "Seniors are excused from warrior duty. Juniors are not. Freshmen and sophomores happily volunteer."

Margaret Pringle grinned at Mary Beth. She sat next to Dennis Green on the other side of their long table for twenty.

"Don't let Mark fool you," Margaret said. "He'd be up there now if he didn't have a reputation to protect. In fact, I believe he was a server last year."

Mark laughed.

"I was."

Mary Beth smiled. She could picture Mark in a loincloth. She could even picture him grunting, groaning, and beating his chest. She had long since ceased to make assumptions about a thoughtful young man who continued to amaze, inspire, and endear.

176

Mary Beth looked at Mark, who looked handsome enough in a blue flowered shirt, and then at Margaret and Dennis, who looked just as smart in matching Hawaiian attire. She wondered if college students had always had this much fun during midterm week.

She adjusted the carnation in her hair when she felt it slip. The flower matched a hot pink floral dress she had purchased for a song six days earlier.

"You look pretty in that dress," Margaret said. "Did you make it?"

Mary Beth laughed.

"I bought it. I couldn't sew a button on a blouse if my life depended on it."

"Did you buy it around here?" Margaret asked.

"No," Mary Beth said. "I bought it in Pasadena last weekend when Mark's mom and I went fabric shopping with my sister. She's going to the prom with Mark's brother tomorrow."

Margaret stared at Mark.

"Let me get this straight. You and Ben are dating sisters?"

Mark smiled sheepishly.

"We have for a month now."

Margaret laughed.

"That sounds positively southern."

Mary Beth ignored the dig. She knew that Margaret meant no offense. She also knew she had a point. Brothers rarely dated sisters, just as boys from 1959 rarely dated girls from 2017.

"It has been interesting," Mary Beth said. "The four of us have been inseparable since we took a road trip to Las Vegas."

"When did you go to Vegas?" Dennis asked.

Mary Beth regretted her comment the second she made it. She didn't want to talk about trips to Nevada any more than she wanted to talk about trips to the fifties.

"We went about a month ago," Mary Beth said.

Dennis turned to Mark.

"How come I never heard about this? You used to tell me everything, buddy. Now I hear you ran off to Vegas with girls you barely knew."

Mark glanced at Mary Beth before proceeding.

"We didn't quite run off with them," Mark said. "Ben and I met Mary Beth and Piper at a gas station in Barstow as we all headed to Nevada in separate cars. When we learned the girls had just moved to California and didn't know the region very well, we naturally offered our services as guides. As fate would have it, they decided to keep us."

Dennis looked at Mary Beth.

"I didn't know you had a car."

Mark jumped in.

177

"She doesn't. She rented a car for the trip to Vegas."

"Is that so?" Dennis asked Mary Beth.

Mary Beth nodded.

"It was a one-time thing. I hope to actually buy a car this month. I don't want to depend on Mark or the bus system every time I need to get around."

"I don't blame you," Dennis said. "What are you looking to buy?"

Mary Beth gave Mark a playful glance.

"I'm thinking about an Edsel."

Dennis laughed.

"You *are* adventurous."

Mary Beth considered keeping the conversation going but decided to let it die. She knew she had dodged a bullet and saw no point in inviting more questions and potential trouble.

She took Mark's hand under the table, gave it a gentle squeeze, and mouthed a "thank you" when he looked her way. Then she settled into her seat as the Tahitian warriors brought the first steaming plates of two-finger poi, lomi-lomi salmon, and haupia to her table.

For the next hour, Mary Beth enjoyed fine cuisine, glasses of okolehao moonshine, and music by a quartet that played everything from "Pearly Shells" to "The Hukilau Song." She spoke to Mark in a soft voice when she saw other couples move on to private conversations.

"Thanks for inviting me," Mary Beth said. "I haven't been to a luau since my parents took Piper and me to Hawaii when I was twelve. This is really fun."

"It is," Mark said.

Mary Beth looked at her date.

"I could get used to this, Mark."

Mark returned her gaze.

"I already am."

"I know," Mary Beth said. "It seems we're both on the same page."

"Do you want talk about it?" Mark asked.

"I think we should."

"OK."

Mark sipped the last of his okolehao, wiped his mouth with a napkin, and tossed the cloth on his plate. Then he got out of his chair and helped Mary Beth do the same.

"What are you doing?" Dennis asked.

"We're going for a walk," Mark said.

"Do you want some company?"

"No. Not this time. Mary Beth and I need to sort some things out."

"Suit yourself. Have fun."

178

Mark nodded but did not respond. He instead escorted Mary Beth past three other tables, the musicians, and the remains of the sacred pig to the back of the fraternity house. A moment later, the couple walked out the front door, stepped onto a noisy street, and considered their options.

"Where do you want to go?" Mark asked.

"Let's go someplace quiet."

"This is Los Angeles. No place is quiet."

Mary Beth smiled.

"Let's just walk."

"OK."

Mary Beth thought about what she wanted to say as the two moved slowly toward a campus that was both shutting down and coming to life. Those who worked at the university and lived someplace else hurried to cars, buses, and peaceful weekends. Those who lived on the campus or in nearby fraternities and sororities hurried to parties, functions, and other social gatherings.

"What are you thinking?" Mary Beth asked.

"I'm thinking we have a problem and need to find a solution," Mark said.

"*Is* there a solution?"

"There has to be."

"What if there isn't?" Mary Beth asked. "I can't stay here. You can't leave. You have family and friends. You have a *life*. You have the same things here that I have in 2017."

Mark stopped and faced Mary Beth.

"Are you saying it's hopeless?"

"No, Mark. That's not what I'm saying. I'm saying I don't have a solution. I'm saying there may not *be* a solution."

Mark gazed at Mary Beth for several seconds but did not speak. He just looked at her with eyes that reflected sadness, hopelessness, and a trace of anger. "Let's find a place to talk," Mark said.

Mary Beth nodded.

"OK."

The two needed only a minute to find a suitable venue. They walked to a shady spot between two academic buildings, turned to face each other, and resumed their difficult discussion.

"I'm sorry for snapping at you," Mark said. "I'm just frustrated. I'm used to solving problems. It's easy to do in engineering classes. It's not easy to do with you."

Mary Beth smiled.

"Is that your way of saying you like me?"

Mark brought his hands to her face.

"It's my way of saying I love you."

"I love you too," Mary Beth said.

Mark leaned forward and gave her a tender, lingering kiss. Then he gazed at her for a few seconds, smiled, and laughed.

"I think I've loved you since you confronted me outside the time tunnel. I can still picture the smirk on your face when you asked if we were 'having fun yet.'"

"I don't smirk, Mr. Ryan. I grin slyly."

Mark laughed.

"I stand corrected," he said. "I fell in love with a grin."

"I suppose that's better than falling in love with a classroom observation of the *Mona Lisa*," Mary Beth said. "That's what Piper did."

"I don't follow."

"Ben made a comment in their art history class on Monday. He said the reason *Mona Lisa* is smiling is because she's sending a message to men who mess up with women. She's sending a message of 'hope and forgiveness.'"

Mark laughed.

"He said no such thing."

"Oh, yes he did. He uttered those exact words in front of the whole class," Mary Beth said. "He looked Piper in the eyes when he did it too."

"What did she do?"

"She melted like butter in a pan. She's in love, Mark. She's just like the rest of us. She's in a spot with no way out."

Mark sighed.

"Have you paid your rent this week?"

Mary Beth nodded.

"I've paid through the end of the month."

"That's good," Mark said.

"The rent is not the problem though. Neither is money," Mary Beth said. "The problem is that we can't stay here forever. As much as I want to, we can't. At some point, we have to go."

Mark met Mary Beth's gaze.

"Can you give me a few days to think of something?"

"I can. I can give you a week if you need it."

"What about Piper?" Mark asked. "Would she be willing to do the same?"

"I don't know. She may be willing to give you a year, for all I know. I have no idea where her head is right now. She's been a different person this week."

Mark nodded. "Give me a week then. If I can't think of something by next Friday, I'll take you through the tunnel myself."

"That's fair," Mary Beth said. She kissed him and took his hand. "Now let's enjoy the rest of the evening."

41: PIPER

The setting was unlike any Piper had ever seen. Sometime between her last physical education class on Thursday morning and her first twentieth-century prom on Saturday night, the Midway High School gymnasium had become a place of magic.

Five *thousand* balloons clung to the ceiling. Crepe streamers hung from the balloons. Photo booths and food stations, reflecting a medieval theme, lined two walls. Perry and the Paychecks, a local dance band, played fifties favorites to three hundred couples in pressed suits, fluffy dresses, and fancy shoes. "A Knight to Remember" had become a night to remember.

Piper embraced it all as she sat with Ben, Wayne, Sally, and several others at one of sixteen tables that lined the bleacher wall and faced the stage. She had decided to rest only after dancing for nearly an hour to "Jailhouse Rock," "Tutti Frutti," "Rock Around the Clock," "Johnny B. Goode," and other songs that defined a generation.

"I'm in heaven," Piper said.

Ben smiled.

"I've been there for a month."

Piper pondered the comment, waited for Wayne and Sally to turn their attention elsewhere, and then looked at her date. She saw pure contentment.

"I'm sorry I put you through all that misery," Piper said.

Ben sighed.

"That's all right. I deserved it."

Piper laughed.

"Is this the boy with more girlfriends than my area code?"

"No," Ben said. He chuckled. "I killed him last week."

Piper studied his face.

181

"You *have* changed."

Ben looked at her thoughtfully.

"I've come to my senses, Piper. I don't want to lose you."

Piper flinched when she heard the words. She heard determination, not resignation, in Ben's voice and wondered how much longer he could keep his hope alive. She wondered how long *she* could put off the inevitable. She clasped his hand under the table and thought of other things.

She didn't find that very hard to do. She had pondered a lot in just the past ten hours and had accumulated enough food for thought to fill a supermarket.

Piper had started the day with a trip to a Pasadena beauty parlor and continued it with stops at a florist, a department store, and the Painted Lady. Thanks to Mark Ryan, her daytime chauffeur, she had been able to do everything she needed to do to prepare for an important date.

Ben had spent the first part of the day fishing with a friend. Told by his mother to leave the house and not return before two, he did as instructed. He went to the Santa Monica Pier and came back at three smelling like mackerel, but he was more than ready to greet his Cinderella when Mark and Mary Beth delivered her in an Edsel at five after five.

After a dozen motherly hugs, photographs, and the exchange of corsages, Ben drove Piper in his freshly cleaned T-Bird to a Chinese restaurant in Pasadena, where they enjoyed dinner with Wayne, Sally, and three other couples. They arrived at the high school at eight fifteen.

Piper turned her attention to others when Perry and the Paychecks took a break and scores of couples left the floor for refreshments, restrooms, and fresh air. She could not help but admire the effort her classmates had put into the dance, the evening, and themselves.

Piper sat up and straightened her strapless dress, a powder blue cascade of tulle, taffeta, and lace that Donna had put together in just three days. She wondered whether she would ever again look as good as she did tonight. She wondered whether she would ever again *feel* as good.

She wallowed in the good feeling for a moment and then turned to the handsome young man in the white jacket, dark slacks, and bow tie. She sensed that his mind was elsewhere.

"What are you thinking?" Piper asked.

Ben smiled.

"I'm thinking about a conversation I had with your favorite person."

Piper stared at her date.

"You spoke to *Vicki?*"

"No," Ben said. "Vicki spoke to me. She walked up to me when you and Sally went to the restroom and started talking. She wanted to get some things off her chest."

"Do I want to hear this?"

"I think so."

"What did she say?" Piper asked.

"She said she likes you."

"Vicki Cole likes *me*?"

Ben nodded.

"She said she misjudged you. She said she misjudged *us*. She said she has never seen two people look happier than we did when we walked through the door tonight."

Piper furrowed her brow.

"Do you think she meant it?"

"I dated Vicki for eight months, Piper. I know her as well as anyone. I know when she means something," Ben said. "She likes you. She respects you too."

Piper smiled.

"I guess I should be thankful."

"You should," Ben said. "Vicki doesn't like or respect many people."

Piper thought about the comment for a moment and considered a reply. She started to say something about respecting Vicki too but stopped when she saw a familiar face approach. She had not seen the teacher since he had returned her art history exam on Friday morning.

"I see that class is still in session," Sam Ginsberg said to Ben, Piper, Wayne, and Sally. "How are my students doing this evening?"

"I'm doing well, Mr. Ginsberg," Piper said.

"Me too," Wayne added.

"Me three," Sally said.

The teacher looked at Ben.

"How about you?"

"I'm enjoying myself," Ben said.

"That's good."

"Do you have chaperone duty tonight, Mr. Ginsberg?"

"Indeed, I do, Ben. I volunteered my services tonight. So did my wife," Ginsberg said. He turned to a slender redheaded woman. "Nancy, this is Ben Ryan, Piper McIntire, Wayne Bridges, and Sally Warner. Each is a student in my art history class. Students, this is my wife, Nancy."

The five exchanged greetings.

"Sam has told me about all of you," Nancy said.

"I hope good things," Ben said.

"Of course."

Ginsberg smiled.

"Ben is the student who made the astute observation about the *Mona Lisa*."

"Is that so?" Nancy asked.

Ben grinned.

183

"I'll say anything for an A."

Nancy tilted her head.

"So you don't believe what you said?"

Ben ditched the grin. He looked at Piper lovingly, took a deep breath, and then returned to the woman with the pointed question.

"I didn't say that, Mrs. Ginsberg," Ben said. "When I said the *Mona Lisa* was sending a message to men, I meant every word. I think she was telling us there is nothing an apology or a bouquet of flowers or a kind gesture can't fix."

"That's a beautiful thought," Nancy said. "I can see you mean it."

"I do, ma'am."

Nancy smiled at Piper.

"Hold on to him, dear. They don't come that way out of the box."

Piper giggled.

"I'll do my best, Mrs. Ginsberg. Thank you."

Nancy nodded.

"I think we've explored this subject to everyone's satisfaction," Sam Ginsberg said. He smiled at his pupils. "I hope you all enjoy the rest of the evening."

"Thanks, Mr. Ginsberg," Ben said.

The teacher waved at the four and then guided his wife toward other tables, other students, and other opportunities to engage in small talk. The couple found a receptive audience at nearly every table. Chaperones had a way of getting and holding people's attention.

Piper used the downtime to relax and take it all in. She praised herself for giving Ben another chance and giving the fifties another week. If she remembered nothing else about this moment and this night, she would remember that she had found the experience she had sought.

Piper looked at Ben as Perry and the Paychecks returned to the stage, picked up their instruments, and gave them a test. She spoke when he met her gaze.

"Did you really mean what you said in class?"

"Yes, Piper. I did," Ben said. "I know people think I said it just to impress you, but I didn't. I said it because I believe it. Even if it sounds silly, I believe it."

Piper touched his forearm.

"I don't think it sounds silly."

Ben laughed.

"I'm glad *someone's* in my corner."

Piper gazed at the boy she had misjudged more times than she could count. She vowed to never again doubt his words or his intentions. She lost herself in happy thoughts until her BFF snapped her out of a daze with an untimely observation.

184

"Hey, you two. The band is playing again," Sally said. "Let's get out there and dance."

Piper looked at Sally.

"We'll be there in a minute."

"OK."

Sally grabbed Wayne's hand and pulled him onto the dance floor. More than thirty couples had already started swaying to "Smoke Gets in Your Eyes."

Piper turned to Ben and saw that he had drifted to another place. She clasped his hand, lifted it above the table, and kissed it.

"We're in a pickle, aren't we?" Piper asked.

Ben nodded.

"Yes, we are."

"Are you going to be all right?"

Ben looked at Piper.

"I'll be fine."

"Ben?"

"Yeah?"

Piper took a breath.

"I don't want this to end."

42: MARY BETH

Los Angeles, California – Tuesday, April 28, 1959

Mary Beth took the plate off the shelf, studied it for a moment, and then looked at the man who had driven her to Ling's Antiques. She didn't care much for his silly grin, but she appealed to him anyway. She didn't have a choice.

"Are you sure your mother will like this?" Mary Beth asked.

"I am," Mark said. "She's collected that stuff for years."

Mary Beth glanced again at the Flow Blue Chinese porcelain plate, considered the pros and cons of getting something else, and finally decided to stick with the dish. She liked the floral patterns on the earthenware plate and ultimately decided that Donna Ryan would too.

Mary Beth brought the plate to the front counter, handed it to a clerk, and waited patiently as he placed the dish in a box. Then she gave the man a twenty, collected her change, and led Mark out the door and onto the sidewalk near the corner of Broadway and Second Street.

"I hope you're right about the plate," Mary Beth said. She put the gift in her handbag and looked at Mark. "I don't want to disappoint your mother after all she has done for us."

"You won't," Mark said. "Trust me on this. She would be happy if you gave her a box of Cuban cigars. She's that kind of person."

"I hope so."

"What do you want to do now?"

"I don't know," Mary Beth said. "Suggest something."

Mark smiled.

"How about the opera?"

Mary Beth laughed.

"We're not *dressed* for the opera."

"Are you sure?"

"I'm positive."

Mary Beth was too. She knew that no opera house in the world would admit a man in a fraternity sweatshirt or a woman in a plain cotton dress.

"Then I guess we're out of options," Mark said.

"I'm never out of options with you," Mary Beth said with a bit of sass. She smiled at her playful companion. "Do we have time to explore?"

Mark nodded.

"We have an hour. Tom said the car would be ready at three."

The couple had left the Edsel with Tom Schmidt, a Ryan family friend and an auto mechanic who specialized in brake repairs. He operated a shop several blocks away.

"Let's walk then," Mary Beth said. "You can give me a tour of the neighborhood."

Mark chuckled. "What makes you think I know the slums?"

"Call it intuition."

"Your intuition is right."

"Then let's go," Mary Beth said.

"OK."

Mark took Mary Beth's hand and led her up Second Street and into Bunker Hill, a historic district that divided downtown Los Angeles and the west side of town. He stopped when she stopped, released his hand, and pointed to something that looked like an escalator.

"What is *that*?" Mary Beth asked.

Mark laughed.

"It's Angels Flight. It's a railway that takes people up the hill."

"It's a *railway*?"

Mark smiled. "That's what city officials and business leaders call it. They call Angels Flight the shortest funicular railway in the world. I call it the lazy man's way to Olive Street."

"Where are the cars?" Mary Beth asked.

Mark pointed to the top of the hill.

"There's one right there. The other must be out of service."

"Have you ever ridden it?"

Mark nodded. "Dad used to take Ben and me down here two or three times a year. He wanted us to see Bunker Hill before the bulldozers got to it. You won't recognize this place in ten years."

"What's going on?" Mary Beth asked.

"The city is moving forward."

"Please tell me it will save the houses."

Mark laughed. "Are you kidding? The houses will be the first things to go. That's why Dad snapped up the place in West Adams. He knew that Victorian mansions in Los Angeles would soon be as rare as California condors. He was a strident opponent of this kind of progress."

"I can see why," Mary Beth said. "I don't like it either."

"It is sad. I'll give you that."

"Is anyone trying to stop it?"

Mark nodded.

"A few neighborhood groups have filed lawsuits and started petitions, but they haven't had much success. They won't either. When 'progress' goes up against sentiment, progress wins every time. It's just the way of the world – or at least the world I live in."

Mary Beth glanced at her guide.

"I live in this world too."

"I guess you do," Mark said. He smiled and reclaimed her hand. "Let's go."

"OK."

The two headed southwest, down Hill Street, and commenced a circuitous tour of one of the oldest parts of Los Angeles. For the next thirty minutes, they strolled past dilapidated mansions, warehouses, and shops and soaked up a neighborhood that was changing before their eyes.

As they did, they talked about progress, conservation, and the City of Angels' glorious past. They conspicuously avoided time travel, dilemmas, and their own uncertain future. Mark seemed particularly eager to avoid the elephant in the room. He spoke to Mary Beth as if she were a permanent part of his life and not a time tourist lingering in a state of limbo.

"We should come back on a Saturday," Mark said as they turned off First Street and started down Grand Avenue. "Most of the stores hold sales on weekends. I'll bet you could buy plates like the one you bought for half price."

"Then let's do it," Mary Beth said. She waited for him to meet her gaze. "Let's come back every weekend for the next month. We have the time."

Mark chuckled.

"I guess we do. Shall we keep walking?"

Mary Beth nodded.

"I want to see the rest of this street."

Mark acknowledged the request with a nod and then led Mary Beth into the heart of the historic district. He did not stop until they reached a busy block that was filled with honking cars, hurried pedestrians, and a wide range of commercial activity.

"Do you see anything you like?" Mark asked.

"I see a *lot* I like," Mary Beth said. She released Mark's hand and gave her surroundings a 360-degree inspection. "I just love the architecture. It's so much different than what I'm used to. It's a shame that so many of these buildings will go."

"It is."

"I have a question though."

188

Mark turned his head.

"What's that?"

"Why are there so many thrift stores? I've seen at least a dozen in the last twenty minutes," Mary Beth said. "There's even one across the street. It seems out of place."

"You're right. There are a lot. Why? I'm not sure," Mark said. "I do know that at least some of the stores have doubled as betting shops over the years."

Mary Beth cocked her head.

"Betting is illegal in California."

Mark laughed.

"Tell that to the people across the street. The FBI raided their shop last year. They said it was a front operation for organized crime."

Mary Beth glanced again at the store and saw three frowning men in suits and fedoras walk out the front door. Each looked like an extra from a gangster movie.

"Mark?"

"Yeah?"

"I think it still is," Mary Beth said.

"What?"

"I think the shop is still a front."

Mark looked across the street.

"It's him!"

Mary Beth's heart raced when she saw that one of the men had a deformed ear. It nearly exploded when she saw him look her way.

"He sees us!" Mary Beth said. She saw the man reach inside his jacket and touch something strapped to his chest. "He has a gun, Mark. He has a gun!"

OK. This is real.

Mark didn't wait for another hint. He grabbed Mary Beth's hand, pulled her back from the curb, and led her away from the chaotic scene.

Mary Beth wanted to sprint but could barely even walk. She bumped into people right and left as she followed Mark down the crowded sidewalk.

"Move faster!" Mark said. "We have to get out of here."

Mary Beth clutched her handbag, picked up the pace, and followed Mark closely as they weaved between people blocking their way. She looked for a policeman but found nothing but shoppers, businessmen, and others who had no idea a lethal pursuit was under way.

Then she looked over her shoulder and saw that things had gone from bad to worse. Ear Man had crossed the street behind them and was moving their way at a rapid clip.

"He's right behind us, Mark."

Mark did not look back. Apparently convinced that the situation had, in fact, deteriorated, he tightened his hold on Mary Beth's hand and plowed through pedestrians like a running back.

As she pushed her way forward, Mary Beth thought about Piper, their parents, and all the people she knew in 2017. She feared for the first time that she would never see them again. She feared she would not see the end of the *day*. Mark and Mary Beth said nothing as they raced toward Fourth Street, a busy intersection, and a difficult decision. They could stay on Grand Avenue, where they were more likely to run into a policeman, or take their chances on a side street and perhaps lose their pursuer.

Mark appeared to consider these choices when they reached Fourth Street and heavy traffic that impeded their progress. He picked the first option when the traffic cleared.

"Let's go," Mark said.

The two crossed Fourth Street just as Ear Man reached the intersection and encountered a new stream of cars that blocked his way. For a few seconds, it appeared as though the time travelers had gained an edge and perhaps a measure of hope. Then everything changed again.

Mary Beth peered across Grand Avenue and saw a new threat. Ear Man's two acquaintances had joined the hunt. The hunters eyed their prey as they stepped forward.

"I see the others," Mary Beth said. "We're not going to make it!"

Mark scanned the vicinity like a fugitive on the business end of a manhunt. When he saw something of interest to the northwest, he looked at Mary Beth with determined eyes.

"Yes, we are. We just have to hurry."

The couple turned their backs on the bad men and sprinted from Fourth and Grand toward Fourth and Hope. As they approached the second intersection, Mary Beth saw what Mark had seen. She saw a cab driver, sitting in a yellow Checker taxi, waiting for a light to change.

Mark reached the vehicle a few seconds later, opened the right rear door, and pushed Mary Beth inside. Then he joined her in back, slammed the door shut, and barked at the driver.

"Go!"

The cabbie looked over his shoulder.

"I'm sorry, folks. I'm done for the day."

Mary Beth peered out a window and saw her pursuers. The hired hands approached from thirty yards out. Ear Man waited on the other side of the light. Each reached inside his jacket. "I have a hundred dollars that says you're not," Mary Beth said. "Now gun it!"

43: MARK

South Pasadena, California – Wednesday, April 29, 1959

Sitting at a table in the lounge of the Chaparral Motel, Mark Ryan scanned three faces and saw sadness, shock, and despair. He had seen all three emotions in the past four weeks but never together and never like this. The situation that faced the two couples was, in a word, hopeless.

"I can't accept this," Ben said.

"You don't have a choice," Mark said. "None of us do."

Mark wanted to sugarcoat things. He wanted to tell his brother and two women he adored that there was a way out, but couldn't do it. After barely escaping with his life in Bunker Hill Tuesday afternoon, he realized that time had run out for all of them. If they did not end this experiment and end it now, someone would get hurt or even killed.

"Do you think the men know where we live?" Piper asked.

Mark shook his head.

"That was our one lucky break. They were never able to tie us to a car. I went back for the Edsel this morning. Tom Schmidt, the guy who replaced my brakes, kept the car in his shop overnight at my request. He didn't ask any questions. He just did it."

"That's something," Piper said.

"It is. It buys us some time, but it doesn't change the big picture. Some very bad people want to get their hands on the sports book. They will kill to get it. I'm sure of that."

"Can't we just send it to them?" Ben asked. "Can't we send it to them anonymously and ask them to leave us alone?"

Mark looked across the table at Ben.

"Who would we send it to? If we mailed the book to the wrong person, we might create even more problems. The guy with the bad ear might kill us out of spite."

191

"Then what should we do?" Ben asked.

"I've already told you," Mark said. "We need to hold the book as a possible bargaining chip and send Mary Beth and Piper home. It's the only thing we *can* do now."

"Can't we explore this more?" Piper asked.

Mark turned to his questioner.

"What's to explore?"

Piper looked to her left, at Ben, and gazed at him for several seconds. Then she took a breath, gave her sister a sad smile, and returned to the man calling the shots.

"There is one thing."

"What?" Mark asked.

"You could come with us," Piper said. "You and Ben could go back to 2017 and stay this time. You could bring your mom and build a new life. We would help you."

Mark looked at Piper like the little sister he never had and always wanted. He could not believe so much wisdom could be packed into such a small frame.

"I've considered that option. I've considered it over and over for the past five weeks, but I keep coming back to the same place."

"What's that?" Piper asked.

"My mother would never go for it," Mark said. "She has a brother in Fresno and a sister in San Diego. She has friends here and a life. So do Ben and I. If we did what you propose, if we followed you to the future and stayed, we would risk a lot. What if things didn't work out between Mary Beth and me or you and Ben? You two could go on with your lives as if nothing important had happened. Ben and I could not do the same. Neither could Mom. We would be stuck in a world we barely understand. We would have to survive without identification and credentials and a *past*. We might end up worse off than we are now."

"You could always return to 1959," Piper said. "You've done it before. No one noticed you were gone the last time. Why couldn't you do it again?"

Mark looked at her thoughtfully.

"I'll tell you why. Geoffrey Bell is why. If we returned to 2017 and stayed more than a day or two, he would control access to the tunnel – not you or Mary Beth or someone we know. He may not want to help us. He may not have the *means* to help us."

Piper tilted her head.

"I don't understand."

"Look at it this way," Mark said. "What do any of us know about the tunnel or the crystals that make it work? We've accessed the portal several times, but can we do so indefinitely? Do the rocks expire like batteries? Does the tunnel? The man who knows for sure died decades ago. It's even

192

possible that the portal and the crystals don't work now. It's possible that you and Mary Beth are stuck *here*. Have you considered that?"

Piper lowered her head.

"No."

"I don't want to give up, Piper. I want to keep Mary Beth. I want to keep *you*. I want to keep both of you in my life, but I don't know how," Mark said. He sighed. "We have to part."

Piper nodded.

Mark surveyed the faces in the room a second time and saw that the gloom had not lifted. He berated himself for letting things go this far. He should have known this would happen. He could see the writing on the wall the weekend the four went to Las Vegas.

"So when *do* we part?" Ben asked. He looked at Mark with eyes that reflected anger, fatigue, and judgment. "Do we do it now?"

"I think we should. We should do it tonight," Mark said. He looked at Piper and then Mary Beth. "We should send you back before any mobsters with guns can harm you."

"What about Mom?" Ben asked.

"She'll be in bed by nine. She won't suspect a thing if we're quiet. She'll just think the two of us came home when we *said* we'd come home," Mark said. "What do you say?"

Ben sighed.

"I say let's get on with it."

"Piper?" Mark asked.

"I agree," Piper said. "We might as well do it tonight."

Mark turned to his right and gazed at Mary Beth. He wanted her thoughts most of all and had been surprised that she had not offered them during the course of the discussion.

"Mary Beth?"

The future medical student took a breath, looked at Piper and Ben with admiring eyes, and then turned to the man at the head of the table. She stared at Mark for what seemed like an eternity before finally saying her piece.

"I agree with almost everything you've said tonight, Mark. We can't stay, you can't leave, and none of us can fix a situation that is broken."

"I thought you felt that way," Mark said.

Mary Beth held up her hand.

"Let me finish."

Mark nodded.

"OK."

"Piper and I came here to have an adventure. We stayed because we fell in love," Mary Beth said. "I don't want to leave in a rush because some bad men chased us through the streets."

193

"What are you saying?" Mark asked.

Mary Beth reached to her left and took his hand.

"I'm saying I want to do this right. I want to withdraw Piper from school, provide people who know us with a story, and give you that book. I want to take a few days to say goodbye to your mother and two young men who have changed my life."

Mark nodded.

"Maybe that's best. Mom is leaving Friday morning to see my aunt. She'll be back Saturday afternoon. You and Piper can come over tomorrow night and say goodbye then. Then we can do our own things on Friday and send you through the tunnel before Mom returns on Saturday."

"I like that idea," Mary Beth said.

"Piper?" Mark asked.

Piper stared blankly into space, as if pondering Mark's proposal, the risks of staying, and other possible courses, and then finally rejoined the others. She took Ben's hand, offered a sweet smile, and slowly turned back to Mark.

"I'm good with that," Piper said. "Let's do it."

44: DONNA

Los Angeles, California – Thursday, April 30, 1959

Donna Ryan looked at the television and then at the couch and tried to decide which was more depressing. She had expected to see forced smiles and genuine frowns on the tube. She usually found sadness in spades on *Playhouse 90*, a drama series that aired every Thursday night. She had *not* expected to find four sorry faces on her sofa.

Of course, she had not expected Mary Beth and Piper McIntire to tell her they would soon leave Southern California for good. She had not expected that at all.

The sisters had made their startling announcement at dinner. They had said they needed to rush back to Germany to be with a mother battling meningitis. The two planned to catch a flight to Frankfurt Saturday morning.

Donna suspected there was nothing she could do to lighten the mood in the living room, but she decided to try anyway. She did not want to spend her final moments with two charming young women staring at a flickering box. She spoke first to Mary Beth.

"Have you heard from your father today?"

Mary Beth turned away from the TV.

"No, Mrs. Ryan, I haven't. He said he would call us again in the morning. He expected to know more about my mother's condition by then."

"Please let me know if there's a change."

"I will. I'll give you an update as soon as I can."

"I appreciate that," Donna said.

"When do you expect to leave tomorrow?" Mary Beth asked.

"I'll leave by seven. I want to make the most of the trip since it will be so short. I typically spend the whole weekend with Phyllis."

195

"Does your sister have a family?"

Donna pondered the question before answering. Didn't most women have families? Maybe they didn't in places like Wiesbaden and Huntsville. Maybe the world was changing.

"She does. Phyllis and her husband have three girls. The oldest is twenty."

Mary Beth looked at Donna with wistful eyes.

"Are you close to your sister?"

"I am now," Donna said. "We weren't that close growing up, because of our four-year age difference, but we've made up for lost ground in the last few years. It's funny how much more you appreciate your siblings as you get older."

Mary Beth smiled at Piper and then at her hostess.

"I can imagine."

Donna let Mary Beth return to *Playhouse 90* and then turned to Piper. She had not spoken to her at dinner and still had many questions about how she was handling this difficult transition. She spoke when the station broke for a commercial.

"Do you plan to go to school tomorrow, Piper?"

Piper turned her head and nodded.

"I want to say goodbye to my friends and teachers."

"I imagine that will be hard," Donna said.

"It will be harder with some people than with others," Piper said. She glanced at Ben. "Either way, I'll survive. I've done this before, Mrs. Ryan. It's part of being an Army brat."

Donna nodded. She could relate. She had moved several times as the daughter of a Navy officer before finally finding a home in San Diego.

"Will you be able to graduate in Germany?" Donna asked.

"I think so," Piper said. "I may have to take a class or two over the summer, but I'll get there. I'm not too worried about it."

"That's nice to hear."

Donna studied Piper for another moment and then moved on to two boys she knew well – or at least *thought* she knew well. As she gazed at Mark and Ben from her upholstered perch ten feet away, she began to wonder whether she knew them at all.

Mark wore the face of a defeated man. He stared blankly into space like someone grappling with a thousand challenges or maybe one intractable problem. He had said little at dinner and relatively little in the past week. For the first time in recent memory, he had kept his thoughts to himself and not confided in a mother who was his mentor and confidante.

Ben wore the face of a miserable man. He stared blankly at the television like someone who could not care less about *Playhouse 90* or *Leave It to Beaver* or *Behind Closed Doors* or any other show that usually grabbed his

196

attention on a Thursday night. He showed signs of life only when Piper clasped his hand and coaxed a smile. He had frowned nearly nonstop since dinner.

My boys are in love.

Donna pondered the sorry situation for a moment and then did the only thing she probably could do to improve matters. She got up from her chair and announced that she was calling it a night. If she did nothing else, she would give the lovebirds a chance to deal with their misery privately and perhaps find a moment of peace in the time that remained to them.

Donna moved toward the sofa as the four young adults rose to their feet. She turned first to the woman with the pretty eyes and the heart of gold.

"Thank you again for the plate," Donna said.

Mary Beth smiled.

"It's the least I could do. I hope you enjoy it."

"I will. I know I will."

Donna stepped forward and gave Mary Beth a warm hug. She was going to miss this girl, she thought. She was going to miss what she had done for her son. She patted Mary Beth on the shoulders, stepped back, and offered the lovely brunette a motherly smile.

"Please keep in touch," Donna said.

"I will," Mary Beth said. "I'll send you a postcard the minute we arrive in Wiesbaden. If I can swing it, I'll attach a box of German chocolates."

Donna laughed.

"You do that."

Donna moved on to Piper. She gave her a hug that was a little more formal but no less meaningful. A moment later, she stepped back and gazed at her with admiring eyes.

"Let me know if you decide to come back," Donna said. "If you return to Los Angeles to attend college or look for a job, just pick up the phone. I will happily provide you with a room or references or anything else you might need."

Piper smiled.

"I appreciate that, Mrs. Ryan. If I come back, I'll give you a call."

Donna nodded and then turned to her sons. Both looked relieved. Neither looked cheerful. Each gazed at her with eyes that reflected affection and gratitude.

Donna spoke first to Mark.

"What are your plans for tomorrow?"

Mark sighed.

"I'm still working that out. I may or may not go to school. I may or may not do anything. It depends on how I feel in the morning."

Donna looked at Ben.

197

"What about you?"

"I *am* going to school," Ben said. "I don't have a choice. I have two tests."

"Don't you have a match too?" Donna asked.

Ben shook his head.

"It was canceled. My day is free after three."

"Then enjoy it. Enjoy the day," Donna said. She looked at Ben and Mark. "That goes for both of you. Do something special with your lady friends. I mean it. I'll take care of the laundry and the dishes when I get back."

"Thanks," Mark said.

Donna nodded but did not respond. She instead kissed her sons good night, smiled at the girls, and then stepped toward an exit that led to a hallway, the stairs, and her bedroom. She turned around when she reached the open doorway and looked at Mark.

"There is a bottle of champagne on the top shelf of the pantry. Your father bought it last year when he went to New York. He bought it for our twenty-fifth anniversary."

Donna took a breath.

"Feel free to enjoy it if you're in the mood for something nice. It will make me happy knowing it didn't go to waste."

"I'll think about it," Mark said.

"You do that," Donna said. "In the meantime, take care of these girls."

"We will."

The matriarch looked at Mary Beth and Piper.

"Thank you again, ladies. Thank you for adding sunshine to our lives and making a difficult time a little more bearable. I will think of you often," Donna said. "Good night."

45: MARY BETH

Santa Monica, California — Friday, May 1, 1959

The ocean churned with a restlessness that almost seemed ordained. Waves rolled in, water rolled out, and sand shifted as two unlikely lovers walked along a quiet beach.

Mary Beth could not help but notice the differences between now and the first time she had dipped her toes in the Pacific Ocean. Five weeks earlier, at Laguna Beach, she had found the water calm, cold, and uninviting. Tonight, in the shadow of the Santa Monica Pier, she found it active, warm, and appealing. It was as comforting as the man who had held her hand on both occasions and made her forget she was the product of another time.

"I wonder where the crowds have gone," Mary Beth said. "I haven't seen more than twenty people since we left the hotel."

Mark smiled.

"I see you missed the bars on the drive in."

"It's seven thirty," Mary Beth said.

Mark laughed.

"I know. It's seven thirty in Santa Monica."

Mary Beth shook her head but did not respond. She saw no point in starting a war of wits on a night she wanted to devote to reflection, remembrance, and romance. So she kept to herself, inspected her glorious surroundings, and soaked up the sights. She found the historic hotels and beachside buildings almost as inspiring as the rapidly setting sun.

"This is so beautiful," Mary Beth said. "Thanks for bringing me."

"You're welcome," Mark said.

"Do you come here often?"

Mark shook his head.

199

"I come here only four or five times a year and almost always to go fishing. Ben and I like to fish off the pier. One can catch a lot with a little patience and decent bait."

"Do you like fishing?" Mary Beth asked.

"I like spending time with my brother."

"I thought so. That's nice."

Mark tightened his hold on Mary Beth's hand as they approached what looked like a gathering of Hells Angels members. More than thirty men in leather jackets or biker vests drank beer and swapped stories around a campfire the size of a tropical hut.

"Just look friendly," Mark said.

Mary Beth laughed.

"OK."

The two smiled and waved to some bikers and ignored the leering stares of others as they moved through the ranks and quickly proceeded to the other side. They passed without incident and resumed their journey down a darkening beach that was once again quiet and secluded.

"Does anyone know we came here tonight?" Mary Beth asked.

"Ben does," Mark said. "So does Dennis Green. I called him this morning and invited him and Margaret to join us for dinner and maybe a walk."

"What did he say?"

"He said, 'Have fun!' They had other plans."

"It's just as well," Mary Beth said.

"Why do you say that?"

"I say it because I want you all to myself tonight."

Mark chuckled.

"That's a good reason."

Mary Beth smiled and then gazed at the soothing sight to her right. Hotels and homes, sitting atop a long, sheer bluff, lit up the east side of the beach like Christmas lights on the eaves of a roof. She took a mental snapshot and returned to her thoughtful companion.

"What are Ben and Piper doing tonight? Or should I ask?"

Mark smiled.

"You can ask. You just may not like the answer."

"What do you mean?" Mary Beth asked.

"They went for a drive," Mark said. "Ben told me he wanted to head up Mulholland Drive after taking Piper to dinner. Mulholland Drive is Make-Out Central."

Mary Beth raised a brow.

"So they plan to park in the dark?"

Mark laughed.

"That's the long and short of it."

Mary Beth smiled.

"I hope they have fun."

Mark cocked his head.

"Is this Piper's protective sister talking?"

Mary Beth looked at Mark thoughtfully.

"No. It's the one who wants her to enjoy her last night here."

Mark shook his head.

"You continue to amaze me."

"I'll take that as a compliment," Mary Beth said.

"You should."

Mary Beth slowed to a stop.

"Can we find a place to sit? My feet are getting tired."

Mark nodded.

"There are some benches on the walk."

"OK."

Mark turned toward the bluff and led Mary Beth to a paved path that ran parallel to the shoreline. They found a small backless bench a moment later, sat down, and directed their attention once again to the churning waves, the sparsely populated beach, and the setting sun.

"Is this better?" Mark asked.

"It's much better," Mary Beth said.

The two quickly settled into a comfort zone. He wrapped his arm around her shoulders. She burrowed into his side. For the next thirty minutes, they did nothing but watch the ocean, keep each other warm, and enjoy each other's company in splendid silence.

Mary Beth used the time to think about forty-two wonderful days. She thought about the trip to Las Vegas, the fraternity functions, and Oscar night in Ben's Thunderbird. She thought about the meaningful dinners at the Painted Lady, dancing to the jukebox, and even encountering Professor Geoffrey Bell's parents at a college lecture. She wallowed in pleasant memories.

Then Mary Beth thought about other things. She thought about time tunnels, men with guns, and pending departures. She thought about losing love for the second time in less than a year.

"You're kind of quiet," Mark said. "Are you all right?"

Mary Beth looked at him through watery eyes.

"I was. Now I'm not so sure."

Mark leaned forward and turned his head.

"What's the matter? Or, should I ask, what else is the matter?"

Mary Beth took a deep breath.

"I was just thinking about irony and bad luck."

"What do you mean?" Mark asked.

Mary Beth wiped away tears.

"I mean I've found what many women don't find in a lifetime. I've found love twice and lost it twice. How rotten is that?"

Mark pulled her close.

"You're where I was last night."

Mary Beth studied his face.

"Where are you now?"

Mark frowned.

"I'm in a place where men find love once, not twice, and spend the rest of their lives in misery when it slips through their fingers."

Mary Beth gently caressed his face.

"You'll find love again."

Mark shook his head.

"You don't know that.

"Oh, yes I do," Mary Beth said. She laughed through her tears. "You look like Warren Beatty."

Mark smiled sadly.

"That's what I'm going to miss most about you. You're an optimist. You find rays of sunshine in the darkest places. You see the best in people. You don't give up."

Mary Beth slipped out of Mark's embrace and turned to face him. She placed both hands on his face, leaned forward, and gave him a soft kiss.

"You're right. I don't give up – and I'm not ready to give up now."

"What does that mean?" Mark asked.

Mary Beth wiped away more tears.

"It means I have another day to think this through, Mark Ryan. I still have one more day to decide what's really important in life."

Mark gazed at her through glistening eyes.

"You can't be serious."

"I am."

"I love you, Mary Beth."

Mary Beth clasped his hands.

"I love you too."

"We should talk about this," Mark said.

"No. I don't want to talk about this any more tonight," Mary Beth said. She caressed his face and kissed him again. "All I want to do now is go back to our room. I want to go back to our room, forget the past, and dream of better things."

46: PIPER

Hollywood, California

Sitting on the warm hood of a 1959 Ford Thunderbird, Piper McIntire nestled into Ben Ryan's side, directed her eyes forward, and gazed at a slice of heaven. From their venue, an overlook on Mulholland Drive, she could see the gleaming lights of Hollywood, the skyline of Los Angeles, and a million stars above. Southern California had never looked so good.

"This place is amazing," Piper said.

Ben pulled her close.

"I thought you would like it."

Piper smiled.

"It's private too. I *really* like that."

Ben laughed.

"That makes two of us."

Piper kissed Ben's cheek and lost herself in the moment. She smiled when Elvis Presley, singing "Love Me Tender," gave way to Buddy Holly and "Maybe Baby" on the radio. Along with the crickets of the Hollywood Hills, Holly's Crickets created a symphony that only lovers could love and time travelers could fully appreciate.

"Do you take dates here often?" Piper asked.

"No," Ben said. "I've been here only five times."

Piper gave him a sly grin.

"Did you bring Vicki?"

Ben blushed.

"Must you know everything?"

Piper giggled.

"Yes."

"OK. If you must know, I'll tell you," Ben said. "I brought Vicki here four times last year. Each time we did nothing more than listen to the radio."

Piper laughed.

"You're a liar."

Ben chuckled.

"Of course I am."

"I shouldn't hang out with a liar," Piper said. "He might tell me all sorts of lies to get all sorts of things."

"He might. He might if he wanted only one thing," Ben said. He took a breath. "If he wanted something else, he might tell you how much he loves you and wants you to stay."

Piper wilted as once again Ben said the right thing at the wrong time. She looked at him until she could look no more. She turned away to hide watery eyes.

"You said we wouldn't talk about that."

Ben pulled her closer and kissed her head.

"I'm a liar, remember?"

Piper laughed and wiped away a tear.

"I know. I've known that for weeks."

"What do you mean?" Ben asked.

"I mean you haven't dated 256 girls. You haven't dated more than twenty. You're not the Romeo you made yourself out to be when I first met you."

Ben laughed.

"Did you dig into my past?"

Piper nodded.

"I dug deep. In my first week of school, I asked more questions about you than questions about civics and literature and math. I talked to some of your dates. I talked to a lot of people."

"What did they say?" Ben asked.

"They told me you were a gentleman and a stand-up guy. One girl, Tammy Price, told me that you serenaded her when she refused to go out with you."

"She did?"

Piper nodded.

"She said you stood outside her window three straight nights and sang "That's Amore" until her father chased you away. I can't say I blame him. I've heard you sing to songs on the radio, Ben. Your voice would frighten Frankenstein."

"I was a desperate man back then," Ben said.

"You serenaded her last *year*."

"My memory is bad."

204

"I suspect it is when it comes to girls," Piper said. "Fortunately for the two of us, my ability to judge character is very good. I figured that any boy who would go to that length to impress a girl couldn't be all that bad. That's why I decided to go out with you."

Ben smiled and shook his head.

"I should have known you were up to something when you started talking to Sally. She said you asked a lot of questions about me the first day of school."

"I did," Piper said. "I considered her a reliable source."

Ben chuckled.

"What else did your 'investigation' of my past turn up?"

Piper brought a hand to her chin.

"Let me think. That *was* a month ago."

"There must be more," Ben said.

"Oh, there is. Most things are just escaping me now."

"Then let them escape. There is no need to round up the usual suspects on our last night together. I want at least part of my past to remain a mystery."

Piper laughed.

"I'm sure you do."

"I'm not kidding," Ben said. "I do."

Piper smiled.

"There *is* another thing. I didn't learn it until recently though."

"What's that?"

"I learned you have a heart."

"That sounds like something my mother would say," Ben said.

"It *was* something your mother said."

"OK. Spill it."

Piper grinned.

"Your mom told me that you once stood up Vicki to date an eighth-grader."

"This sounds bad," Ben said.

"I thought so, too, at first. Then your mom filled me in. She said you did a very nice thing last fall. She said you fulfilled a promise to a neighbor girl in South Pasadena – a *crippled* neighbor girl – by taking her out for ice cream on her fourteenth birthday."

"Don't believe her. Mothers lie all the time to make their children look good. That's how they raise liars like me. You shouldn't take her seriously."

"Your brother confirmed the story," Piper said. "Is he lying too?"

"Yes," Ben said. "My mom raised two liars."

Piper laughed.

"I believe that as much as I believe you picked our restaurant at random."

205

Ben tilted his head.

"I *did*."

"Is that why you asked Sally for advice on where to take me tonight? She told me about your little chat," Piper said. She kissed him again on the cheek. "I appreciate the effort though. Your choice showed imagination."

"So you enjoyed dinner tonight?" Ben asked.

"Do puppies pee on floors? Of course I enjoyed it."

Piper did too. She had enjoyed every moment at Luigi's Grill, a pricey Italian restaurant in Beverly Hills that regularly catered to millionaires, celebrities, and politicians. She had ordered a pasta dish she could not pronounce and goaded Ben into doing the same. By the time the waiter brought out the gelato at eight fifteen, she was ready to kiss every man in the building.

"That's good," Ben said. "I wanted you to enjoy it. That's why I asked Sally for suggestions. I knew she wouldn't steer me wrong. I didn't want to do anything wrong tonight."

"Do you think you've succeeded?" Piper asked.

Ben nodded.

"I think so."

"I do too."

"So what you're really saying is that I can do no wrong."

Piper smiled.

"Don't get carried away. I'm just saying you've had a good night."

Ben chuckled.

"I can't believe this. You just told me I was a gentleman and a stand-up guy, a person who serenades high school girls and takes crippled eighth-graders out for ice cream. Now you're saying I'm just a guy who's had a good night? I'm full of outrage."

Piper laughed.

"You're full of something."

"I mean it, Piper. What's not to like?"

"You mean besides an abject lack of humility?"

Ben nodded.

"Yes."

"All right," Piper said. She looked at the smart aleck. "If you insist on me spoiling a perfectly fine evening by listing your flaws, I'll do it."

Ben lifted his arm from Piper's shoulders, placed his hands behind his head, and reclined against the windshield. He grinned as he prepared to take his medicine.

"Let me have it," Ben said.

"Very well," Piper replied. She swiveled to face him. "First of all, Ben Ryan, you are the most conceited person I have ever met. Yes, you're gorgeous. Yes, you're smart. But that doesn't mean you should *tell* people that. Even Vicki told me she had her fill of you more than once."

"She's lying too. She lies as much as my brother."

"I doubt it."

Ben smiled.

"Is that all?"

"No," Piper said. "That's just the tip of the iceberg."

Ben gestured with his arm.

"Please continue."

"OK. I will," Piper said. She scolded him with a glance. "In addition to being insufferably conceited, you are obnoxious, slovenly, boorish, argumentative, materialistic, and dangerous. Don't think for a minute I've forgotten the night you almost killed me."

Ben frowned and took a breath. He sat up, brushed off his slacks, and slid forward on the hood until he was once again at Piper's side.

"I guess that means you don't like me."

"No, Ben. It means I think you have flaws."

"You've laid out a brutal case, counselor. Even I wouldn't go out with me."

Piper laughed.

"Fortunately for you, I'm a forgiving person."

"So you really think I'm a bad boy?" Ben asked.

Piper nodded.

"I do. I think you're bad and ornery and needlessly difficult," Piper said. She turned to face him. "I also think you're caring, considerate, and way too sexy for your own good."

Ben beamed.

"Now you're talking!"

"Don't get too excited," Piper said. "All I'm saying is that your virtues outweigh your vices."

Ben offered a playful grin.

"What do you think we should do about that, Miss McIntire?"

Piper smiled sheepishly.

"I don't know."

Ben raised a brow.

"We could drive back to the house. I have a big empty room."

Piper looked at Ben thoughtfully.

"You also have a big empty car."

She kissed him softly and sighed.

"Why wait?"

47: DENNIS

Los Angeles, California – Saturday, May 2, 1959

D ennis Green mumbled and moaned when his unfriendly friend jabbed him in the shoulder and told him to wake up. He didn't like waking up before ten on weekend mornings and suspected that the clock had yet to strike eight.

"Stop poking me, Carter. I'm awake," Dennis said.

"I'm glad to hear that," Carter Williams said. "Now throw on some clothes and get your ass downstairs. Some men want to see you."

"What men?"

"FBI agents. They want to talk about Mark."

"What?" Dennis asked.

"Just go downstairs," Carter said. "I'll meet you in the living room."

Carter walked away from the bunk bed, one of ten on the second-floor sleeping porch of Zeta Alpha Rho fraternity, and took his leave. He left his fraternity brother dazed, confused, and more than a little irritated on a morning he should have been none of the above.

Dennis threw back the covers on his bed, swung his legs over the side, and lowered himself to the cold tile floor. He vowed to investigate Carter for criminal harassment if this law-enforcement matter turned out to be nothing more than a case of double parking.

He walked across the porch, pulled a few items from a closet, and headed for the door. Dressed in striped pajamas, a bathrobe, and corduroy slippers, he was ready to take on the world.

Dennis asked himself some questions as he walked down a hallway and then a flight of stairs. Why did the FBI want to talk about Mark? Why did the FBI want to talk about *anyone* in a fraternity on a Saturday morning? Was someone in serious trouble?

Dennis gave the questions a moment of thought and then turned his full attention to the matter at hand. He had a date with J. Edgar Hoover.

The college senior reached the bottom of the stairs a moment later. He turned to his left, walked across a large parlor, and made his way toward an open door. He heard voices even before he passed from the parlor to the living room. He had a crowd waiting.

Dennis felt uneasy the second he stepped into the room. Seven people gathered in a group in front of the console television, including three men in crisp suits and four fraternity brothers in not-so-crisp pajamas. Carter turned his head as Dennis approached.

"Dennis, these are the men I mentioned," Carter said. He turned toward the men. "Gentlemen, this is Dennis Green. He is Mark Ryan's roommate."

Each of the suited men flashed badges. The closest stepped forward.

"Good morning, Dennis. I'm Special Agent Trent Richards of the Federal Bureau of Investigation. These are my colleagues, Agent Frank Dennison and Agent Manny Trujillo."

Dennis shook three hands.

"We're here to investigate a serious matter that may involve Mark Ryan," Richards said. "Do you have a moment to answer some questions?"

"Of course," Dennis said.

Richards, a tall man with a deformed ear, pulled out a pen and a notepad. He scribbled a few notes, glanced at his colleagues, and then smiled at Dennis in a way that left him cold.

"I'm told you're Mark's best friend. Is that true?" Richards asked.

"It is," Dennis said.

"When did you last see him?"

"I saw him yesterday. Is he in trouble?"

"No," Richards said.

"Is he in danger?" Dennis asked.

Richards shrugged.

"I don't know. That's what I'm here to find out."

Dennis nodded.

"How can I help?"

"You can help by telling me if Mark has come in contact with a young woman who recently moved to this area," Richards said. "We believe her name is Colleen Finley."

"I don't know any Colleen."

"I see," Richards said.

"What does Colleen look like?"

"She's about five-foot-five and 120 pounds with long brown hair. She's very pretty and very southern. We think she came here from Huntsville, Alabama."

209

Dennis felt his stomach turn the second he heard brown hair, pretty, and southern. He had no doubt the FBI wanted Mary Beth McIntire.

"Is she dangerous?" Dennis asked.

"We don't know," Richards said.

"What makes you think Mark may be associating with this woman?" The agent stared at the student.

"We have three independent sightings of Miss Finley with a man fitting Mark Ryan's description. They were seen together twice in Las Vegas six weeks ago and once in Bunker Hill last Tuesday. The man with Miss Finley wore a Zeta Alpha Rho shirt."

"There are four Zeta chapters in the area," Dennis said. "Have you checked the others?"

Richards lowered his pad.

"We've checked every one. This is our last stop."

"I see," Dennis said.

Richards studied the collegian's face.

"I sense you know something."

"I might," Dennis said. "But before I say more, I'd like to *know* more. I'd like to know why the FBI is looking for Colleen Finley and why she may be a threat to Mark."

The agent cocked his head.

"It's real simple, Mr. Green. Colleen Finley is a fraud artist. She has defrauded nearly a dozen men out of more than four million dollars in the last three years. Most of her victims have been college men with access to family money. Has your friend come into money lately?"

Dennis sighed.

"He has."

"Please explain," Richards said.

"Mark's father died last fall and left him a large inheritance."

Richards stared at Dennis.

"Do you know where your friend was last night?"

Dennis took a deep breath.

"I know where he is right now. He's at the beach with the woman you want. He's at the Surf Side Hotel in Santa Monica."

48: MARK

Santa Monica, California

The ring of the phone woke Mark with a jolt. Loud, incessant, and obnoxious, it rattled him, mind and body, until he rolled out of bed and picked up the receiver.

"Hello?"

A man spoke over a scratchy line.

"Mark?"

The time traveler put a hand to his temple as he tried to match the familiar voice with the information stored in his head. He couldn't do it.

"Yes, this is Mark. Who is this?"

"It's Dennis."

"Dennis?"

"Yeah, I know. It's early here too."

Mark glanced at the clock next to his bed and then at the woman *in* his bed. Each had a revealing face. Both were alive and ticking at eight thirty.

"What's going on?"

"I don't know. I'm sorry to wake you, buddy, but something happened a few minutes ago that I think you should know about."

"What?"

Dennis sighed loudly over the phone.

"Three FBI agents came to Zeta Alpha Rho and asked questions about a woman who fits Mary Beth's description. They asked a lot questions about *you*."

Mark rubbed his temple.

"FBI agents?"

"That's what they called themselves," Dennis said. "They talked to Carter and Jack and then asked for me. They wanted to know where they could find you."

211

"Did you tell them?"

"I did."

"Dennis!"

"They had badges, Mark. They had information too. They said that Mary Beth is some kind of traveling criminal. They said she's a con artist who steals money from people like you."

"What are you talking about?" Mark asked.

"The agents claimed she's a woman named Colleen Finley," Dennis said. "They said she's scammed millions of dollars from people."

"You don't believe that."

"I don't know what to believe."

"You've met her," Mark said.

"I met a woman who came to California out of nowhere. How well do you really know her?" Dennis asked. "How do you know she is who she says she is?"

"I just know."

Mark did not tell his best friend *why* he knew. He did not want to compound his morning with a time-travel tale that would surely make things worse.

"Is Mary Beth with you now?" Dennis asked.

"She is," Mark said.

"You might want to fill her in then."

Mark glanced again at Mary Beth and saw that she was following the conversation closely. He could see fear and apprehension in her bleary blue eyes.

"Tell me about these agents," Mark said. "What did they look like?"

"I just remember the one. He said his name was Trent Richards. He was tall with black hair and dark eyes. He had a bad ear too. His left ear was messed up."

Mark put his hand over the speaker and turned to Mary Beth.

"Get dressed."

"Why?" Mary Beth asked.

"Just do it," Mark said. "We have to go."

"OK."

Mark returned to Dennis.

"Are the men still there?"

"No," Dennis said. "They left twenty minutes ago."

"Did you name the hotel? Did you tell them exactly where we were?"

"I did, Mark. I didn't think I had a choice. Please tell me these guys are cops."

Mark took a breath.

"I can't, Dennis. I can't."

"Oh, crap."

212

Mark closed his eyes as he tried to process a hundred thoughts. Somehow, someway, the bad men from Bunker Hill had tied him to Zeta Alpha Rho. They knew his name and his present location and would likely figure out the rest before the morning was done.

Mary Beth had no doubt concluded the same. She had already put on the white cotton dress she had worn on Friday and was now busy throwing makeup and toiletries in a bag.

"Did you tell the men I've been living at home?" Mark asked.

"No," Dennis said. "I didn't say anything about your house or your family. I didn't get the chance. They took off the second I named the hotel."

Mark sighed. He was grateful for that. He had only begun to consider what all this meant for Ben and Piper and the mother who would soon return home from San Diego.

"Did you see the car?" Mark asked.

"Did I what?"

Mark cursed the bad connection.

"Did you see the car the men drove?"

"I did," Dennis said. "I saw it plain as day."

"What was it?"

"It was a Lincoln, Mark. They left the lot in a new black Lincoln."

49: BEN

Los Angeles, California

B en huffed as he left his warm bed, a beautiful woman, and the tranquility of a peaceful morning to answer the phone in his mother's room. He wanted to ignore the ringing distraction, but he could not. One could not ignore a device that rang more than twenty times.

He entered the room a moment later, picked up the receiver, and waited to blast the person on the other end. Unless the caller was someone telling him that his mother was hurt or that he had won a valuable prize, he was ready to fire with both barrels.

"Hello?" Ben asked.

"Ben?"

"It's me."

"Thank God you're home," Mark said over the phone. "Where's Piper?"

"She's asleep, Mark. Why are you calling? It's eight forty."

"Listen to me, Ben. Listen real close."

"I'm listening."

Ben felt his stomach twirl as he sat on the edge of Donna Ryan's bed. He detected fear in his brother's voice, along with an unmistakable sense of urgency.

"Look out the window."

Ben lifted the phone off a nightstand and walked to the room's lone window. He opened the blinds, peered through the glass, and looked at the scene beyond. He saw an empty driveway, a quiet street, and a paperboy making the last of his morning deliveries.

"I'm looking," Ben said.

"Do you see a car out front?" Mark asked. "Do you see a black Lincoln?"

"No. I don't. What's going on?"

"I'll explain later. I don't have much time."

"Mark?"

"Just listen, Ben. I want you to lock the front door, wake Piper, and tell her to get dressed. Tell her to gather her things and prepare to go through the tunnel."

"Why?"

"Just do it!" Mark said. "Do it the second I hang up."

"All right. All right."

"Do something else too."

"What?" Ben asked.

"Get the crystal and the key. Then get the book. All three should be in my dresser. Have them ready when we arrive."

"Where are you?"

"We're at the hotel," Mark said.

"What is going *on*?"

"I'll tell you later. Just lock the door and don't open it for anyone but me. I'll honk when we arrive. I mean it, Ben. Don't open the door for anyone."

"I won't."

"I have to go," Mark said. "I'll see you by nine thirty."

Ben sighed when he heard a click and looked again out the window. He saw a neighbor fetching his paper and a red car moving down the street. He did not see trouble.

He suspected that trouble was on the way though. He had never heard his brother speak to him that way. Mark did not make urgent calls to warn about the weather.

Ben returned the phone to the nightstand, walked toward an open door, and stepped into an empty hallway. He resisted the temptation to wake Piper immediately and did what Mark had asked him to do first. He went to secure the residence.

As he walked down the hallway and descended the creaky stairs, Ben pondered not only an urgent phone call but also an incredible evening and an incomparable woman. Even now she seemed surreal. Piper McIntire was a figment of his imagination, a dream, a pleasant apparition that had come into his life on a Saturday morning and would *exit* his life on a Saturday morning. It wasn't fair, he concluded. It just wasn't fair.

Ben reached the entry a moment later, opened the front door, and peeked outside. He saw nothing he hadn't seen before and certainly nothing to give him alarm. He began to wonder whether Mark had overreacted to something. He shut the door, locked it, and moved toward the stairs, a woman he wanted to see, and a conversation he didn't want to have.

As he ascended the steps, Ben thought about Mark and Mary Beth's close encounter with mobsters on Tuesday, the gathering at the Chaparral Motel on Wednesday, and the sense of hopelessness that had gripped four people the rest of the week. He asked himself the obvious questions. Was this really happening? Was it too late to turn back? Were there options that no one had explored? Could he still alter a course that seemed set in stone?

Ben didn't know. He knew only that he had to do what his brother had asked him to do. He had to take prudent measures to protect himself and the woman he loved from a threat that still seemed vague, distant, and strangely unreal. He had to do what he had rarely done before. He had to put aside his own selfish interests and act in the interests of others.

He climbed the stairs, walked down the hallway, and braced himself for a pleasant woman, an unpleasant moment, and a difficult transition. He opened the door to his room a moment later and found the pleasant woman, dressed in a robe, sitting on the edge of his bed.

"I heard the phone ring," Piper said. "Is everything all right?"

Ben shook his head.

"Something is wrong."

"What?"

"I don't know," Ben said. "I just know we have to get dressed."

"It's not even nine."

"I know."

Piper smiled cheerfully.

"Let's make breakfast first."

"We don't have time," Ben said. "We have to get ready. Mark and Mary Beth are coming."

"They left the beach?"

Ben nodded.

"They will be here by nine thirty."

"What's going on?" Piper asked.

"You have to leave, that's what. You have to leave soon. We can't have breakfast. We can't even have the morning."

"Ben?"

"Get dressed, Piper, and then go downstairs. Get your stuff. Get everything you want to take back to 2017," Ben said. He frowned. "It's time to say goodbye."

50: MARY BETH

Santa Monica, California

Mary Beth scanned Pico Boulevard for black Lincolns as Mark drove his Edsel as fast as he could toward the Painted Lady, their siblings, and a rendezvous with 2017. She had advised him to take the more regulated route because she was certain the bad men with guns would take the faster but less direct Olympic Boulevard in their sprint to Santa Monica.

"What time is it?" Mary Beth asked.

Mark glanced at his watch.

"It's five to nine."

"Do you think they know about the house?"

"No. They will by the end of the day though."

Mary Beth frowned as she mentally reviewed the past few days and the past six weeks. It was all coming to an end, she thought. It was all coming to one inglorious end.

She turned to the driver and saw that he, too, had much on his mind. She hated seeing the frown on his face and the fear in his eyes. She hated seeing the sadness.

"What are you thinking about?" Mary Beth asked.

Mark sighed.

"I'm thinking about the book. I asked Ben to retrieve it and have it handy. I wanted him to have something to give the mobsters in case they went to the house first."

"That was smart," Mary Beth said.

"No. It wasn't. I should have told him to burn it."

"Why?"

Mark looked at his passenger.

"Don't you see? Even if we give it to them, they won't let us live. They *can't* let us live. They can't very well make bets with that book knowing that others know of its existence."

Mary Beth battled a wave of guilt as the truth sank in. She was the one who had purchased the book and decided to use it. She was the one who had carelessly tossed a receipt in a garbage can. She had put at least two lives in mortal jeopardy.

"I'm sorry, Mark. I'm sorry for buying that book. I was stupid."

Mark smiled sadly.

"Don't blame yourself. I was stupid long before that. I opened a can of worms when I opened that drawer. I should have left well enough alone."

Mary Beth put a hand on his arm.

"I'm glad you didn't."

"Why do you say that?" Mark asked.

"I say it because your curiosity brought us together. It brought Ben and Piper together. It enriched the lives of at least four people."

Mark laughed.

"You're amazing."

"No. I'm just a person who sees silver linings," Mary Beth said. "I don't regret one minute we've spent together. I hope you feel the same."

"I do," Mark said.

Mary Beth gave his arm a gentle squeeze and then directed her eyes and her attention to the uncluttered road ahead. She welcomed the change. Looking for bad men in black Lincolns beat thinking about a future without Mark Ryan.

"You should call your mother," Mary Beth said. "She needs to know what's going on."

"I know," Mark said. "I've been thinking about her since we left the hotel. I don't know what to tell her."

"Tell her the truth," Mary Beth said. "Tell her everything. You and Ben can't manage this by yourselves. You need her guidance now."

"You're right."

"Is she returning today?"

Mark nodded.

"She'll be home by six."

"Then tell her tonight. Tell her the truth. Tell her everything. Then go to the police," Mary Beth said. "You'll be all right. I know you will."

"I hope so."

Mary Beth started to make another comment but stopped when she saw a black 1958 Lincoln Mark III approach. She tapped on the driver's thigh.

"Mark?"

"I see them," Mark said. "Turn your head. Don't let them see your face."

"I won't," Mary Beth said.

Mary Beth glanced again at the Lincoln and then slowly turned her head toward the front passenger window. She fixed her eyes on a bank and then a five-and-dime store.

She sensed Mark's anxiety as the Edsel and the Lincoln entered a busy intersection, passed each other under a yellow light, and then continued in opposite directions. She sighed when she glanced at the side mirror and saw the black car slowly move away.

Mark let out a breath.

"I think we made it."

Mary Beth smiled when she saw relief on Mark's face but frowned when she heard a squeal. She looked out the back window just as the Lincoln completed a U-turn.

"They saw us," Mary Beth said. She turned to Mark. "Step on it!"

Mark did just that. He stepped on the accelerator and flew through the next intersection as the men in the Lincoln waited for traffic to clear. By the time his pursuers were able to find an opening, run a red light, and begin the chase, he had a healthy lead.

"Where are they?" Mark asked. "I can't see them."

Mary Beth swiveled in her seat and peered again through the back window. This time she did not turn away. She focused on the black Lincoln weaving around cars two blocks back.

"I see them. Go faster, Mark. Go faster!"

"I'm trying."

Mark did more than try. He ran the next two lights and then pulled away when he hit an unregulated stretch between La Cienega Boulevard and Le Brea Avenue. For more than a minute, the Edsel put serious distance on the Lincoln and gave its occupants a measure of hope.

Mary Beth took a deep breath when she saw other cars fall in behind the Edsel and provide a buffer between the hunters and their prey. They were going to make it, she thought.

Then, just that quickly, their fortunes changed. The time travelers came upon an elderly couple crossing the street at an intersection. The delay allowed the men in the Lincoln to regain lost ground, come back into view, and resume a deadly chase.

"I see them again," Mary Beth said. "Can you go faster or turn off?"

Mark looked in the rear-view mirror.

"I can do both. Hold on!"

Mark hit the gas again and kept his foot on the pedal as he put some distance on the men in black. Then he turned right onto Crenshaw Boulevard, drove south a few blocks, and turned right again. He zigzagged through the heart of West Adams for the next few minutes in a desperate and ultimately unsuccessful attempt to ditch his pursuers and buy much-needed time.

"Drive past the house, Mark. Do it twice if you have to," Mary Beth said. "Make some noise. Make it now. We have to let Ben and Piper know we're here."

Mark did as instructed. He drove toward the Painted Lady's block, approached the mansion from the west, and accelerated as he passed the house. He turned sharply at the end of the block.

"Do you have your crystal?" Mark asked.

Mary Beth nodded.

"It's in my purse."

"Hold onto it. Hold it tight. We may need it."

Mark turned sharply two more times and made another pass at his home. This time he honked as he approached the mansion. This time Mary Beth saw Ben and Piper in front of an open door. Both waved as if trying to signal their presence. The strategy had worked.

"I saw them, Mark. I saw them," Mary Beth said.

"So did I."

"Is this the last pass? Is this where we get out?"

Mark nodded.

"Let's hope the third time's a charm. I'm going to pull up in front."

"OK."

Mary Beth held onto her door as Mark circled around the block a final time. She looked out the back window and saw that the Lincoln had closed to within a hundred yards.

"Hurry! Please hurry!"

Mark checked his mirror, flipped up the sun visor, and slowed down as he prepared to make one more turn. Then he fishtailed onto the last street, accelerated past six or seven parked cars, and squealed to a halt along the curb in front of the Painted Lady.

"Get out!" Mark said. "Get out and run for the door!"

Mary Beth grabbed her purse, threw open her door, and exited the Edsel. As she did, she heard a car skid around the corner, sideswipe another vehicle, and approach at a rapid clip. She glanced at the door to the mansion and saw Ben and Piper frantically wave her forward.

Mary Beth ran straight for the door and made it about halfway up a plush front lawn when she heard a shot, a thud, and a groan. She looked back and saw a man pointing a handgun out the front passenger window of a Lincoln that had stopped on the far side of the street. Then she turned her attention to the sidewalk, saw Mark lying face down on the ground, and screamed.

"Mark!"

Mary Beth felt her heart race as she sprinted toward Mark and saw three men in dark suits and fedoras exit the dented Lincoln. She could not believe it had come down to this. She could not believe that her six weeks in heaven had come down to six seconds of hell.

Her mind raced as she approached the sidewalk. Was Mark hurt? Could he walk? Could he make it to the house? Could she do anything to help him?

Mark quickly rendered the questions moot. When Mary Beth reached his side, he lifted his head, looked her in the eyes, and then scrambled to his feet.

"I'm fine," Mark said. "Run!"

Mary Beth did not wait for further instruction. She did not wait for *Mark*. She turned to face the Painted Lady, clutched her purse, and ran toward the open door with reckless abandon.

Mark threw his arm around her waist and pushed her forward as they sprinted across the lawn and moved toward the door, their siblings, and safety. He screamed at Ben and Piper to go inside as they approached the small front porch and then urged Mary Beth to do the same.

Mary Beth stumbled slightly as she heard two more shots, regained her balance on the porch, and followed Ben and Piper into the mansion. She let out a breath when she heard Mark enter the residence behind her, slam the door shut, and lock it.

Mark turned around, stepped away from the door, and scanned the faces in the entry as if conducting a head count. He stared at Ben.

"Do you have the rock?" Mark asked.

"Yes," Ben said.

"Do you have the key?"

"Yes."

"What about the book?"

"I couldn't find it."

Ben barely got the words out when danger arrived in spades. One mobster kicked the front door. Another broke a window in the living room. The man at the door advised one of his peers to circle around to the back of the house. They clearly intended to finish the job.

"It doesn't matter," Mark said. "We have to go. Everyone head to the basement!"

Mary Beth felt fear as she followed Piper and Ben down a dark hallway and a dull pain as they passed through the door to the basement. She placed her hand on the small of her back and felt a wet, sticky substance. She looked over her shoulder as she descended the stairs.

"Mark?"

"I see it," Mark said. "Just keep going. We can't stop."

Mary Beth tightened her hold on her purse as she entered the basement and moved with the others toward a distant door. She didn't make it halfway before she started to wobble and fade.

"Mark?"

"Yeah?"

"I'm getting weak," Mary Beth said.

"I've got you."

Mary Beth heard Mark's words but could not process them before her journey to the door, the tunnel, and the future became a jumbled blur of voices and actions. She felt Mark pick her up and carry her into the tunnel. She did not feel much of anything else. The dull pain in her back had spread to the rest of her body and left her numb, stunned, and semiconscious.

She looked up at the tunnel ceiling as a string of blue and white lights came to life, flickered, and transformed a gloomy chamber into a comforting space. She reached out, touched Mark's face, and noticed tears in his eyes. She felt sadness and happiness and a strange sense of peace.

Mary Beth clung to those feelings as Ben opened the outer door and Mark carried her up several steps to a familiar backyard. She became conscious of muted daylight, chirping birds, and soft, soothing rain. This is where it had begun, she thought. This is where it would end.

Mary Beth relaxed when Mark carried her to the middle of the yard and let her mind drift when he gently lowered her to the damp grass. She smiled weakly as Mark supported her head, Ben pulled off her shoes, and Piper spoke frantically into a cell phone.

She embraced the warmth of three people she loved and then lifted her eyes to the sky. She felt rain strike her cheeks and a breeze ruffle her hair. She felt all this and more as a quiet spring morning kissed her goodbye, the pain went away, and her splendid world went black.

51: PIPER

Los Angeles, California – Friday, June 2, 2017

iper tried to focus as she held her cell phone in one hand and Mary Beth's wrist in the other. She wanted to do a thousand other things, including cry, but she knew she couldn't do anything until she put her grievously wounded sister into an ambulance.

"Yes," Piper said into the phone. "She still has a pulse. It's steady but weak. Please hurry. I don't know how much longer she can hang on."

Piper looked at Mark and Ben and saw two men in shock. Mark knelt to her right. He supported Mary Beth's head in his lap. Ben knelt across from Piper. He pressed a wadded handkerchief against a hole in Mary Beth's back as she lay, eyes closed, *on* her back. Both Mark and Ben stared blankly into space.

Piper let her own mind drift when the dispatcher stopped talking. She thought of the trip to Las Vegas, the prom, Ben's tennis matches, and Donna Ryan's goodbye hug. She thought of everything but her dying sister until the dispatcher spoke again and brought her out of a daze.

"Did you say she was shot in the back?"

"Yes. I did," Piper said. "She was hit just above the waist."

The dispatcher typed the information.

"Is there an exit wound?"

Piper released her sister's wrist and brushed a hand across her abdomen.

"I don't think so," Piper said. "Please hurry!"

"The ambulance will be there soon, ma'am. Please stay on the line."

Piper shook her head. What did the dispatcher think she was going to do? Hang up and have a drink with the boys? Then she remembered that the dispatcher did not *know* about the boys. She would have to deal with that problem soon enough.

223

"How is her pulse?" Mark asked.

Piper brought a finger to her lips and shot him a glance that he clearly understood. Then she reclaimed Mary Beth's wrist, waited a moment, and whispered an answer to Mark.

"It's getting weaker."

Mark nodded and returned to Mary Beth. He brushed her long hair away from her face and then stroked her cheeks with the back of his hand.

Piper admired his devotion to her sister. Even Jordan Taylor had not attended to Mary Beth as thoughtfully and completely as this quiet engineering student from the 1950s. She wondered what would happen to Mark when he returned to his own time. She wondered what would happen when he resumed his life without the woman he loved.

The dispatcher again interrupted her thoughts.

"Ma'am? Are you still there?"

Piper pressed the phone to her ear.

"I'm still here."

"The ambulance and a police unit should be there shortly."

Piper turned her head. She heard two faint but distinct sirens in the distance.

"I hear the sirens now."

The dispatcher responded.

"That's good. I'll stay with you until they arrive."

"Thank you," Piper said.

"You're welcome."

Piper hit the mute button and turned to Mark.

"You have to go. You both have to leave now."

"Why?" Mark asked.

"You don't belong here," Piper said. "The police will ask questions. You don't want to answer them now. You won't want to answer them later."

"We'll be fine," Ben said.

"No, Ben. You won't! Trust me. You have to leave."

"We can't leave now."

"Yes, you can. Go now. Find a place to stay, get something to eat, and call me later. Call me tonight," Piper said. She gazed at Ben. "Do you remember my number?"

Ben nodded.

"I do."

Piper reached forward and touched his arm.

"Then call tonight."

"All right."

"Now go."

Mark gently lowered Mary Beth's head to the lawn as Ben withdrew his hands from her back. The two stood up a moment later, gazed at the bleeding woman, and then turned to Piper.

"Take care of her," Mark said.

"I will," Piper replied. She took a breath. "Now please go."

Mark nodded and then led Ben across the yard to the closed front gate. They opened the gate, entered the side yard, and disappeared from sight a few seconds later.

Piper hit the mute button, switched to speaker mode, and placed the phone on the grass. She did not hear a dispatcher clamoring to be heard. She did not hear anything except sirens, a barking dog, and Mary Beth's labored breathing.

She tried to think of a story as the vehicles drew near. How did she explain a gunshot on a tranquil Friday morning? How did she explain a gunshot to the *back*? The police would have questions. So would her parents. So would the Bells.

Piper thought about the matter and then set it to the side. She ignored the sirens, the dog, and the dispatcher who asked if she was "still there." She ignored them all. At eight fifteen on June 2, 2017, she cared only about her sister, best friend, and hero.

Piper checked Mary Beth's pulse again, placed her soft purse under her head, and gently stroked her face. When she was convinced she had done all she could do for her badly wounded sister, she did something for her badly wounded soul.

She placed her head on Mary Beth's chest and thought of their many happy times together. She thought of their fights, their struggles, and their shared journey to the past. She thought of all the things she would miss if her sister didn't make it. Then she closed her eyes and cried.

52: BEN

Ben returned the phone to a new friend, thanked him for letting him use it, and then walked across a room toward Mark and a conversation he had dreaded for hours. He had dreaded the conversation because he had feared he would have to deliver bad news.

Fortunately for Ben Ryan, brother, survivor, and time traveler, he did not have to deliver bad news. At nine o'clock, near the end of the longest day of his life, he had the pleasure of delivering *good* news. He did so with a hug and a smile.

"She's going to make it," Ben said. "She'll be in the hospital a few more days, but she's going to make it. She's going to live, Mark. She's going to be all right."

"What do you know?" Mark asked. He wiped away a tear. "There *is* a God."

"Let's sit down. I'll tell you the rest."

"OK."

Ben and Mark walked to a table, one of eight in the dining room of the La Brea Avenue Mission, and sat down on opposite sides. They looked at each other for a moment, like siblings often do in times of crisis, and communicated their thoughts with gazes instead of words.

"How are you doing?" Ben asked.

"I'm better now. I'm a lot better," Mark said. "What did Piper say?"

"She said that doctors operated on Mary Beth shortly after she arrived, removed the bullet, and 'patched her up in time for lunch.' She actually said that."

"I believe it."

"She was lucky. The bullet just missed her spine."

"Did it hit any organs?"

Ben shook his head.

"Like I said, she was lucky."

"What's she doing now?" Mark asked.

"She's resting."

"Does she remember what happened?"

"I don't know," Ben said. "She hasn't done much all day except sleep and babble. She talked about 'Mark,' 'Ben,' and 'Mr. Ear' when she came out of surgery."

Mark took a breath.

"What about Piper?"

"What *about* Piper?" Ben asked.

"What has she said? I'm sure she's talked to the police."

"She has. She has twice."

Mark studied his brother's face.

"What did she tell them?"

Ben rested his head on his hands.

"She told them a story they don't believe."

"What do you mean?" Mark asked.

Ben looked around the room before answering. He didn't think any of his fellow travelers at the homeless shelter cared a whit about shootings, even in Los Angeles, but he didn't know for sure. He decided to lower his voice and choose his words carefully.

"Piper told the police she thinks Mary Beth was shot by someone trying to enter the house through the backyard and the door to the basement."

"Go on," Mark said.

"She said she heard a popping sound about eight this morning, peeked out the window, and saw someone flying over the fence in back. She went out to investigate, saw Mary Beth sprawled on the lawn, and called for help."

"That sounds like a good story to me."

"There are some problems though," Ben said. "There are a lot of problems, in fact."

"Such as?"

"The first is that no one else heard a shot. No one else saw a man in the backyard or even the neighbor's backyard. No one heard or saw anything unusual this morning except for a lady across the street. She saw two young white males walk along the side of the house and exit the scene in a hurry. Know anyone who fits that description?"

Mark frowned.

"What are the other problems?"

Ben paused again when two homeless men sat down at a nearby table. The two were among the first people Mark and Ben had met after coming to the shelter. The time travelers had come to the mission after learning that outdated identification and twenty dollars would not get them a room at even the most inexpensive motel in the area.

227

"Mary Beth's attire is one problem," Ben said. "She wore a fifties dress. She didn't bring a fifties dress to Los Angeles and apparently didn't buy one here either. Piper told police she didn't know where she got the dress. She just said Mary Beth has done a lot of shopping lately."

Mark sighed.

"Is there more?"

"There is plenty more," Ben said. "The police seem baffled that the burglar shot Mary Beth in the back, not the front, and that the bullet didn't leave an exit wound. They have already sent the bullet to a forensics lab for examination. These guys are better than Joe Friday on *Dragnet*."

"Please tell me that's all."

"I wish I could, but I can't. The biggest problem is that the police haven't yet spoken to Mary Beth. They will probably do so tomorrow. That means Piper and Mary Beth have just hours to get their stories straight. Let your imagination go wild with that."

Mark took another breath.

"We've got a problem then."

"*We* don't," Ben said. "Piper and Mary Beth do. We don't exist, remember?"

"What about the witness?"

"I guess she didn't get a good look at us. The police gave Piper a generic description of two young white males. Piper told them she didn't see anyone fitting that description."

"When can we see them?" Mark asked.

"That's another problem. We may not get the chance *to* see them. Mary Beth's parents have attended to her all day. They haven't left her room once. Then there are Professor and Mrs. Bell, the people who presently own the mansion. They just returned from Santa Barbara, where they have been the past week. They will no doubt want to visit. They will no doubt have questions."

"Are they at the house now?"

"I think so," Ben said.

"That means we will have to trespass to go back to 1959."

"I know."

"We've got problems," Mark said.

Ben nodded.

"I know."

53: MARY BETH

Saturday, June 3, 2017

Ten minutes after waking up from her third nap of the day, Mary Beth looked at the lunch she wanted to eat and then at the sister she didn't want to talk to. She decided the sister was more important. When one had to compare notes before talking to police investigating a shooting, one sometimes had to make sacrifices.

She pushed away her lunch tray, clicked off the television in her hospital room, and turned to face Piper. She frowned when she saw determination and restlessness in her eyes.

"We're in a spot, aren't we?" Mary Beth asked.

Piper forced a smile.

"Yes, we are."

Mary Beth sighed.

"Have you spoken to the boys?"

Piper nodded.

"Ben called me last night. He and Mark are staying at a homeless shelter on La Brea Avenue. They didn't have the money or the ID to stay anywhere else. It's funny what you forget when you're being chased by mobsters in the 1950s."

Mary Beth responded with a sad smile. She had forgotten a lot of things in her final minutes in 1959. She had forgotten to change into 2017 attire and grab some belongings she had left in the Painted Lady. She had forgotten to tell Mark that she loved him.

"How are they?" Mary Beth asked.

"Ben is stressed," Piper said. "He's stressed about their predicament. He knows the Bells are back and that he and Mark no longer have easy access to the property. He's also worried about us. So is Mark. I guess he

229

couldn't even function yesterday. He loves you so much, Mary Beth. I could see it in his eyes when he was holding you on the lawn."

"I don't remember that. I don't remember anything after we entered the basement."

"I'm not surprised. You lost a lot of blood."

Mary Beth turned her head in both directions.

"Where are Mom and Dad?"

"They went to have lunch with the Bells," Piper said. "They will be back by two. That gives us less than an hour to get our stories straight."

"When are the police coming?"

"That depends on you. Dad told a Detective Peterson that he would call him today when you were able to talk. *Are* you able to talk?"

"I'm able," Mary Beth said. "Whether I'm willing is another matter."

"You don't have a choice. The police want a statement. You'll have to tell them something before we leave Los Angeles."

"I know."

"That's why I didn't go to lunch with the others. I knew I wouldn't get another chance to tell you what I've already told the police."

Mary Beth frowned.

"Please don't tell me I was shot by a burglar."

Piper nodded.

"You were shot by a burglar around eight o'clock yesterday morning."

"Piper!" Mary Beth said. "They won't buy that."

"They have to. I've already told them that I heard a pop in the backyard around eight, looked out the kitchen window, and saw someone climbing over the back fence. Then I said I ran out of the house and found you lying on the lawn."

"Did you describe the burglar?"

Piper shook her head.

"This is where you have some latitude. You can say a ninja warrior shot you, so long as you can say it to a detective without laughing. Just don't say your assailant looked like either Mark or Ben. They were seen leaving the property at the time of the shooting."

"What do you suggest I do?" Mary Beth asked.

"I suggest you say as little as possible. Say that you heard a disturbance in the backyard and went out to investigate. Say you saw someone of medium height and weight who was dressed from head to toe in black and wore a mask. You don't know the age, race, or even the gender of the burglar. You just know the person pulled a gun when you caught him or her in the yard and fired at you when you ran back toward the basement door."

"They won't buy that."

"Of course they won't," Piper said. "The police *already* think I'm hiding something. We just need to make sure they don't suspect we're hiding two

230

boys from 1959. We need to tell them something that will allow us to get out of here and leave all this behind."

Mary Beth sank when she heard the words. She wanted to leave the shooting behind, but she wasn't sure she wanted to leave Los Angeles. She didn't want to leave Mark and Ben stranded in 2017 without money or resources or the means to get home. She didn't want to leave *Mark*.

"Do you want to leave?" Mary Beth asked.

Piper sat up in her bedside chair.

"What do you mean?"

"I mean do you really want to leave this behind? Do you want to leave Ben?"

"What do you think?"

"I think you still want to find a way to make this work," Mary Beth said. "Don't think for a minute I wasn't watching you this week. You're as miserable as I am."

"You noticed?"

"You've been miserable since we decided to leave."

Piper frowned.

"Even if I have, what's the point of prolonging this? Mark and Ben can't stay. They have a mother back in 1959, in case you've forgotten. We have a mother and a father here. We have a life here. Do you want to throw that away for a guy?"

Mary Beth smiled and put her hand on Piper's arm.

"It's funny."

"What's funny?" Piper asked.

"I'm older than you," Mary Beth said. "I've done more, seen more, and learned more, but I'm the one who's acting like a love-struck teenager. You're acting like the adult."

Piper returned the smile.

"Appearances can be deceiving."

"I don't follow."

"I've had crazy thoughts all day, Mary Beth. I've thought about putting Mark and Ben in a hotel and then bringing them to Huntsville. I've thought about skipping college and running off with Ben. I've thought about spending every penny in my savings to keep this going."

Mary Beth laughed.

"What's stopping you?"

Piper sighed and smiled sadly.

"Do you really have to ask?"

Mary Beth shook her head.

"No."

"So what do we do now?" Piper asked.

Mary Beth gave Piper's arm a gentle squeeze.

231

"We say goodbye – again. We tell the boys how much we love them and send them back to the past. Then we get on with our lives and hold on to our memories."

Piper gazed at her sister.

"That's a very adult thing to say."

"It's a very practical thing to say," Mary Beth said. "We don't have any options."

"I agree."

"Can you sneak them in here before we leave?"

"I think so," Piper said. "I know so."

Mary Beth smiled.

"Then do what you can to make it happen. I want to see both of them before we leave Los Angeles. I want to say goodbye the right way."

Piper took her sister's hand.

"I'll do what I can."

"Thanks," Mary Beth said. "You're the best."

54: MARK

Monday, June 5, 2017

Mark held the device to his ear and tried to hear Piper's answer. He knew that the cell phone was state of the art for 2017, but for this call, it worked no more effectively than a tin can at the end of a waxed string. He stepped outside the homeless shelter and then repeated his question. "Can you hear me now?" Mark asked.

"I can hear you," Piper said. "I can hear you much better."

"Thank God. I was getting ready to break this thing."

"Don't do that. You have enough problems."

Mark laughed.

"Tell me about it. We're down to our last five dollars."

"You won't be for much longer."

"What do you mean?"

"I mean we're going to give you some money. We still have nearly half the money we won in Las Vegas," Piper said. "We think you'll need it. We want you to put it to good use."

"That's Mary Beth's money, not ours. We can't take it."

"She wants you to have it, Mark. *I* want you to have it. You'll need it."

Mark could not disagree. He and Ben would need every cent if their stay in 2017 turned out to be a long one. He tried not to think about that possibility.

"Is Mary Beth free?" Mark asked. "Can she talk now?"

"She can't. She's in her room. She's with my folks."

"Will they be there all day?"

"No," Piper said. "That's the good news. Mom and Dad are leaving at one. They are going to lunch and then to a store. Mary Beth and I gave them a long list of things to buy. If we're lucky, they will be gone at least two hours. You can see us after they leave."

233

"What about the nurses? Will they let us in?"

"They will if you identify yourselves as cousins. They let a cousin see the patient in the next room, but they refused a group of friends. For some reason, they draw the line at family."

"Then I guess we're cousins today."

"You can even say you're *kissing* cousins. Mary Beth would like that."

Mark laughed. He would miss Piper almost as much as her sister. He digested all that she had told him and then turned his attention to another matter. "Has Mary Beth spoken to the police?" Mark asked.

"She has," Piper said. "She talked to a detective on Saturday."

"Does he believe your story about a burglar?"

"I don't think so. He pressed us hard for a description of the assailant and rolled his eyes when we gave him Zorro. He also questioned our timeline, the sequence of events, and our general attention to detail."

"He's suspicious," Mark said.

"He's *very* suspicious. The only thing he doesn't suspect is that I shot my own sister."

"That's comforting."

"It's unnerving," Piper said. "I've lied more times to the police than Al Capone. If they ever find out I'm lying, I'll have bigger things to worry about."

"It won't come to that."

"I hope not. I want to spend the next year in a dorm and not a prison."

Mark laughed and shook his head as he held the tiny phone to his ear. He appreciated Piper's humor almost as much as her courage. She had taken some big risks in the past few days and had come through for at least three people.

"What do your parents think of all this?" Mark asked.

"They haven't said much," Piper said. "They were in shock, like the rest of us, most of Friday and didn't say anything substantive until Saturday afternoon."

"What did they say then?"

"They asked me if I was lying."

"Are you kidding?" Mark asked.

"No. I'm not. One reason they doubt my version of events is because it's at odds with a recording of my call to the dispatcher. The recording apparently picked up a second voice when I attended to Mary Beth. The detective asked me about it twice. I told him both times that I was alone with Mary Beth from the time I called to the time the ambulance arrived."

Mark's admiration for Piper increased again. He wondered how many times he could thank someone who had made so many tough decisions in the span of a few days.

"What do your parents think now?" Mark asked.

234

"I don't know. They haven't said much more about the case. They are almost completely focused on Mary Beth's recovery and returning to Alabama."

"What about the Bells? Have you talked to either of them?"

Piper paused before answering.

"I have. I spoke to Professor Bell briefly, by phone, on Saturday."

"What did he say?" Mark asked.

"He didn't say much," Piper said. "He asked me how I was doing. Then he asked me, point blank, if Mary Beth and I had entertained any male visitors Friday morning."

"What did you tell him?"

"I told him we hadn't. I didn't know what else to say. I can only imagine his reaction had I told him the truth."

"You did the right thing," Mark said.

"I hope so. I just can't figure out why he asked the question. It's not like Mary Beth or I know any guys we could have called over at eight in the morning."

"Did he let the matter drop?"

"That's the thing," Piper said. "I don't know."

"What do you mean?"

"I mean Professor Bell wants to speak with me again later today."

"Will he be there when we're there?" Mark asked.

"He shouldn't. He said he would visit the hospital around three."

"Then we will definitely be there by one. What do you want us to do when we arrive?"

"Go to the large waiting room on the second floor," Piper said. "Keep a low profile and don't tell anyone you know Mary Beth or me. I'll come for you as soon as I can."

"OK."

"There's one more thing."

"What's that?" Mark asked.

"The Bells will leave their house around two thirty and not return until at least six. They plan to take my parents and me out to dinner after they see Mary Beth. Give some thought to going back to the mansion then. It may be your best chance to enter the property unseen."

"I understand."

"Mark?"

"Yeah?"

"Tell Ben I miss him," Piper said.

"I will."

"I'll see you at one."

55: BEN

Ben sipped bitter coffee from a paper cup, gathered his thoughts, and then gazed across an outdoor picnic table at a brother who had the answers to his questions. He continued with the questions as soon as a noisy garbage truck pulled away from the La Brea Avenue Mission.

"Did Piper say more about the shooting?" Ben asked.

Mark shook his head.

"She won't either. She's tired of talking about it. She just wants to go home."

"Did she say that?"

"She did in so many words.

"I refuse to accept this," Ben said.

"You have to accept it. *I* have to accept it. Piper and Mary Beth have lives here. They have friends and family here. They have a future here. We don't. We live in 1959."

"We could live here. I know we could."

"We could," Mark said. "We could live the rest of our lives without a mother too. Do you want to give up Mom and all our friends and relatives for Piper?"

"No."

"We don't have a choice, Ben. We have to go back."

Ben couldn't disagree. He knew deep down the gig was up. He lived in the age of Sputnik, Edsels, and *I Love Lucy*. Piper lived in the age of Voyager, Teslas, and *Game of Thrones*. He had seen the program advertised on the sides of buses all weekend.

"So what's next?" Ben asked.

"We go to the hospital at one. We see the girls for an hour or two, say our goodbyes, and then return to the house as fast as we can."

"Why the hurry?"

236

"The Bells will be gone from two thirty to six," Mark said. "Piper said the professor and his wife plan to visit the hospital around three and then take the McIntires to dinner. That means we'll have a few hours to access the property, enter the tunnel, and go home."

"That's plenty of time."

"It is."

"It seems so simple," Ben said.

"It won't be."

"What do you mean?"

Mark looked away and stared at the street for a moment. When he finally looked again at his brother, he did so with eyes that revealed fear, worry, and sadness.

"Think about it, Ben. What did we leave three days ago?"

"We left a house full of mobsters."

"What will we return to?"

Ben sighed.

"I get it."

"Piper is going to give us the rest of the Vegas money. She wants us to put it to good use. I think the only we way can do that is to buy a gun this afternoon."

"You think we'll need one?"

Mark nodded.

"We may need two. When we go back through the tunnel, we will go back to the house as we left it. It will be nine thirty on May 2, 1959. One man with a gun will be trying to kick in our door. A second will be trying to break through a window. A third will be roving the grounds. We may have to shoot our way out of our own home."

"Did you lock the door in the hallway?"

Mark shook his head.

"The men will have unrestricted access to the entire house. We may walk into an ambush the second we open the door from the tunnel to the basement."

"We can't win a gunfight with mobsters," Ben said.

"We probably can't," Mark said. "If it comes to that, we'll be dead within a minute."

Ben pondered that cheery prospect as two police cars sped by on La Brea Avenue. Suddenly he had more to think about than a hospital visit, a painful goodbye, and a broken heart.

"What are the alternatives?"

"There are none," Mark said. "There are none if we want to see Mom again. We have to go back. If we can find a place to hide in the house, even for a few minutes, we might have a chance. The men will have only minutes

237

to find us before the police arrive. I'm sure our neighbors called the cops when they heard the first shot."

"We're in a mess, aren't we?"

Mark chuckled.

"Think of it as a challenge."

"I prefer challenges on the tennis court," Ben said.

"I'm sure you do."

"Did Piper say anything else to you?"

"She did," Mark said.

"What?"

"She said, 'Tell Ben I miss him.'"

Ben smiled sadly.

"I guess that's something."

"It is. I know it doesn't seem like much, but it is. Piper will never forget you. She'll think of you and your time together for the rest of her life."

"You seem sure of that."

"I am."

Ben gazed at his brother.

"Mark?"

"Yeah?"

"Do you have any regrets?"

"What do you mean?" Mark asked.

Ben sighed.

"Do you regret opening that drawer?"

"No," Mark said. "That's the funny thing. I don't."

Ben smiled.

"I believe you."

"I wouldn't trade the last six weeks for anything, Ben. I'm happy for the first time in years. I have a purpose. I'm alive," Mark said. He put his hand on his brother's arm and laughed. "Now I just have to find a way to stay that way."

56: MARY BETH

Mary Beth gazed at her "kissing cousin" through glistening eyes, gently squeezed his hand, and laughed when her nose began twitch. Even in a hospital room filled with the odors of cafeteria food, bodily fluids, and disinfectants, she could pick up a whiff of La Brea Avenue.

"You *smell*," Mary Beth said.

Mark chuckled.

"I haven't had a shower since yesterday."

"That's all right. You look like a dream. That's all that matters."

Mary Beth soaked up a sight she hadn't seen in more than three days. She didn't care that Mark Ryan hadn't had a shower. She didn't care that he hadn't changed his clothes. She cared only that he was here, at her side, on what would likely be a difficult day.

"How are you feeling?" Mark asked.

"I'm feeling pretty good," Mary Beth said. "It's amazing what painkillers can do."

Mark smiled.

"Are you going to be able to walk out of here tomorrow?"

"I hope so. I took a few steps this morning without falling."

"That's good."

Mary Beth smiled and shifted her attention to the far side of her room. She saw Ben and Piper sitting in facing chairs, holding hands, and gazing at each other with sad eyes. They had done little else since Mark and Ben had entered the semi-private chamber at a quarter past one.

Mary Beth studied the teens for a moment and then returned to Mark. She noticed that he seemed happy but physically spent. She wondered how *he* had survived the weekend.

"Did you walk here?" Mary Beth asked.

Mark shook his head.

239

"We took the Metro. It was kind of nice."

"Was it nicer than your Edsel?"

"*Nothing* is nicer than my Edsel."

Mary Beth laughed.

"Your brother might disagree."

"He does," Ben said from twelve feet away.

Mary Beth looked at the tennis ace.

"Are you eavesdropping, Ben?"

"No. I'm gawking at your sister."

Mary Beth giggled. She started to say something to Piper but stopped when she saw her sibling pick up her buzzing cell phone. She watched with interest as Piper stared at the screen.

"Is something up?" Mary Beth asked.

"I don't know," Piper said. "I've been summoned to the waiting room."

"Are Mom and Dad back?"

"No. I have to go though."

"OK."

Piper released Ben's hands and rose from her chair. Then she looked at Mary Beth with eyes that revealed concern, curiosity, and perhaps a trace of anxiety.

"I shouldn't be long," Piper said.

Mary Beth nodded.

"Take your time."

"I just might."

"What about me?" Ben asked.

Piper smiled.

"You're coming with me."

Ben laughed.

"You're the boss."

Piper grabbed Ben's hand and pulled him from his chair. Then she opened the door, motioned for him to walk out first, and glanced again at her sister.

"Don't go anywhere."

Mary Beth smiled.

"I'll do my best.

Piper gazed at Mary Beth and Mark and then followed Ben into a hallway that had become busier and noisier in the past half hour. Then she shut the door and left a college graduate from 2017 and a college senior from 1959 to themselves.

"I wonder what that was about," Mark said.

"I don't know," Mary Beth said. "Maybe she wanted privacy."

"I hear that's in short supply."

"You have no idea."

240

"That will change soon enough," Mark said.

"I imagine it will."

"What are your plans for the next few days?"

"I'll fly back to Huntsville tomorrow, of course. Then I'll probably rest another week on the couch at home," Mary Beth said. "I doubt my parents will let me do more than watch TV, eat ice cream, and play with my cell phone."

"I played with one this morning at the homeless shelter. One of the residents let me borrow his to call Piper and play a few games. It's an addicting device."

"That's the understatement of the century."

"What do you mean?" Mark asked.

"I mean that's all anyone does in this time. They make calls and send texts and play games with their phones, but they don't personally interact. That's the thing I miss most about the fifties. People actually talked face to face. They did stuff together."

"You sound wistful and nostalgic."

"I am," Mary Beth said.

"Would you go back if you could?"

"I might. Depending on the circumstances, I might."

"Would you go back if you could take your parents, your sister, and maybe a half dozen other people?" Mark asked. "Would you go back today?"

"I'd go back in a heartbeat."

"Are you serious?"

"I am," Mary Beth said. "If I could bring my closest relatives and maybe a few other things, like a modern medical guide, a history book, and my grandma's banana cream pie recipe, I would go back this very minute."

Mark looked at her with moist eyes.

"That's what I needed to hear."

"Don't cry. I know it's hard. I've done nothing but cry and mope and feel sorry for myself the past two days. I want things to be different. I just don't know how to fix this."

"I know."

"Are you ever going to tell your mom the truth?" Mary Beth asked. "Are you going to tell her that Mary Beth and Piper McIntire were more than just two girls with fashion sense?"

Mark took a deep breath.

"I might. I might break open a bottle of whiskey some Saturday night and tell her everything. I think she would like hearing more about you. She adores both of you."

Mary Beth met his gaze.

"I'm going to miss our conversations."

241

"You'll find someone to talk to," Mark said.

"I'm sure I will. Whether I find someone who listens is another matter. You're the best listener I have ever known, Mark Ryan."

"I try."

Mary Beth started to respond but paused when her nurse, a young African-American woman, came in the room, picked up her tray, and left. The nurse left the door open.

"What about you?" Mary Beth asked. "What are your immediate plans?"

"I'll finish school. Then I'll look for a job," Mark said. "I would still like to get on at JPL. I think my mom would like that. She would like me close."

Mary Beth clasped his hand.

"What about personally? Are you going to be all right?"

Mark forced a smile.

"Is anyone all right after losing someone like you?"

"That doesn't sound reassuring," Mary Beth said.

"I'll be fine," Mark said with manufactured cheer. "If I can get through the next twenty-four hours, I'll have the best life your Vegas winnings can buy."

Mary Beth smiled.

"Did Piper give you the money?"

Mark nodded.

"She did. Thanks."

Mary Beth paused to consider his words.

"Mark?"

"Yeah?"

"What did you mean when you said, 'If I can get through the next twenty-four hours'?" Mary Beth asked. "Are you expecting some trouble?"

"I don't know," Mark said.

"Those men won't still be there, will they?"

"They might."

"What will you do if they are?"

"You don't want to know."

"Mark, what are you—?"

Mary Beth stopped when her cell phone buzzed. She picked up the device, read a text from her mother, and dropped the phone to the floor.

"What's the matter?" Mark asked.

"My parents are coming back."

"What?"

"They forgot something. They just left the restaurant."

Mary Beth pressed her temples as her head started to pound.

"I can leave and come back," Mark said.

242

"No. I don't want you to leave," Mary Beth said. "I want to know what you're going to do if those men are still at the house."

"You don't want to—"

"Mark!"

"We're going to get a gun, Mary Beth."

"No!"

"We *have* to!" Mark said.

A familiar voice rang out.

"You don't have to do a thing."

Mary Beth glanced at the door and saw a ghost.

"Mrs. Ryan?"

Donna Ryan smiled at her son as she entered the room.

"You don't have to do a thing, Mark."

"Mom?" Mark asked. "How did you get here?"

Professor Bell, Ben, and Piper followed Donna into the room. Bell grinned. Ben beamed. Piper smiled through a veil of tears.

"I'll explain the how and when and why in due course, Mr. Ryan," Bell said. "I'll explain it all. I'm Geoffrey Bell, by the way. It's nice to meet you."

Mark hesitated.

"You too."

Mary Beth gripped the sides of the bed as her head started to swim and her body grew weak. She looked at Bell, Donna, and finally her sister.

"Piper?"

Piper stepped forward. She stopped at the edge of the bed, took Mary Beth's hand, and spoke to her sister in a soft, loving voice.

"They get to stay, Mary Beth. They get to *stay*."

Mary Beth gazed at Piper and then at Mark. She looked to him for answers but saw only bewilderment, enlightenment, and finally a smile.

In a matter of seconds, hopes had replaced fears, happiness had displaced sadness, and a never-ending nightmare had become an impossible dream. Mary Beth pulled Mark in, gave him a hug, and then turned to face the others.

This was real, she thought. It was real. She smiled and took a breath. Then she wiped away a tear as a burden lightened, the truth took hold, and a trickle became a flow.

57: MARK

Mark looked at three things and tried to decide which was more impressive: his host, his beloved, or the view from Geoffrey Bell's seventh-floor hotel room. All three inspired.

Bell continued to deliver. For nine days he had helped Donna, Mark, and Ben adjust to both 2017 and the sovereign state of Alabama. He had seen to their needs, dealt with their concerns, and answered several of their many inquiries. He planned to answer the rest of their questions and offer them a glimpse of the future today.

Mary Beth continued to amaze. She had recovered from her nearly fatal wound and resumed a wide range of activities in her hometown of two hundred thousand.

She sat next to Mark on one of the two sofas in Bell's suite. Ben, Piper, Donna, and Jeanette Bell occupied the other. Each managed cups of coffee that sat on tables in front of the couches.

Professor Bell did not sit. He stood in front of a picture window that offered a glorious view of a 363-foot-high rocket. The Saturn V Dynamic Test Vehicle, the signature exhibit of the U.S. Space and Rocket Center, loomed over its lush surroundings a quarter mile away.

"Do you like the view, Mark?" Bell asked.

Mark laughed.

"I think you know the answer, Professor."

Bell smiled.

"I do. I know the answers to many questions, including questions you have asked for days. I intend to answer those questions this morning and perhaps make some sense of a situation that remains unsettled and fluid."

"I appreciate that," Mark said.

"Have all of you had breakfast?" Bell asked.

244

Mark and Mary Beth nodded. Donna and Ben did the same. Mrs. Bell, an attractive redhead with a warm smile, simply looked at her husband with amusement.

"I haven't," Piper said. She glared at Mary Beth. "My sister yanked me out of the house before I even had a chance to grab a glass of orange juice."

Bell laughed.

"I left some pastries in the kitchen. Please help yourself."

"I may do that," Piper said. "Thank you."

Bell looked at the group as a whole.

"Does anyone want to get things rolling?"

"I do," Mary Beth said. "Why are my parents not here?"

Bell smiled.

"The answer to that question is as simple as is it complicated. I did not ask your parents to join us because I don't want them to know about the tunnel. That is particularly true with your father. As a military man, he might feel obligated to report our little secret to the government. The government could then confiscate my property and use time travel for ignoble purposes."

"I understand," Mary Beth said.

Bell looked at the other couch.

"Do you have something, Ben?"

"I do. I'd like to know how you knew we were in trouble," Ben said. "It's not like we sent any signals or left any clues."

Bell chuckled.

"You did though. You left a big clue. I knew something was up the moment I walked through my home a few hours after the shooting and noticed a newspaper on a living room table. It was a copy of the *Los Angeles News* from March 21, 1959."

"I'll bet Piper left it there," Ben said.

Piper glared at Ben.

"I'll bet Piper did too."

Mark laughed. He loved watching Ben and Piper bicker almost as much as he loved watching them shower each other with affection. He had no doubt they would find a reason to stay together long after this difficult transition was over.

"I'm glad you *did* leave it there," Bell said to Piper. "Your 'carelessness' is the reason we are all safe, sound, and gathered here today. We all owe you a debt of gratitude."

Piper grinned.

"Thank you, Professor."

Mark looked at his host.

"How did you figure out the rest? How did you know the newspaper wasn't something Mary Beth or Piper had borrowed from a library or bought at a curio shop?"

"I didn't," Bell said. "I didn't at first. So I did some research. I went to the public library, dug up some microfilm, and started reading newspapers from the spring of 1959."

"What did you learn?" Mark asked.

"I learned a lot of things, including one thing I already suspected," Bell said. "I learned that time flows in streams that often diverge and sometimes combine. In the first running of the twentieth century, you and Ben did not encounter men with guns on May 2, 1959. You did not entertain two young women from 2017. As best I can tell, you spent a quiet, uneventful weekend at home with your mother. You did not, to my knowledge, make the news."

"Are you saying we changed history?"

"That's exactly what I'm saying. You certainly changed the history of my house. When Jeanette and I purchased the Painted Lady in 2000, I inquired about its past. I wanted to know, among other things, if the mansion Percival Bell had built in 1899 had any skeletons in its closets. I learned it did not. I was told that the most eventful thing to happen at the house was a small fire in 1988. I knew nothing about mobsters or a shooting or a family named Ryan."

"I see."

"I uncovered a different history when I went to the library twelve days ago. I learned not only about your family but also about a violent incident on May 2, 1959. I learned from news articles that three gunmen chased four young adults into the mansion and left minutes later in a black Lincoln. The adults, including residents Mark and Ben Ryan, were never seen again. Nor was the owner of the house. Your mother returned to the mansion later that evening from a trip to San Diego, but she too disappeared. She vanished before the police could ask her a single question."

"What did you do then?" Mary Beth asked.

"I dug deeper. I learned as much as I could as quickly as I could because I suspected that lives were in danger," Bell said. "It was then I concluded that at least one of the young people in this room had discovered the tunnel and used it to travel through time."

"How did you know that Mark and Ben had come with Piper and me to 2017? How did you know they were even *alive*?"

"I didn't. I guessed as much after speaking to Piper and reading the police report. The report mentioned a male voice in the background during Piper's emergency call. I concluded that the voice belonged to either Mark or Ben and that both had accompanied you to 2017."

"How did you save Mrs. Ryan?" Piper asked.

"I saved her by traveling to the past. I reprogrammed a portal I have used many times to take me back to the early afternoon of May 2, 1959."

"Why then?"

"I selected that time of day because I knew no one would be home. I knew from reading official sources that the cops had finished inspecting the mansion at noon. I also knew that Donna had not yet left her sister's home in San Diego. So I called her from a house phone, asked to meet her at a nearby restaurant when she arrived in Los Angeles, and went from there."

Piper looked at Donna.

"You agreed to meet a total stranger?"

Donna smiled.

"I agreed to meet a man and his wife at a safe public place. Professor Bell introduced himself as one of Mark's instructors and said he needed to speak to me privately – and at the earliest opportunity – about a matter of great importance. So I drove straight to the restaurant."

Piper tilted her head.

"I would *never* do that."

"Of course you would," Mary Beth said. "You ran off to Vegas with two boys you didn't know from a hole in the ground. You would meet a professor in a New York minute."

The Bells, Mark, and Ben laughed heartily. Mary Beth grinned. Piper sulked. Donna smiled warmly at Piper and placed a hand on her knee.

"I understand where you're coming from," Donna said. "I really do. People don't trust each other like they did sixty years ago. From what I have learned about this time, they don't trust each other like they did *ten* years ago. Times have changed."

Mary Beth looked at Donna.

"So what happened at the restaurant?"

"The professor told me everything," Donna said. "He said he was a time traveler from 2017 who had come to 1959 to save me and my boys."

"Why would you believe him?" Mary Beth asked.

"He showed me newspaper articles. The first, from May 4, 1959, reported Mark and Ben's disappearance. The second, from May 5, 1959, reported mine."

"That's all it took?"

Donna nodded.

"I believed the professor. I trusted his wife. I looked them both in the eyes and saw their fear and concern. It's hard to fake that."

"What happened then?" Mary Beth asked.

"We waited until dark and then drove to the mansion. We wanted to make sure we could enter a crime scene without drawing a lot of attention. I knew at least one of my neighbors would watch the house closely. He was that kind of person."

"Was anyone there when you arrived?"

Donna shook her head.

"The house was empty. It was also a mess. The men who chased you into the mansion had broken windows, overturned furniture, and pulled out drawers."

"What did you do then?" Mary Beth asked.

"I went through the place. I grabbed a large handbag from a closet, walked into every room, and looked for small belongings I could take to 2017. This was where my faith in Professor and Mrs. Bell was tested the most."

"What do you mean?"

"I mean I gathered more than photos and items with sentimental value. I collected jewelry, cash, and stocks and bonds from a safe in my bedroom. I put myself in a vulnerable position at a time I was distraught and not thinking clearly."

"Did you call anyone?"

"No," Donna said. "That was the hardest decision of all. I wanted to call my brother and my sister and tell them goodbye, but I couldn't bring myself to do it. I didn't know what to say. I also didn't know if I would ever return. That was still up in the air."

Mary Beth took Mark's hand. She looked at him with great affection and then turned to the woman to whom she owed so much.

"So you gave up your siblings for your sons?"

Donna took a deep breath.

"That's one way of looking at it. I look at it differently. I gave up maybe twenty more years with my siblings, whom I love dearly, for a lifetime with my boys."

"There's more to it though," Mary Beth said. "I can see it in your eyes."

"There *is* more. There is much more," Donna said. "Truth be told, I did not want to stay in 2017. I told the Bells I wanted to get the boys and bring them back to 1959. I wanted to deal with the hoodlums through the police and try to resume life as we had always known it."

"So what changed your mind?"

"*You* did. So did Piper."

"I don't understand."

"Then let me explain. I did a lot of thinking between the time I traveled through the tunnel and the time I met you at the hospital. I thought about how miserable Mark and Ben were the night you said goodbye. Then I thought about how happy they might be if I gave them a chance to be with the women they loved. So I decided to stay."

Mary Beth offered a tearful smile.

"Thank you."

"I would do it again, dear," Donna said. "I wouldn't even hesitate."

248

Mary Beth nodded but said no more. She wiped a tear, leaned into Mark's side, and let the group conversation head into a different direction.

Ben looked at Professor Bell.

"What about the mobsters?"

"What about them?" Bell asked.

"Were they ever arrested?"

"They weren't in your case. They *were* arrested and prosecuted in another case. Tommy "The Handler" Parkinson, the man with the bad ear, was convicted of homicide in 1962. His associates went to prison the next year on racketeering charges. All three were part of a crime syndicate that operated in Los Angeles, Las Vegas, and Phoenix."

"So Ear Man was a killer?" Ben asked.

"Ear Man was a killer. Your family was lucky," Bell said. "Parkinson and his men would have killed all of you to obtain the sports book Mary Beth told me about."

"What happened to the book?" Piper asked. "Did anyone find it?"

"I don't know," Bell said. "None of the news stories mentioned the book. Nor did Parkinson or his associates at their trials. It's probably stuck in a drawer somewhere."

Mark laughed.

"What's so funny?" Bell asked.

"I was just thinking that's how all of this started," Mark said. "I opened a stuck drawer one day and found time-travel instructions from Percival Bell. They came with two clear crystals and a key to the basement door."

"Do you have the items with you?"

"I still have one crystal and the key."

"Where is the other crystal?" Bell asked.

Mary Beth tentatively lifted her hand.

"It's at home. I put it with my seashells."

Several people laughed.

"I'm happy you found a place for it, but I'll need to collect it before I leave," Bell said. He smiled at Mark. "The same goes for yours."

"You can have it," Mark said.

The group laughed again.

Bell stepped to the windowsill, picked up a cup of coffee, and took a sip. He studied the others, looked at them with satisfaction, and resumed the conversation.

"Are there any more questions?" Bell asked.

"I have one," Mark said.

"What's that?"

"Did your father ever time travel?"

Bell cocked his head.

"Why do you ask?"

"I'm just curious. When Mary Beth and I were back in 1959, we attended a lecture, a lecture on time travel, and spoke to a couple named Joshua and Julia Bell."

"You met my parents?"

"We did," Mark said.

"What did you talk about?"

"We talked about time travel."

The others laughed.

"That makes sense," Bell said. He smiled. "How did you meet?"

"Your father approached us after the lecture," Mark said. "He liked the questions Mary Beth had asked the speaker and wanted to get her thoughts on the subject. Then he told us he had a diary and some letters from his grandfather that suggested *he* had traveled through time."

"I see."

"Do you know anything about that?"

"I know quite a bit," Bell said. "I inherited the diary and the letters from my father when he died in 1996. It was then I learned the secret *you* learned by opening a drawer."

"Did your father do anything with the documents? Did he travel?"

"He did not. Unlike you and me and Percival Bell, he was a cautious man. He respected knowledge and power and handled both with great care."

"I sensed that," Mark said. "I also sensed that someday he would share the documents with someone who *could* do something with them. It appears he did in a roundabout way."

Bell nodded.

"Do you have any more questions?"

"No," Mark said. "I'm done."

"How about the rest of you?" Bell asked. "Do *you* have more questions?"

Four people shook their heads.

"Let's move on, Geoffrey," Jeanette said. She smiled at Donna, Mark, and then Ben. "I think our fifties family is more interested in tomorrow than yesterday."

"Then let's shift gears," Bell said. "Let's go from the past to the future and discuss how we're going to integrate the three of you into the twenty-first century."

58: MARY BETH

Gulf Shores, Alabama – Sunday, October 8, 2017

On the fifth day of her engagement to Mark Ryan, Mary Beth McIntire walked west along a white sandy beach and noticed that God had misplaced the setting sun. He had placed the orange ball along the coast, not away from it, and dropped it near Biloxi.

"It's different here," Mary Beth said. "It *feels* different."

"It should," Mark said. He smiled. "It's Alabama."

She spanked him with an open hand.

"You know what I mean."

Mark laughed.

"I think I do. But maybe you should explain."

"All right, smart guy, I will," Mary Beth said. She smiled and shook her head. "It feels different here because it feels permanent."

"Isn't that a good thing?" Mark asked.

"It is if things remain permanent."

"You lost me between 'different' and 'permanent.'"

Mary Beth forced a smile as they proceeded toward a collection of beachside cottages and an uncertain future. She resumed the conversation a moment later.

"I worry about change," Mary Beth said. "I worry about losing what I have, including the people I love."

Mark tilted his head.

"Everyone worries about that."

"I know. But not everyone obsesses about it. I've obsessed lately."

"Is there a reason why?"

Mary Beth nodded.

"Today is the first anniversary of Jordan's death. I didn't bring it up earlier because I didn't want to spoil our weekend, but I've been thinking about it all day."

"Do you want to talk about it?" Mark asked.

Mary Beth smiled.

"I would rather talk about football."

Mark laughed.

"Then talk about football."

"I would if I thought it would help."

"Do you think about Jordan a lot?"

"I have today. I'm a little crazy about dates and anniversaries. Last October 8 was Jordan's twenty-fourth birthday. It was also the fifth day of our engagement," Mary Beth said. She glanced at Mark. "Today is the fifth day of *our* engagement."

Mark smiled.

"I get it now. You're obsessive, crazy, *and* superstitious."

Mary Beth glared at Mark.

"Don't forget homicidal. I'm in a killing mood right now."

Mark laughed.

"I'll be good."

Mary Beth shot a playful grin.

"You better."

Mark and Mary Beth said no more for the next five minutes. They walked in splendid silence as the crowds thinned, the sun dropped, and a not-so-crimson tide rolled in.

Mary Beth enjoyed every second. She used the time to ponder and reflect. She let her mind drift when Mark took her hand, laced his fingers through hers, and pulled her close. She thought about other walks on other beaches. Nineteen fifty-nine seemed so long ago.

"You're quiet all of a sudden," Mark said.

"I'm just thinking again."

"Can I ask about what?"

Mary Beth smiled.

"You can. I'm no longer homicidal."

Mark laughed.

"That's a relief."

"I'll bet it is," Mary Beth said.

"So what's on your mind now?"

"I'm thinking about how lucky I am to be here."

"I can't argue with that," Mark said. "There were several times that last day I didn't think we would make it. We were lucky to escape the mob."

"I don't mean just that. I mean other kinds of luck. I wouldn't be here today, walking with you, if several things hadn't fallen into place back there."

"I don't follow."

"Think about it," Mary Beth said. "We're here because Piper left an old newspaper on a table and charged her phone the day I was shot. We're here because Ben asked her to the prom. We're here because your mother gave up her siblings. We're here because *you* didn't give up on *us*."

"Do you think about that a lot?"

"I think about it all the time. It's another reason I'm a little nutty today. I wonder when my luck will run out – or my lucky charm will run away."

Mark leaned toward Mary Beth and kissed her cheek.

"I'm not going anywhere. That's why I put a ring on your finger. I wanted to tell you in the clearest possible way that I'll be here tomorrow and the next day and the next."

"I know."

Mark smiled.

"See? You're better already."

Mary Beth laughed.

"Why do you put up with me?"

"I 'put up' with you because you're a wonderful human being," Mark said. "I 'put up' with you because you're smart and kind and beautiful. Don't think for a minute I've overlooked that."

Mary Beth smiled.

"You're talking like a guy again."

Mark chuckled.

"Just don't lump me with my brother."

"I won't," Mary Beth said. "Your mother broke the mold with Ben."

"Yes, she did."

"How is he doing anyway? Is he adjusting to college life?"

"I should ask *you* that," Mark said. "You talked to his roommate this morning."

"Piper is not his roommate. She's his dorm mate."

"That's what I call a distinction without a difference."

Mary Beth laughed. She couldn't disagree. Though Ben and Piper occupied different rooms in the same dormitory complex at UCLA, they were, for all practical purposes, roommates. They had become best friends and more since moving to Westwood in August and starting college careers in the city that had brought them together.

Piper had decided to attend college on the West Coast in late July. She told her parents she had developed a weakness for sunshine, beaches, and Thai cuisine. She told Mary Beth she had developed a weakness for brown-eyed boys with killer smiles.

Brody and Colleen McIntire gave Piper their blessing despite numerous misgivings. They suspected that her decision to trade Knoxville for Los Angeles had less to do with academics and ambience than a young man she had met at a Huntsville shopping mall.

Mary Beth and Piper had introduced Donna, Mark, and Ben to their parents at a church picnic on June 18. Each followed a script they had helped to create in two days in a hotel suite. With the help of a physics professor and his resourceful wife, the girls had managed to fully integrate a fifties family into the digital world in less than a week.

The colonel and his wife had warmed immediately to Donna and had done all they could to welcome her to Alabama. Brody helped the widow repair and furnish a three-bedroom Victorian she had purchased in Five Points, a historic district in Huntsville. Colleen went out for coffee with her new friend at least twice a week.

Brody also warmed to Mark and leapt at the chance to find him a job. He introduced the recent college graduate to his colleagues at the Marshall Space Flight Center and then to his friends in Huntsville's engineering community. The flight center snapped up the quiet Californian before Geoffrey Bell could even manufacture his bachelor's degree.

Mary Beth smiled as she thought about bogus credentials and her visit to Midway High School. She wondered if Principal Raines had ever requested Piper's records. She wondered what West Germany had sent in reply. Then she felt a twinge of envy.

Like Mark and Ben and unlike Mary Beth, Piper had actually attended school in the spring of 1959. She had passed tests, passed notes, and passed people in the hallway. She had strolled at a hop, made out at a drive-in, and redefined the *Mona Lisa*. She had attended the prom.

It did not matter that Piper had not marched in Midway High School's graduation or appeared in its yearbook. She had been a vital part of something real. Now that member of a high school Class of '59 was a member of a college Class of '21. It was enough to make one's head spin.

Mary Beth pondered the irony of it all. She was the only one of the four young people who was doing what she had planned to do a year ago. She was taking classes at the University of Alabama School of Medicine and preparing for a new life with the man she loved.

She thought about how quickly her relationship with Mark had formed and blossomed and wondered whether it had developed *too* fast. Love, her grandmother once told her, was a crock-pot stew and not a microwave meal. It required time and care. It punished expedience.

Mary Beth walked with Mark down the quiet beach until they reached the Bon Secour National Wildlife Refuge. The undeveloped marsh between Gulf Shores and Gulf Highlands was the only undeveloped stretch of the

Fort Morgan Peninsula. It was a perfect place to rest, get someone's undivided attention, and put one last matter to bed.

Mary Beth stopped when the beach became more grass than sand. She glanced at the setting sun as it said good night to Alabama and then turned to face her fiancé.

"Can I ask you a question?" Mary Beth asked.

Mark smiled.

"I believe that's allowed when you're engaged."

Mary Beth stared at Mark.

"Can I ask you a *serious* question?"

"You're wearing a bikini, Mary Beth. You can club me with a bat if you want."

She laughed.

"I just lumped you with Ben."

Mark chuckled.

"I was afraid you would do that."

He placed his hands on her shoulders and met her gaze.

"What do you want to ask me?"

Mary Beth took a breath.

"Are you happy?"

"What are you getting at?"

"It's a simple question, Mark. Are you happy? Are you happy here? Are you happy with your life? Are you happy knowing you will never again see the world you left?"

He put his hands to her face and gave her a long, tender kiss.

"I am," Mark said. "I'm very happy."

"OK."

"That's it?"

Mary Beth nodded.

"That's it."

Mark laughed.

"I thought you were going to ask something big."

Mary Beth looked at him thoughtfully.

"I did."

Mark smiled and shook his head.

"I may never understand you."

"That's all right," Mary Beth said. She took his hand and smiled. "You have years to figure me out."

Made in United States
Orlando, FL
07 August 2022

20683255R00157